Jonas Mills Bundy

The Life of General James A. Garfield

Jonas Mills Bundy

The Life of General James A. Garfield

ISBN/EAN: 9783337416607

Printed in Europe, USA, Canada, Australia, Japan

Cover: Foto ©Raphael Reischuk / pixelio.de

More available books at **www.hansebooks.com**

THE LIFE

OF

GEN. JAMES A. GARFIELD.

BY

J. M. BUNDY

ILLUSTRATED.

NEW YORK:

A. S. BARNES & CO.

111 & 113 WILLIAM STREET.

1880.

CONTENTS.

—•••—

THE LIFE

OF

GEN. JAMES A. GARFIELD.

CHAPTER I.

GARFIELD'S NOBLE ANCESTRY.

"In this world all is relative. Character itself is the result of innumerable influences, from without and from within, which act unceasingly through life. Who shall estimate the effect of those latent forces enfolded in the spirit of a new-born child—forces that may date back centuries and find their origin in the life and thought and deeds of remote ancestors—forces, the germs of which, enveloped in the awful mystery of life, have been transmitted silently from generation to generation, and never perish! All-cherishing nature, provident and unforgetting, gathers up all these fragments, that nothing may be lost, but that all may ultimately reappear in new combinations. Each new life is thus the 'heir of all the ages,' the possessor of qualities which only the events of life can unfold."—*Garfield's Eulogy on General George H. Thomas.*

JAMES ABRAHAM GARFIELD is the natural and worthy heir of a noble lineage. It is true that his ancestors, so far as traceable, have been people of moderate, and generally lowly, position and circumstances. Their names have not been found in Court Chronicles or books of the Peerage, across the water; nor have they, with a few exceptions, figured conspicuously in American records, fleeting or permanent. But if virtue, courage, adventurousness of spirit, independence, and loyalty to God, truth, and country, constitute nobility of character, and prove nobility of blood, the men and women whose strong characteristics have descended to the greatest of the Garfields were people of a "rare strain of blood," to use the expressive language of the turf, where only actual qualities of race are considered. There is nothing "lucky" or "accidental" about either the character or the career of the next President of the United States. The most wonderfully developed specimen of American man- hood in this country has come to his present commanding posi- tion as legitimately, by the help of as favorable influences, and by virtue of as inexorable laws, as the big pines of the Yo- semite.

Let us look into this as far and as clearly as dim or scanty records and traditions will enable us to see.

It is tolerably certain that the male ancestor of the American Garfields was one of that picked company of men, women, and children, who came over in the ship which bore Governor Win- throp to the Massachusetts shores, and it is absolutely certain that this ancestor, Edward Garfield, was one of the one hun- dred and six proprietors of Watertown, now a lovely suburb of Boston, for he is so recorded in 1635. It is undoubtedly true --for all the circumstances prove it--that Edward Garfield was one of those men whose religion was so heroic and practical that they coolly and patiently encountered the dangers and priva- tions and sufferings that would have appalled nine tenths of Norman William's adventurous, freebooting founders of the nobility of conquered England, and with notions as much higher than those of the Norman robbers as the heavens are higher than the earth. But in Massachusetts, in the seven- teenth century, a quiet and sustained heroism was so common that individual heroes rarely got special mention. So, all that is known of Edward Garfield is that he lived to be ninety-seven years old, thereby, according to Carlyle's maxim, showing much virtue, and setting an example to his descendants which has been well observed.

Going backward from Edward Garfield, authentic history finds little to stand on, in the pursuit of his ancestry, and speculation has been wild and vague. There is a controversy as to whether the Garfields were of Saxon origin, coming over from Germany to England, or whether they are pure Welsh. General Garfield himself is a strong evidence of the former theory. When he talks German, as he does fluently and well, no stranger would doubt his being a pure-blooded German. He has the fair Saxon complexion and the Saxon temperament and *physique*. But this is not conclusive, though strongly presumptive. Among the few ancestral facts, however, that are on record in England, are those found in the "Herald's Visitation to Middlesex," about the middle of the seventeenth century, in which are recorded the family arms and crest of the Garfields of Middlesex, one of whom had the name of Abraham, which has kept reappearing in the family in this country, though sometimes shortened to Abram. This Middlesex settlement of the Garfields is pretty strong confirmation of the theory of their Saxon origin.

Returning to Edward Garfield, he had a son Edward, who had a son Benjamin, who had a son Thomas. Benjamin showed the warlike spirit that has been natural to the race, as well as civil ability. He was a captain in the Indian wars and a representative from Watertown, in the " Great and General Court of Massachusetts," probably a big-hearted and big-brained man. Doubtless more of this stock were of the same sort, though recordless. At all events, five generations of the Garfields, including the first Edward, are buried in and around Watertown. " Their record is on high."

The sixth Garfield in line of descent was Solomon, the great-grandfather of General Garfield, of whom more presently. His brother Abraham had his chance to show Garfield blood, by risking the loss of it in the fight at Concord Bridge, which was the Sumter tocsin of our Revolutionary ancestors, and afterward was one of the signers of the curiously framed but tremendously suggestive affidavits sent to the Continental Congress, to prove that these cool-blooded heroes acted on the defensive. Of Abraham Garfield we hear no more. Solomon Garfield was, however, destined to make history. As one of the self-crowned " sovereigns" who wanted to carve his sover-

eignty out of the then wild and " Western" forest beyond
the Hudson, he " moved " with his family into what was then
known as " The Wilderness" of New York, and helped to
" settle" what is now known as the town of Worcester, in this
State. This was as heroic and manhood-developing a business
as killing Indians or fighting " red-coats."

Solomon had there in his " clearing" a son named Thomas,
from whom and his wife, Asenath Hill, was begotten, in December, 1799, Abram, or Abraham, Garfield, the father of General
Garfield. The father spelled his Christian name sometimes in
one way and sometimes in the other. He never disgraced
either phase of that patriarchel name. So much for the male
line of the family.

The ascent through the lineage of General Garfield's heroic
mother, Eliza Garfield, will show an equally noble " strain of
blood " and greater distinction. Eliza Ballou, as she was before she married Abram, or Abraham, Garfield, came of that
purest, highest, most intelligent and enduring race of involun-
tary colonists who were ever expelled for their religion from
France—the Huguenot fugitives from the inconceivably foolish
" Edict of Nantes." It seems as though God had determined
that the Old World should send to America the very choicest of
seed for the propagation of a nation. Among these Huguenot
" settlers" was Maturin Ballou, the founder of the American
family of Ballous. Coming here for religious liberty, he and
his associates were naturally drawn to Rhode Island, the home
of the man who had made the greatest pronunciamento of
religious liberty up to that time—Roger Williams. Maturin
Ballou " settled " in Woonsocket, in Rhode Island, and he and
his descendants, for several generations, enjoyed there to perfection the liberty they crossed the seas to find. James Ballou, the father of General Garfield's mother, also enjoyed the
bold and adventurous spirit of his race, being taken up as a boy
into the wilderness of New Hampshire, where his father cut out
for his family a home in the forest, in Richmond, just north of
the Massachusetts line. By marriage in New Hampshire this

branch of the Ballous became "connected" with the large
Ingalls family, of which General Rufus Ingalls is an able representative.   From James Ballou and Mehitabel Ingalls was
born Eliza Ballou, General Garfield's mother.

She was born in Richmond, Chester County, New Hampshire, on the 21st of September, 1801, in the same town where
Hosea Ballou, the founder of Universalism in this country, and
a relative, was born.   The Ballous, according to all traditions,
have been small in stature, and have been called a "French
pony breed"—which means compactness and toughness of fibre,
moral, intellectual, and physical ; great nervous energy, combined with endurance, and a fine texture of organization
throughout.   Eloquence and the gift of poetry came naturally
to the family.   Silas Ballou, a brother of General Garfield's
grandfather James, was the author of over a score of hymns in
the Universalist "collection" of his time.   It will be seen that
the General came honestly by his oratorical powers, imagination,
and finer sentiments, from his mother's side of the family, while
he inherits the great physical development and strength, and
the accompanying good-nature, generosity, and sense of humor
that have characterized the Garfields.   General Garfield's
father was a man of prodigious strength.   He was famous as a
wrestler, and never met his match, though men would come for
miles from all around to wrestle with "Abe Garfield," as they
called him.   His grandfather, Solomon Garfield, was offered a
grindstone weighing five hundred pounds if he would carry it
home.   He put it on his shoulders and carried it home, a mile's
distance, without even availing himself of the privilege of leaning against a fence.   This feat was performed in Worcester,
N. Y., and while I was at Mentor a Worcester born man called
who gave the tradition as being fresh to this day.   All other
stories about the Garfields confirm the accepted theory that they
have been distinguished for their physical strength and for
their generosity, warm-heartedness, and dashing courage, but
without much tendency to intellectual feats.   General Garfield
believes that he is the second Garfield who ever graduated from

a college. The dynamic forces that were to take him out of
the range of all previous Garfields lay coiled up in the fine,
sensitive, religious, intellectual nature of his mother, who was
most fortunately situated for the development of whatever was
purest, best, and noblest in her, and prepared for the great mission she was to fulfil—a mission which she is far from believing to be ended.

When Eliza Garfield was eight years old, in the wild New
Hampshire " clearing," her father died, and her mother taught
her a lesson of heroic faith and vigor by taking the four little
children and moving into the newly settled community at
Worcester, New York, where Heaven had ordained that the
destinies of the Garfields and Ballous should form a junction.
Among her playmates for five years was Abram Garfield, her
future lover and husband. But her eldest brother James, after
whom the General was named, had had his ideas enlarged and
his adventurous spirit quickened by service in the war of 1812,
and so, when the war closed, he was wild with the notion of
moving to " the new West," as forest-covered Ohio was then
called. He induced his mother to take her children there, and
they all went fearlessly out, to conquer a new home. It was in
1814, and their destination was Muskingum County, near
Zanesville, in Central Ohio. The tedious journey took six long
weeks.

Now for Abram Garfield, an orphan, and bereft of the little
Ballou girl, his playmate. He was " bound out " to service with
a Mr. James Stone, who brought him up, but he broke his fetters at eighteen, and, keeping the Ballou girl in his heart all the
while, he set out for the Ohio wilderness, found his " better
half," and made her legally such by proper ceremony, when he
was nineteen and she a year younger. The building of the Ohio
Canal by the State gave a fine chance for the enterprising young
giant, whose will power, energy, and decision were as strong as
his tremendous muscles. A born master of men, " smart,"
active, and keen-witted, he found a place as superintendent on
the canal work, and soon got to taking contracts, which for

some time were profitable. A sudden rise of prices broke him, but he paid in full, and struck out for the wilderness of Orange, fifteen miles from Mentor, taking a half-brother with him. There was but one house within seven miles of them. They erected a log-cabin and both lived in it until another was built, and then went to work to cut a hole in the forest. There, on the 19th of November, 1831, James A. Garfield, the youngest of four children, was born.

CHAPTER II.

JUDGED by mere outward appearances, the advent of this robust, big-eyed, Saxon man-child, in a little log-cabin, in a small hole in the dense forest of Orange, Ohio, was not a particularly fortunate entrance into the world. But if my readers have sympathized with the views briefly outlined in the pre-

BIRTHPLACE OF JAMES A. GARFIELD.

ceding chapter, they will agree with me that such a birth, amid precisely such surroundings, was of great good omen to the child, who was to bear all the burdens and sorrows and struggles of that hand-to-hand fight for existence and development which is the blessed fate of nine tenths of the boys and men who make the Republic what it is. But this is only a

negative view. Positively, the being born of such a father and
such a mother, in the Orange woods, at that time, was a most
auspicious ordering of destiny. Not only was the daily fight
for a living heroically and joyously borne by the father, but
with religious cheerfulness by the mother. The whole atmosphere of life in that little "clearing" was pure, noble, and inspiring.

But when the bright young boy was but eighteen months old
this little home of happy labor and hope was darkened by a
sudden, unexpected, and, in fact, needless, calamity, which
seemed to cloud all its future. A fire broke out in the woods,
which was approaching Abram Garfield's "clearing," near his
wheat. With all his tremendous physical energy he fought
that fire all day long, by ditching, clearing away the leaves,
or other methods. By doing the work of ten ordinary men he
saved his crop and diverted the fire. He came in at night,
heated and exhausted, and got suddenly chilled. For a day or
two he suffered intensely, when a quack doctor came along and
said, "You are in danger, Garfield," and put a blister around
his throat, which drew every particle of inflammation in his body
into Garfield's throat, and the glorious man choked to death at
thirty-three, in the fulness of his magnificent strength. He had
fought fire like a Viking. He died like one. Immediately
before his death he got up and walked across the room, looked
out at his oxen and called them by name, went back and sat
down on the bed, and said, "Eliza, I have brought you four
young saplings into these woods. Take care of them." And
he died, sitting up against the head of his bed. That is the
sort of stock that James A. Garfield comes from. But events
were to prove that the Ballou stock was of a sort even more
heroic, because of a finer and higher "strain."

Widow Garfield's situation and that of her "four saplings"
seemed well nigh hopeless to the neighbors. Not so to her,
however. Her mother had taken four fatherless children out
into the wilderness of New York. She would maintain for her
four children what the giant force of her husband had cut out

of the Orange woods. She would not " put her children out,"
as the neighbors insisted. No one else should raise that brood
but herself. She was entitled by law to $120, as a " year's
support," which she could hold as against any creditor.
But even in her desperate situation she scorned to take this
entirely just advantage. She paid off all the debts, sold fifty
acres of land, which was mortgaged for purchase-money, and
saved thirty acres on which to support herself and her children.
Thus she began to wrestle with life, with four children to take
care of—Mehitabel, aged seven ; Thomas, a boy of nine years ;
Mary, seven years old ; and James, then, as I have said, eighteen months old.   •

Only those who have lived in new settlements can comprenend
how the Widow Garfield got along. A few incidents, out of a
multitude, must illustrate. Abram Garfield had " got in" a
good crop of wheat, all secured by fences except about a hundred rails. There were, in readiness for splitting into rails,
great chestnut " cuts," and a few days after the funeral Widow
Garfield took her son Thomas out to the pile of " cuts" and
with his help split the needed rails herself—the plucky little
woman. She was a first-rate seamstress, and would go to the
shoemaker's and make clothes for his children, while he, in
return, would make shoes for her children. By the time that
Thomas got to be a lad of ten or twelve he was able to ride a
horse to plough corn, and earned twenty or twenty-five cents a
day, paid in wheat or any other " produce." He was a true
" father's boy," and seemed inspired with an idea of self-sacri-
ficing labor, that gave him almost the spirit of a mature man
and the sense of responsibility for the support of the family.
The sisters also were helpful, in all ways. The widow had a
few sheep. She and her daughters carded the wool, wove the
cloth, and made all the garments that could be made of wool.
So, in all sort of ways the busy little household managed not
only to exist, but to live well, as they thought.

But this did not satisfy the Widow Garfield. She wanted
mental and spiritual nurture for her children ; so, when a log

school-house was to be put up she tendered a little corner of her farm for a site, and so got what she desired within easy distance for young James, who, at the early age of three, went to school in that little log hut, not because he was sent, but because of his own longings. At the end of the first term he received a New Testament as a prize for being the best reader in his class of little boys. The school-house was plain and rough enough. The scholars sat on split logs, hewed a little on the top, four pegs put on the round side and supporting the benches. At first the teacher was very ordinary, but Eastern schoolmasters or "school-ma'ams" came along and did better. Little James went to school summers and winters, loving all his studies, and working hard. Text-books were few and of all sorts, but faithfully learned, which was the main thing. James, for instance, whose prodigious memory developed early, learned Webster's spelling-book almost by heart by the time he was eight years old. In fact, up to that time the main things he had learned were reading, spelling and writing—learning the language at the natural period for learning it.

Even when James, with his rapid growth, at the age of ten, had become able to work, his fatherly brother Thomas insisted on the former going to school. The mother, with her intense New England spirit, was, of course, glad to see James " getting along in his books " as rapidly as possible. In fact, the feeling of the whole family seemed to be, " Whatever else happens, James must go to school ;" and as for James, it is the common local tradition that even if he knew that study would never prove useful to him he would have pursued it for the love of it. In fact, he was seeking in all directions for books to read. Of course there were few to be had in the scattered homes of Orange, but these he got at and devoured. The old " English Reader" filled him with delight, and he can now quote from it, from memory, by the page.

Simultaneously with this tropical growth of intellect, under circumstances not so unfavorable as might be thought, was the growth of religious faith and sensibilities, under the teaching,

influence, and direction of his mother, who was what is called
a "Campbellite." And this requires a brief digression. It is
not creditable to the people of other sects that they know so
little of the real character of the class of Christians known as
"Disciples," who number nearly three quarters of a million of
good people, principally in Ohio, Indiana and the South, and
are called "Campbellites." They are mostly plain and unedu-
cated people, but their creed is one to which other Christians
seem quite generally tending. Briefly, it is merely a protest
against imposing, as a condition of church membership, any
human formula of divine truth. The belief in the New Testament and in the divine character of Christ and his atonement,
and in immersion as the proper mode of baptism, is all there is
of the so-called "Campbellite" faith. In practice they are
very simple and apostolic. Laymen can preach, and preaching
is not regarded as an isolated and peculiar profession. As for
Alexander Campbell, the founder of this sect—for it is as secta-
rian as any "denomination," and bigoted on the subject of
baptism—he was one of the few recent great "Fathers of the
Church" who have left their impress on vast numbers of people.
A prodigy of learning and polemical power ; distinguished for
the rare combination of a subtle metaphysical brain with keen
practicality which seems peculiar to the Scottish thinkers ;
bold, independent, and masterly in all ways—his grip on his
large army of followers is as strong as Theodore Parker once
said that of Calvin was on New England orthodoxy. But it is
not "a cold clutch." It is that of a beloved and full-blooded
master. The influence of this grand and powerful nature on Garfield's early career was strong and educational. It began when he
was very young, coming first through his mother, who, with her
husband, had been converted to the "Disciples" faith shortly
before James was born—converted by the preaching of a man
named Bentley, who had built a mill and a store two or three
miles from the Garfield homestead. He preached all through
that country, and kept his business going all the time. There
was something very primitive, plain, powerful, and convincing

about the utterances of these unordained "Campbellite" preachers.

The Widow Garfield was a great Bible reader, and taught her children to read it. She regularly walked to her "Disciples" meeting-house, three miles away, every Sunday for years, and took the children with her. Later a church was organized in the little school-house on her land. In all ways she impressed religious truth on her children, and kept them not only from bad habits but from bad thoughts. Anything that approached impurity of life and speech, in any degree, was hateful to her beyond expression. In that household there was a sort of flaming sword swinging constantly against all forms of indecency and immorality. Yet the Widow Garfield was the farthest possible from what might be called the sanctimoniousness of religion. She did not bring any of its forbidding aspects into the family. She was not merely a cheerful, but a jolly woman, a woman of great "heartiness," an exquisite singer, and had a memory almost marvellous. It is General Garfield's belief that she could have sung for forty-eight hours consecutively, from her large repertory, if her strength could have held out that long. She knew an infinite variety of songs—hymns, ballads, and the war-songs of 1812, such as those describing the fight of the Guerriere and the Wasp and Hornet, and all those naval engagements. Whenever the children were depressed or dull she would sing and fill their hearts with vigor and cheer. She was full of life and of a cheerful and robust morality that knew no taint.

But to return to James, who kept on going to school and de-vouring what story-books he could pick up. He and his cousin, Harriet Boynton, read "Robinson Crusoe" over and over again. He read and mastered "Josephus" when he was about twelve, and was wild over a story of the adventures of a man travelling down the Mississippi. When he was about fourteen he read Goodrich's "History of the United States," and so thoroughly were all its facts impressed on his plastic mind that he can now quote freely its statistics of the American and British losses in most of the battles recorded. Having so few books, the study of them was intensified. Even a so-called poetical " History of the United States," by a fellow named Eggleston, was committed to memory. But the exciting romance of " Jack Hallyard " set the boy's imagination on fire and enkindled the passion for the sea that was to be worked out on the tow-path of a canal, and the story of " Alonzo and Melissa" captivated his

GARFIELD AT 14 YEARS (FROM A MINIATURE).

imagination. Most of this reading was done at night, after his mother had retired, and with her permission.

But all this did not interfere with rapid and thorough work in school. By the time James was fourteen he had completed Pike's Arithmetic and got into Kirkham's Grammar. Then came Denham's Arithmetic, which he mastered, and about that time he began " declamations" at school. All this while, too, he made himself useful at home, not only by doing " chores," but by work on the farm of all sorts, including mowing. At fifteen he was a large boy, strong and athletic, inspired, too, by the traditions of his father's wrestling. He was too thoroughly good-natured to be quarrelsome, but he had imbibed the notion, not that it was a disgrace to be an orphan, but that other boys who had fathers and " big brothers" had, somehow, an advantage over him and were inclined to " run over" him, and every sign of this he resented, and fought instantly and " to hurt," no matter against what odds of strength or numbers, until he got the name of being " a fighting boy," which was a great grief to his mother.

By the time he was fifteen he had absorbed a large amount of peculiar literature. Two sorts of books had a special fascination for him—those that had accounts of wars, especially American, and those that described sea life in any form. About that period he began to " work out" away from home, especially in summer. When he was fourteen or fifteen he worked at boiling " black salts," from the ashes of burned logs. He got nine dollars a month and was boarded. Then he worked in " haying" a season, and took a two-year-old colt for pay —money being rarely paid. All he earned went into the common stock. It was the pride and joy of all the children to get " Mother" something, if they could, but it was not much that she would suffer them to do in this way. She was very simple in her tastes and attire, although she always had the " knack" of putting on things that would look well.

In the summer when James was sixteen he worked at haying at " full men's rates," a dollar a day, which was the largest pay he ever got for his manual labor. When the haying was over he went to Newburgh, now a part of Cleveland, and found that his father's brother Thomas wanted some wood chopped. James took the contract to chop a hundred cords, four-foot wood, at twenty-five cents a cord, a formidable undertaking for the most resolute boy. He stuck to it manfully until the last cord was chopped. He could " put up" readily two cords

a day, so that he cleared about half a dollar a day, as he was
boarded. This long and hard job was done near Newburgh,
on a height whence he could see the fascinating blue waters of
Lake Erie, and, in his intervals of rest, as he would straighten
up, he could see that blue segment of the lake, and occasionally
a steamer, and all his wild notions of seafaring life that the
books had enkindled set his fancy on fire. His wood-chopping
seemed dreadfully dull and prosaic, but he had a feeling that
it was disgraceful to back out of anything he had undertaken,
and he stuck to his task.

As soon as it was done, however, he went to Cleveland, bent
on shipping as a hand before the mast. He boarded a vessel,
found some drunken sailors, and a captain who looked a
drunken beast ; was shocked, and turned away and walked off
— partly disillusionized, not wholly. He happened to meet a
cousin whom he knew merely by sight, and who was running a
canal-boat. The cousin asked him if he did not want to drive
horses for him. The offer was accepted, for it flashed on young
Garfield's quick mind that he could make the canal work a
primary school, the lake the academy, and the ocean the
college. So began his canal-boat experience, which has been
sufficiently and in some cases extravagantly exploited. It
came along naturally, without accident or any merely wild
notion of adventure, and James went through it rough and
tumble, like the brave and lusty youth he was, for three
months, when he got paid ten dollars a month and board. Not
through any fault of his own, he had several fights, and invariably came off better than his antagonist. The one feature of this
singular experience which was of special value to him afterward, was his learning to steer, and something about the navigation of the Ohio River—an experience that served him in the
army, when he saved his command in eastern Kentucky from
starving, by piloting a boat sent for supplies, when no professional on hand would undertake the perilous duty. He
stood at the wheel for forty-four hours out of forty-eight,
and saved his boat from being wrecked. When he re-

turned to his command with a load of supplies his men were eating their last crackers.   Until this time his wise and devoted wife was never able to understand why Providence had put her James through his canal experience.   Then she said—as though everything in his life ought to have some great significance— "I see what your life on the canal meant, now."   With which wise wifely view all sensible people who realize Garfield's great mission will agree.'

Providence having quite other ends for young Garfield to achieve than could be accomplished even on the ocean, that had been his ultimate conception of an arena for his energies, his canal experiment resulted in an attack of fever.   He was carried home to his mother almost delirious, and there, for five months of illness, her wise and long-reaching love began to mould his destiny, by gentle and insidious, but holy, craft, to higher uses than he had dreamed of.   She knew well enough that it would not do for her to stand right in front of that strong will of his.   She did far better.   She had no word or look of reproof for his having gone off and incurred a serious illness, in gratifying what she regarded as a foolish and wicked love of adventure.   She was merely the incomparable nurse—quiet, patient, loving.   As soon as James got able to read she scoured the neighborhood for books that would lead his mind into wholesome channels.   She got a school-teacher by the name of Bates, now a prominent preacher, to come over and see him, and the teacher would instruct him in the new problems in arithmetic, and so occupy his mind.   Bates became an intellectual stimulus to the sick boy that long winter.   The mother had conspired with Bates to get him to want to go to the Geauga Seminary, not far away, and both worked artfully together to that end. Finally, as the opening of the school term drew near, the astute mother said, "James, you are not fit to go back to the lake now.   You health is too much broken.   You will break right down again.   Thomas and I have talked it over, and we have raised seventeen dollars, which will be pretty nearly enough to pay the necessary money expenses of your going over to Chester

to school." She had also arranged with her sister to have two of her boys go, so as to have the three " club together" and board themselves with the supplies they could take. " But," she adroitly added, " if you feel still determined to go on the lake, why, go over there to school this year, and by that time I hope your health will be restored. Then, if you go to work in haying or carpentering"—for James had already learned the latter in building a house for his mother—" you will make enough to go in the fall term, and then I think you can teach district school ; and, if you want to, you can sail on the lake summers, and when the lake is frozen over you can teach school."

She knew how to guide her young Viking without showing her purpose. The idea of earning something and being some-body came in on him like a passion, for he had felt bitterly his dependence, and all his hard earnings had gone to pay doctors' bills, even his colt. Against this penniless dependence his whole soul revolted. And so the mother conquered, and the destiny of the son, from that date to now, has been rapidly upward. To Geauga Seminary he would go, and " Mother" Garfield's heart was full of joy.

CHAPTER III.

Thus, in the spring of his eighteenth year, March, 1849, James and his two cousins, well provisioned, went ten miles over to Chester, to get all they could out of the Geauga Seminary, an institution founded and supported by the "Free Will Baptists." They rented a room with a cook-stove and two beds, in a cheap old house, partly tenanted by a poor widow, who contracted to do their cooking and washing at very low rates. The academy itself was considerable of an institution for the time and place, and was enriched by the possession of a library of about one hundred and fifty volumes, which latter fact startled and delighted young Garfield. But he soon made another discovery in the school, the importance of which dawned on him only very gradually, and which turned out to be the greatest discovery of his life-time. He found there a modest, studious, somewhat reserved girl, of about his own age, named Lucretia Rudolph. He only met her, however, in recitations, and as he felt "green" and awkward, and she was absorbed mostly in her studies, the acquaintance was, for some time, without opportunities or provocations for anything more.

When the term closed James went to work haying, and took a job with a carpenter. There was a house to be built in Chester, and he got the job of cutting out the siding at two cents a board. He went back to the fall term and fought his way through to the end of the year, paying all his expenses, and having a few dollars left. He then presented himself for examination, to get a certificate to teach school, which he readily obtained, and taught his first district school, beginning two weeks before he was eighteen. He received twelve dollars a month and "boarded around."

He had some tough customers to manage in this school. There were several boys in it with more brawn than brains, who conceived it to be their chief duty and pleasure to bully the schoolmaster. He labored under the special disadvantage of teaching in the school district next to where he had been born and brought up, and where everybody knew him as " Jim" Garfield. The winter before the teacher had been turned out by the boys—that is, his position was made so hot that he was glad to leave. There was constant skirmishing between the " big boys" and young Garfield for about a fortnight, until one of them flatly refused to obey, and Garfield whipped him. As the mutineer was returning to his seat he caught a heavy billet of wood, and turned, without Garfield's knowledge, when the latter heard a shriek from the scholars, looked around, and saw the big club, held in both hands, falling on his head, with a force that might well have proved fatal, had not Garfield thrown up his arm and warded it off. His arm was nearly broken, but with the other he threw the mutineer so that he fell on his back ; then jerked him on his feet, seized and threw him, put his knee on his breast and hand on his throat, and said, " Now, sir, I shall whip you until one of two things occurs : either till you die or until you absolutely submit to the order." Then he gave the scholar a series of heavy blows until he surrendered. And as there were several large boys who seemed to be in conspiracy with the flogged ringleader, Garfield added, " If there is any scholar here who expects, at any time, to make any sort of disturbance, come on now and settle here." The school was quiet and orderly for the rest of the winter. It was " Jim" Garfield no longer, but " the master."

During that winter Garfield did a good deal of reading. Pollock's " Course of Time" impressed him very much, and he learned it nearly all by heart. It was during that winter that he fell under the influence of a " Disciples" preacher who held forth in the little school-house. The preacher was a good solid old man, the incarnation of good sense, and had something about him that touched the young school-master. For some years previous the latter had been somewhat " offish" on the subject of religion ; felt the irksomeness of its pressure, and absented himself from church. A strange feeling came over him that this plain old preacher had come to get hold of a life that was likely to run to waste. The preacher touched his sympathies and moved his heart. He " came out," made a profession of religion, and was baptized in the faith of his mother. He was then a few months past eighteen. To use the General's own language : " Of course, that settled canal, and lake, and sea, and everything." A new life, with new thoughts and ambitions, dawned on him. He resolved at once that he would have the best education that it was in the power of work to give. With this high purpose he went back to Chester and began his new life. He remained there during the spring and next fall, making four terms at Chester, and taught again the next winter, getting $16 a month.

By that time the institution at Hiram, which was the product, mainly, of the educational zeal and liberality of the " Disciples," was being started, and the fresh enthusiasm it called out drew Garfield to it, as, later on, the Republican Party, in its fresh enthusiasms, called him to it.

CHAPTER IV

HIRAM, and the institution which has been known under the successive names of the "Hiram Eclectic Institute" and "Hiram College," deserves a separate chapter. The spontaneous outgrowth from a community that was exceptionally devoted to every attainable means of intellectual and religious culture, it also largely owed its inspiration to that great-minded teacher and apostle, Alexander Campbell, who was not only an educational zealot, but whose original and powerful mind impressed itself on all his more enlightened followers as no other mind, in recent times, that I know of, has impressed itself. Hiram, from the beginning, was more a hive of busy, earnest, and co-operative workers after knowledge than a mere "institute," or "college." To Garfield it offered opportunities and incitements to development of both brain and heart such as no other place would have given. He could there be both pupil and teacher. An atmosphere of wholesome and cheerful religious enthusiasm and of pure domestic life pervaded the place. There, too, he came to know thoroughly the hard-working and proficient student who was to be his wife.

He had studied Latin two terms—that is, he had gone painfully through the paradigms of the grammar and the rules, which he had mastered, but had not gone into any reading book. He had gone through algebra, natural philosophy, and botany, and had collected a fine herbarium. He had also pursued other studies, including a term of Greek.

When young Garfield first went to Hiram, he had studied Latin grammar so far that he understood the conjugations and declensions, but had not learned the construction of sentences. He had his option between entering a primary class and going over the work which he had already done, or of going into an advanced class, which would compel him at once to begin the translation of Cæsar's Gaul. Quite naturally, he chose the more difficult task. But when he looked over the first lesson of translation, about six lines, he realized for the first time what an unknown quantity the work of translation was. But he sat down to face this difficulty with that quiet, bull-dog tenacity and purpose which has so often pulled him through. Immediately after supper he took a candle and his text-book and went up to the recitation room in an upper story, so as to wrestle alone with this new task. He had four room-mates in the room which he occupied in the basement. Sitting down in front of a table with his Cæsar, he began his attack by getting from a glossary the signification of each word. But this did not solve the problem. So he wrote out each word on a separate piece of paper, and arranged and rearranged these slips very much as he might work any other puzzle. Finding that one signification would not answer, he wrote down all the various significations of each word, which, of course, increased his difficulties in something like a geometrical ratio. But he kept sullenly and determinedly at it, and worked away hour after hour without moving or looking away from his task, until, about midnight, it was accomplished. Then for the first time he came back to self-consciousness. He found that he did not know where he was or how he had come there. His candle was making its last expiring flickers. But one by one recollections of his home, of his journey to Orange, and of his coming to Hiram, came back to him, and he then realized that he was a student at Hiram, and that he had conquered the most appalling task of his life.

It has been said that "there are some women whom to know well is a liberal education." The truth of this has been illustrated in the biographies of many great men. It is known by every man who has had any considerable acquaintance with men of decided force and elevation of character. When this sort of "liberal education" comes at the plastic and forming period of

the life of an ingenuous young man whose nature is receptive
and impressionable, and whose energies and ambitions are enkindled by the pure tuition of a noble and religious woman, of
great brains and attainments, the results are such as can be
attained through no other process.

It was Garfield's good fortune to have such a woman as
teacher, counsellor, fellow-student. and friend at the most critical and forming period of his life. She was so much his senior
in years, had such elevation and decision of character, and was
so resolute of purpose to maintain the " maiden widowhood "
occasioned by the death of her affianced before marriage, that
the closest intimacy of friendship with young Garfield could not
be in the slightest degree misunderstood, even by the gossips.
This woman, Miss Almeda A. Booth, achieved a position in
the " Western Reserve" something like that which was held
by Margaret Fuller in New England, so far as regards multifa-
riousness of intellectual acquisitions, decision of character, and
influence over intellectual men.

The range of her studies and the zeal with which she pursued
so many branches of knowledge were fully as notable as Margaret Fuller displayed. The divergence in their paths was favorable to the peace and usefulness of Miss Booth, whose religious
faith never wavered nor ceased to sustain her, and who found
happiness in the profession of teacher, to which she consecrated
her whole life, without reserve, doubts, or weariness.

A few of the more ambitious and hard-working students at
Hiram found themselves drawn by this noble teacher into an
intimacy with Miss Booth which was in the highest degree
honorable and fruitful of good to both parties. Chief among
them was Garfield, whose touching and heartfelt tribute to his
friend of friends—delivered at Hiram College, on the 22d of
June, 1876, and covering forty pamphlet pages—is a worthy
memorial, eloquent in the sincerity of its sadness, in its por-
trayal of a finished career, and in its allusions to his own indebt-
edness to the departed. The very " dedication" on the front

leaf of the pamphlet tells the whole story so suggestively that I give it in full, viz. :

To the thousands of noble men and women, whose generous
   ambition was awakened, whose early culture was guided,
   and whose lives have been made nobler by the thoroughness of her instruction, by the wisdom of her
   counsel, by the faithfulness of her friendship,
   and the purity of her life, this tribute to
   the memory of
   ALMEDA A. BOOTH
   is affectionately dedicated.

Garfield came to the "Eclectic," as a student, in the Yale Term of 1851. He was then nineteen years of age—large and stalwart of form, an athlete in proportions, and consumed by a general ambition to learn everything that could be learned. But he describes his own appearance, at that time, by the words "pulpy," and "green." In his eulogy on Miss Booth, describing his own feelings, he says :

"I had never seen a Geometry ; and, regarding both teacher and class, with a feeling of reverential awe for the intellectual height to which they had climbed, I studied their faces so closely, that I seem to see them now, as distinctly as I saw them then. And it has been my good fortune, since that time, to claim them all as intimate friends."

In the Spring Term of 1852, Garfield and a fellow-student were appointed to aid Miss Booth in writing a colloquy for the public exercises at the end of the school year. Miss Booth at once directed the work, gave all sorts of suggestive hints, criti- cised the parts, trained the speakers, and put it on the stage, so that its success was marked. Says he, of this work :

"My admiration of her knowledge and ability was unbound- ed. And even now, after the glowing picture painted upon my memory in the strong colors of youthful enthusiasm has been shaded down by the colder and more sombre tints which a quarter of a century had added, I still regard her work on that occasion as possessing great merit."

Other dramatic co-operative efforts naturally followed this success, and disciplined, enlivened, and cultivated the amateur dramatists. In the Fall Term of 1852 Miss Booth and Garfield were members of a class in Xenophon's Anabasis, but near the close of this term both Miss Booth and himself became teachers, and could only keep up their studies outside of class hours. "In mathematics and the physical sciences," says Garfield's eulogy, "I was far behind her ; but we were nearly at the same place in Greek and Latin, each having studied it about three times. She had made her home at President Hayden's almost from the first, and I became a member of his family at the beginning of the Winter Term of 1852–3. Thereafter, for nearly two years, she and I studied together and recited in the same classes (frequently without other associates) till we had nearly completed the classical course."

From a diary which Garfield kept, he was able to state what Miss Booth accomplished in the classics, in the two years referred to above, in his eulogy. As they pursued their studies together, his statement of her achievements is a faithful record of his own. In the Winter and Spring Terms of 1853 they read Xenophon's Memorabilia entire. So zealous were some of these Hiram students that a dozen of them—of course including Miss Booth and Garfield—hired a professor for a month of the summer vacation, and a "Literary Society" was formed. Bearing in mind that Garfield is giving the list of his own studies at this period, we quote from his eulogy, as follows :

"Miss Booth read thoroughly, and for the first time, the ' Pastorals ' of Virgil—that is, the Georgics and Bucolics entire— and the first six books of Homer's Iliad, accompanied by a thorough drill in the Latin or Greek grammar at each recitation. I am sure that none of those who recited with her would say she was behind the foremost in the thoroughness of her work or the elegance of her translation.

"During the Fall Term of 1853, she read one hundred pages of Herodotus, and about the same amount of Livy. During that term also, Profs. Dunshee and Hull, and Miss Booth and I, met, at her room, two evenings of each week, to make a joint translation of the Book of Romans. Prof. Dunshee contributed his studies of the German Commentators, De Wette and Tholuck ; and each of the translators made some special study for each meeting. How nearly we completed the translation I do not remember ; but I do remember that the contributions and criticisms of Miss Booth were remarkable for suggestiveness and sound judgment. Our work was more thorough than rapid, for I find this entry in my diary for December 15, 1853 : ' Translation Society sat three hours at Miss Booth's room, and agreed upon the translation of nine verses.'

" During the Winter Term of 1853-54, she continued to read Livy, and also read the whole of ' Demosthenes on the Crown.' The members of the class in Demosthenes were Miss Booth, A. Hull, C. C. Foote, and myself.

" During the Spring Term of 1854, she read the ' Germania and Agricola ' of Tacitus, and a portion of Hesiod."

It was under the peculiar circumstances existing at Hiram that Garfield came to become what is called a " preacher." Teachers and pupils were nearly all " Disciples." They held what were called " social meetings," at which some of the " elders" or leaders of the church would open with prayer, and call on the young men who were church-members to speak. They early recognized in young Garfield a sort of vigor and force of expression and facility of speech, and naturally called on him, so that it finally came to be understood that he was expected to speak on every occasion. But at first he did so with great diffidence. He felt awkward, and felt a sense of his inferiority in culture to many of those around him, but he persevered, and, what with his practice in debating societies, gradually got to think freely on his legs, and developed such power that often, when the preacher at church did not feel like speaking, he would call on " Brother Garfield." This, among the " Disciples," was entirely natural. It did not signify or imply any intention to recognize him even as an incipient " preacher," in the common ecclesiastical sense.

To review the tremendous work done by Garfield at Hiram, before going to college. He began at Hiram in the fall of 1851, with but twenty-four weeks of Latin and twelve weeks of

Greek. He taught for two winters in the district school. After the first term he taught constantly from three to six, and later, the whole six classes, so that he could only study nights and mornings. In June, 1854—less than three years after he went to Hiram—he not only had fitted himself to enter college, but had completed two years of the college course, so as to be admitted in the junior class in Williams, in full and good standing. He not only paid his way as he went, and supported himself, but had " saved up" about $350. If there is any precedent for such achievements I never saw or heard of it.

It is impossible to overestimate the forming character of the studies thus athletically pursued, at such a period of Garfield's life, with such singular enthusiasm and in such inspiring and elevating and refining companionship. Such a combination of circumstances, influences, and associations was far more valuable to the formation of the tastes, tendencies, aspirations, sentiments, and principles of the future soldier and statesman than the most famous universities of the world could have supplied. Mind and heart were simultaneously quickened and developed. The whole man was made more manly by submitting to the influence and instruction of a noble woman.

It is to Garfield's high credit that he grows more and more proud of the education which this woman filled with her own spirit. Of her and her influence he speaks as unreservedly as did John Stuart Mill of that of his wife, as to which, in his eulogy of Miss Booth, Garfield says :

" I should reject his opinion on that subject as a delusion, did I not know, from my own experience as well as that of hundreds of Hiram students, how great a power Miss Booth exercised over the culture and opinions of her friends."

NOTE.—Certainly it was not one of the least important of the experiences of Garfield as professor at Hiram that there came to him just such a pupil as Burke A. Hinsdale, who was to become his *protégé* and intimate friend. Mr. Hinsdale thus describes the first acquaintance :

" To me, General Garfield is no more than he was before his nomination at Chicago. My acquaintance with him began in November, 1853. Then it was that, a gawky boy, the smell of the furrow upon my garments, I first appeared in

Hiram. He soon made the capture of my heart. At that time the leading Hiram men were called Philomatheans, from the society to which they belonged. In an address delivered in 1875, speaking of the old Hiram days, I said : 'Henry James (an old Hiram man) speaks of the Philomathesians as " wonderful men," mentions those that he thought the " master spirits," and adds : "Then began to grow up in me an admiration and love for Garfield that has never abated, and the like of which I have never known. A bow of recognition, or a single word from him, was to me an inspiration." The exact parallel of my own experience. Garfield, you have taught me more than any other man, living or dead ; and when I recall those early days, when I remember that James and I were not the last of the boys, proud as I am of your record as a soldier and statesman, I can hardly forgive you for abandoning the academy for the field and the forum ! ' And the cheers with which the old chapel rang as I read the paragraph showed that a heart chord had been struck."

The half brotherly and half fatherly affection of Garfield for Hinsdale grew with the years, and no father could have taken a more constant and affectionate interest in Hinsdale's whole subsequent life then Garfield did. But this implied no lack of independence on Hinsdale's part, for it is equally creditable to both that he felt free to criticise Garfield at all times, and that Garfield rather encouraged the criticisms that came from a younger man, who was not only absolutely loyal to him, but to truth and conscience. To no other human being, save his wife, has Garfield written so long, so frequently, with such absolute freedom and with such fulness. Mr. Hinsdale—or President Hinsdale, I should say, for he is Garfield's worthy successor in the presidency of Hiram College—has preserved every scrap of paper he has received from his great friend. To his great liberality, confidence, and devotion to Garfield, I am indebted for the absolutely unrestrained use of his whole collection of letters from Garfield, about 400 in all. They include a correspondence lasting from 1857 to the eve of the Chicago Convention. Most of them Hinsdale had not looked at for many years. That he should fearlessly submit them to the scrutiny and use of a stranger is an ultimate proof of the absolute knowledge he had that there was nothing in the most hasty and confidential notes of Garfield that would not bear inspection and the light. How many of our public men would be willing to have such a correspondence exposed to even a private view ?

CHAPTER V.

In selecting a college wherein to pursue the last half of the usual curriculum, Garfield, as usual, acted with great care and judgment. He would naturally have drifted to Bethany, the college in Western Virginia founded by Alexander Campbell, and sustained by the "Disciples," if he had been a drifter ; the exact reverse of which he was, as is shown by the following letter, written about that time by Garfield, which I find in Whitelaw Reid's "Ohio in the War," viz. :

"There are three reasons why I have decided not to go to Bethany : 1st. The course of study is not so extensive or thorough as in Eastern colleges. 2d. Bethany leans too heavily toward slavery. 3d. I am the son of Disciple parents, am one myself, and have had but little acquaintance with people of other views ; and, having always lived in the West, I think it will make me more liberal, both in my religious and general views and sentiments, to go into a new circle, where I shall be under new influences. These considerations led me to conclude to go to some New England college. I therefore wrote to the Presidents of Brown University, Yale, and Williams, setting forth the amount of study I had done, and asking how long it would take me to finish their course.

"These answers are now before me. All tell me I can graduate in two years. They are all brief business notes, but President Hopkins concludes with this sentence : 'If you come here, we shall be glad to do what we can for you.' Other things being so nearly equal, this sentence, which seems to be a kind of friendly grasp of the hand, has settled the question for me. I shall start for Williams next week."

It was a wise choice. First, because Williams was a small rural college, where a poor young man could get along and be respected, but mainly because its whole spirit was that of the great man who was then its President, Mark Hopkins, who was in the full vigor of his powers—a man unique in college history for the union of philosophic breadth, wide attainments, generous manhood, and capacity to communicate. He was quick to

recognize "the making" of a great man in the awkward
young Western giant who came to his care, and there sprang up
between teacher and pupil a friendship that has grown to this
day.

In preparing this chapter in regard to Garfield's Williams
experience I gratefully availed myself of the kind offer of
Colonel A. F. Rockwell, an able and accomplished officer in the
Quartermaster's Department of the United States Army, who
was a classmate of Garfield at Williams, and has ever since been
an intimate friend and correspondent. Colonel Rockwell proposed to send, and did send, a circular letter to each of the sur-
viving members of the class, asking for such reminiscences as
might be interesting and appropriate for this book. The letters which follow, from Garfield's classmates, all came in response to Colonel Rockwell's letter. Afterward, knowing the
intimate personal relations between Cyrus W. Field Esq., and
both ex-President Hopkins and President Chadbourne, I asked
Mr. Field to write to both for such letters as they might choose
to send me.

These letters, taken together, present such a complete picture
of Garfield, as a Williams student, that they need very little, if
any, connection or comment. I give first the letters of Dr.
Hopkins and President Chadbourne, as follows :

REMINISCENCES BY EX-PRESIDENT HOPKINS.

WILLIAMS COLLEGE, July 17, 1880.
MAJOR BUNDY.

Dear Sir: You ask some account of the college life of Gen. Garfield. I remember no incidents worthy of note, but some characteristics may be given.
Anything that may aid the people in forming a judgment of his fitness for the
office to which he is nominated they have a right to.

My first remark, then, is that General Garfield was not *sent* to college. He
came. This often marks a distinction between college students. To some, college is chiefly a place of aimless transition through the perilous period between
boyhood and manhood. Without fixed principles, and with no definite aim, with
an aversion to study rather than a love of it, they seek to get along with the least
possible effort. Between the whole attitude and bearing of such, and of one
who *comes*, the contrast is like that between mechanical and vital force. In
what Gen. Garfield did there was nothing mechanical. He not only came, but

THE LIFE OF GEN. JAMES A. GARFIELD. 33

made sacrifices to come. His work was from a vital force, and so was without fret or worry. He came with a high aim, and pursued it steadily.

A second remark is that the studies of Gen. Garfield had breadth. As every student should, he made it his first business to master the studies of the class-room. This he did, but the college furnishes facilities, and is intended, especially in the latter part of its course, to furnish opportunity for gaining general knowledge, and for self-directed culture. To many, the most valuable result of their college course is from these. What they have affinity for they find, and often make most valuable acquisitions in general literature, in history, in natural science, and in politics. Of these facilities and of this opportunity Gen. Garfield availed himself largely. Of his tendency toward politics in those days we have an illustration in a poem entitled " Sam," which he delivered while in college, and in which he satirized the Know-Nothing Party. He manifested while in college the same tendency toward breadth which he has since, for it is well known that he has been a general scholar and a statesman rather than a mere politician.

And as Gen. Garfield was broad in his scholarship, so was he in his sympathies. No one thought of him as a recluse, or as bookish. Not *given* to athletic sports, he was fond of them. His mind was open to the impression of natural scenery, and, as his constitution was vigorous, he knew well the fine points on the mountains around us. He was also social in his disposition, both giving and inspiring confidence. So true is this of his intercourse with the officers of the college as well as with others, that he was never even suspected of anything low or trickish ; and hence, in part, the confidence I have always felt in his integrity. He had a quick eye for anything that turned up with a ludicrous side to it, and celebrated a trick the Freshmen played on the Sophomores by a clever parody of Tennyson's " Charge of the Light Brigade," published in the *College Quarterly*. Respecting always the individuality of others, and commanding without exacting their respect, he was a general favorite with his associates.

A further point in Gen. Garfield's course of study worthy of remark was its evenness. There was nothing startling at any one time, and no special preference for any one study. There was a large general capacity applicable to any subject, and sound sense. As he was more mature than most, he naturally had a readier and firmer grasp of the higher studies. Hence his appointment to the metaphysical oration, then one of the high honors of the class. What he did was done with facility, but by honest and avowed work. There was no pretence of genius, or alternation of spasmodic effort and of rest, but a satisfactory accomplishment in all directions of what was undertaken. Hence there was a steady, healthful, onward and upward progress, such as has characterized his course since his graduation. If that course should still be upward, it would add another to the grand illustrations we have already of the spirit of our free institutions. * * *

PRESIDENT CHADBOURNE'S LETTER.

WILLIAMS COLLEGE, Williamstown, Mass., July 9, 1880.

General Garfield graduated from Williams College in 1856. He evidently came to college for a purpose, and nothing turned him from that purpose. He recognized the fact that the professors were placed over the college to instruct and govern the students. He gained from them all the good he could, and those now living remember him as a noble man even as a student. He then gave promise of what he has since become—that is, a man equal to any emergency, a man of strong convictions of duty and unflinching courage. There are no stories to be told of him of insubordination to law, neglect of work, or indulgence in stale college tricks—those things he left to other men. Hard work, a genial nature, and manly spirit gave promise of that growth of character and constantly increasing influence which all have witnessed since Gen. Garfield became prominent in public life. It is pleasant for instructors to see their pupils come to honor, but when, as in this case, the honors seem to be so natural a result of wise, energetic action begun in college days, they are in duty bound to present such examples to those just beginning life. Few can have the opportunities for the kind of success achieved by Gen. Garfield, but had no political honor ever have come to him, he would have been a power for good in the world.

P. A. Chadbourne.

LETTER FROM THE HON. C. H. HILL.

33 School Street, Boston, June 23, 1880.

I think at that time he was paying great attention to German, and devoted all his leisure time to that language. In his studies, his taste was rather for metaphysical and philosophical studies than for history and biography, which were the studies most to my liking, but he read besides a good deal of poetry and general literature. Tennyson was then and has ever been since one of his favorite authors, and I remember, too, when Hiawatha was published, how greatly he admired it, and how he would quote almost pages of it in our walks together. He was also greatly interested in Charles Kingsley's writings, particularly in Alton Locke and Yeast. I first, I think, introduced him to Dickens and gave him Oliver Twist to read, and he roared with laughter over Mr. Bumble.

We belonged to the Philologian Society, one of the two great literary societies of the college, and it was at his suggestion that I attended its weekly meetings regularly, and almost always took part in the debate. I think he was considered our best debater, although we had several who were very good. Garfield had always been a Whig of the Seward and Wade school, and until the organization of the Republican Party, in 1856, men with his opinions, during our college days, were in a sort of political limbo, for he would have nothing to do with the Know-Nothing Party, which then seemed to be carrying everything before it, and attracted large numbers of young men, but whose principles he strongly condemned, and he had no liking, of course, for the Democracy. The great political questions of the day—the treatment of Kansas, the dangers from the influx of foreigners and from the Roman Catholic Church, the constitutionality of Personal Liberty Bills, the Crimean war, and the desirability of an elective judiciary—were eagerly debated in the Philologian, and he invariably took part, except during the period when he was President of the society. Two members of the Convention at Chicago which nominated him for President were active members of the society, Mr. W. S. B. Hopkins, of Worcester, Massachusetts, and our classmate, General Ferris Jacobs, of Delhi, N. Y.

Other prominent debaters were the lamented Dr. Dimmock, of Adams Academy, Quincy; ex-Senator Hitchcock, of Nebraska; E. L. Lincoln (now deceased); S. B. Forbes, and Charles Marsh, of the Class of 1855, and Charles S. Halsey, Edward Clarence Smith, C. D. Wilber, and others whom I do not now recall, of our own class. In all these debates, I should say that he was distinguished for moderation—not always, perhaps, in expression, but in opinion. His instincts were conservative. I remember distinctly that he was, when he came to college, a fervent supporter of an elective judiciary, but in preparing himself to take part in a debate on that subject, he studied himself over to the opposite side of the question, and began his speech by frankly admitting that he had within a week entirely changed his opinions on this subject.

In 1870, I was appointed Assistant Attorney-General of the United States, and for five winters my rooms were in the same street with Garfield's house at Washington, and but a few doors from it, and either at his house, or at the Capitol, I saw him almost daily. I think, in college, he looked forward rather to a professional and judicial career than to a political one, but I perceived that his intellectual growth since he left college had been a steady and consistent expansion of what he was as a young man. His political opinions, as they showed themselves in our conversations, were what they appear, I think, in his speeches—broad and conservative—those of a party man who, however, looks beyond party, and of a practical statesman who deals with existing facts, and does the best with them, rather than those of a political doctrinaire. His consistent and unflinching support of honest money, and constant enforcement of the duty of maintaining the national honor by paying the creditor according to his contract, reminds me of one trait in his character. Although a poor boy, and a very poor man in college, and although he has been comparatively poor ever since, I never perceived in him the slightest tincture of bitterness or envy toward those who were better off than he was, or of dislike for the rich because they are rich. In my long intimate companionship with him, I am certain he would more than once have betrayed some such feeling had he entertained it, and I know I should have noticed and remembered it. At Washington, he was always delighted to see old college friends, and talk over college days, about which his memory is wonderfully retentive. Two other members of our class, Mr. Gilfillan, Treasurer of the United States, and Colonel Rockwell, resided in Washington at the time, and formed a nucleus for class meetings whenever an old classmate turned up. Toward Williams College he has always entertained a most filial affection, and ever speaks with deep feeling of the benefits which he derived from his two years' residence there, and especially from the instruction and influence of Dr. Hopkins, the President, who during his thirty years' tenure of that office impressed himself as strongly upon the young men under his charge as any college instructor the country has ever seen, and who has old pupils on the Supreme Bench of the United States, in both Houses of Congress, and in other positions of trust and influence throughout the land.

I remain your obedient servant,

CLEMENT HUGH HILL.

J. M. BUNDY, ESQ.

LETTER FROM THE REV. JAMES K. HAZEN.

PRESBYTERIAN COMMITTEE OF PUBLICATION,
1001 MAIN STREET,
RICHMOND, VA., June 22, 1880.

The warm personal regard and affection I have for Garfield lead me to respond with alacrity, though I fear I can furnish you little that will be valuable for the purpose which you have in view.

We expected much of Garfield when in college, and predicted for him a seat in Congress within less than ten years of his graduation (he reached it in seven), but, so far as I know, our class prophecies did not point to a Presidential candidacy ; if they had, our memoranda would doubtless have been very full.

It was my privilege to board at the same table with Garfield during our Senior year, and I have a very vivid recollection of our daily conversations upon the various subjects of study that engaged our attention, but particularly upon the Shorter Catechism.

It was the custom then, and perhaps is still, in old Williams, for the Senior Class to devote Saturday morning to an exercise in that time-honored standard of the Calvinistic faith, under the instructions of President Hopkins, and, though holding a different type of theology, none of our class entered into the study more heartily than Garfield. It suited his metaphysical turn of mind.

In the discussions that followed, as we went from the class-room to our dinner-table, I was always impressed with the keenness of his criticisms, though my faith in the old Catechism and its doctrines was not shaken, and with the straightforward fairness and the hearty respect which he accorded to views which he utterly refused to accept. It occurs to me that in this we have a characteristic feature of the man, which has more than once been prominently manifested in his political career.

The occurrences of the last few days have recalled to my mind very vividly the beginning of the campaign of 1856, twenty-four years ago. The first Presidential candidate of the Republican Party, John C. Fremont, was nominated shortly before our graduation. A college ratification meeting was held, on receipt of the news, and, among others of the Senior Class, Garfield spoke. Probably this was his first Republican speech, and I can testify that it was enthusiastic and eloquent.

He had turned his attention to politics before this somewhat, having delivered, on the occasion of the Adelphic Union Exhibition, 1855, a poem, entitled "Sam," which may be found in Vol. III., No. 1, page 25, of the *Williams Quarterly.*

Of the heartiness and cheeriness of his manner as a friend and companion, I have the pleasantest recollections, and I can recall nothing whatever that in the slightest degree mars this impression.

Strong, however, as was my attachment to Garfield during our college life, it has been greatly strengthened by incidents that have since occurred.

It was my fortune to be the only one of my classmates on the losing side in the late war. Going South very soon after graduation, it has been my home ever since. In 1871 or 1872, some fifteen years from the time we graduated, business called me to Washington, and I found there several of my classmates and college acquaintances occupying various positions of honor and responsibility, but none of them recognized me as I met them, and I was under the necessity of introducing myself. Not so, however, with Garfield. On the morning of my arrival a friend had given me a seat on the floor of the House at the opening of the session. Shortly afterward Garfield came in from the opposite side of the hall, and approaching his desk, which happened to be just before the one I occupied, he recognized me the moment he entered and greeted me at once with my old college nickname, "Rex." I mention this as indicating the possession of one of those faculties which men of high position have found it necessary to cultivate. But what I designed to mention especially in connection with this was the warm welcome I received to his home, and the many kindnesses experienced then and on subsequent occasions, many of them prompted, as I am disposed to think, by the very fact that I was regarded in the light of "an erring brother." Yours, very truly,

JAS. K. HAZEN.

LETTER FROM THE REV. JOHN TATLOCK.

HOOSICK FALLS, N. Y., June 25, 1880.

Mr. Garfield displayed in college that perfect self-possession, that entire command of his powers and of his mental resources, which afterward made him successful in the field and a ready and powerful debater in Congress.

Of his boldness and facility in turning to account vague scraps of information, which more timid men would fear to use, and which less able men could not use, I recall an illustration:

In his Junior year he was engaged in a public debate between representatives of the two literary societies. The speaker who preceded him on the opposite side produced an elaborate illustration from " Don Quixote." Garfield, in reply, raised a laugh against his opponent by comparing him to the knight attacking the windmill. " Or rather," said he, " it would be more appropriate to say that the gentleman resembles the *windmill* attacking the knight."

At the supper following the debate Garfield was rallied on his extensive acquaintance with the classics. He laughingly replied that he had never read " Don Quixote," and had heard only an allusion to the mad knight's assault upon the flying arms of the innocent mill. . . .

To this I will only add that he was a man of a sweet, large and wholesome nature, and endeared himself the most to those who knew him best.

Yours truly, JOHN TATLOCK,
Classmate of Gen. Garfield, and Co-Editor with him.

LETTER FROM MR. SILAS P. HUBBELL.

CHAMPLAIN, CLINTON COUNTY, N. Y., June 28, 1880.

Garfield entered our Junior Class in fall of '54. He brought with him from Ohio another student, Charles D. Wilbur, who joined our class at same time, and between them there seemed to be a strong attachment. They roomed together in South College, and, as we termed it, were college chums. Wilbur unfortunately was lame and limped badly, and required the ⟨illegible⟩

stout cane. They were always together, and Garfield's kindness to his crippled chum was very noticeable. The pair in their daily walks to and from the recitation-rooms and about the college grounds excited the eager gaze and curiosity of their fellow-students, from their quaint and odd appearance and evident unfamiliarity with college ways and doings.

Besides, the contrast in the appearance of the couple was very striking—Garfield of large frame, looming up six feet high, strong and healthy, and looking like a backwoodsman, and Wilbur, with a pale, intellectual cast of countenance limping along beside him.

They made no attempt to conform to the ways and peculiarities of college life, or to ingratiate themselves with the students. They both seemed to be in dead earnest, striving to get an education, and to be entirely engrossed in their studies and college duties.

Their position at first was a very isolated and peculiar one, and which was somewhat enhanced by a whisper that soon circulated among the students that they were *Campbellites*. Now, what that meant, or what tenets the sect held, nobody seemed to know, but it was supposed to mean something very awful. But they continued on pursuing the even tenor of their way, unmoved by the stares and criticisms of their companions. After a time this feeling passed away, and Garfield, by his successful attainments and straightforward, manly course, commanded the respect and admiration of his class and of the whole college.

College life, as everybody knows, is a world in miniature; we had our elections, our debates, our caucuses, our anxieties and ambitious desires. There were two large debating societies in the college, one the Philologians, the other the Philotechnians, and a strong rivalry existed between the two societies. Garfield joined the Philologian Society, and took great interest in its welfare. He very soon took prominence as a debater, and by his ready wit and intimate knowledge of the subject discussed generally won his side of the case. He was a very hard student, and he never would speak or enter into the debate unless he had thoroughly mastered the subject beforehand. The subjects discussed in these meetings were of a varied character, but he always spoke on the side of right and freedom, and in behalf of the people and against oppression of all kinds. In October, 1855, in the public debate between the two societies held in the college chapel, he was one of the persons elected to represent his society in the debate. The subject for discussion was, "Was the Feudal System Beneficial?" The negative was supported by Garfield, and by his animated, earnest, and convincing arguments, and enthusiastic denunciations of the oppressions of the system, he won the hearty applause of his auditory. At the beginning of the Senior year he was elected President of the Philologian Society by a large majority, and won the admiration of all by his knowledge of parliamentary tactics, and the ease and grace with which he presided over the assembly.

At the commencement of Senior year Garfield was elected one of the editors of the *Williams Quarterly*, a periodical conducted by the students, and won an honorable distinction in our literary world by his contributions to the magazine. Some of his essays at the time were very noticeable, one in particular I now remember, entitled "The Province of History," which showed a depth of research and broad, far-reaching views as to the province of history which was not expected of an undergraduate at college. This article appeared in the number for June, 1856, and placed Garfield at the front in regard to literary attainments.

Garfield early joined the Mills Theological Society, which represented some of the best men in college. They held meetings every week, had a very fine library, embraced among their members a great deal of the best culture and talent in the college. It was unsectarian in character, and wielded a powerful influence for good over the whole college.

Garfield successively filled the offices of Librarian and President of the society, and by his urbanity, innate kindliness of nature, and good sound judgment in the management of its affairs, won the respect and esteem of all its members. Garfield was quiet and undemonstrative in his religious habits. There was no cant about him. But he impressed all with his deep sincerity and honesty of purpose. He lived the life of a true Christian.

I well remember commencement day at "Old Williams," when our class graduated. Garfield took one of the highest honors of his class, called the metaphysical oration. The subject of his oration was "Matter and Spirit." The audience were wonderfully impressed with his oratory, and at the close there was a wild tumult of applause, and a showering down upon him of beautiful bouquets of flowers by the ladies, a most fitting end to his arduous, self-denying college course and a bright augury for the future.

I remain respectfully yours, SILAS P. HUBBELL.

LETTER FROM MR. LAVALETTE WILSON.

HAVERSTRAW, N. Y., June 28, 1880.

Mr. Garfield even then showed that magnetic power which he now exhibits in a remarkable degree in public life, of surrounding himself with men of various talents, and of employing each to the best advantage in his sphere. When questions for discussion arose in the college societies, Garfield would give each of his allies a point to investigate ; books and documents from all the libraries would be overhauled, and the mass of facts thus obtained being brought together, Garfield would analyze the whole, assign each of his associates his part, and they would go into the battle to conquer. He was always in earnest and persistent in carrying his point, often against apparently insurmountable obstacles, and in college election contests (which are often more intense than national elections) he was always successful.

He showed perfect uprightness of character, was religious without cant or austerity, and his influence for good was widely felt. I never heard an angry word or a hasty expression, or a sentence which needed to be recalled. He possessed equanimity of temper, self-possession, and self-control in the highest degree. What is more, I never heard a profane or improper word or an indelicate allusion from his lips. He was in habits, speech, and example a pure man.

Arising, some may say from his own early struggles, but as I believe from his native nobility of character, was his sympathy for the suffering or depressed or humble. He would find out their wishes and desires, their best points, and where their ability lay, and encourage them to advancement and success. Not even now has he any of that inapproachability and hauteur which too often accompany great talents and high position. He is a democrat in the high-est sense of the word; no matter how humble a position a person may hold, how unfashionably dressed, how countrified in appearance, or lacking in knowledge of the usages of polite society, he will feel at ease in Mr. Garfield's presence, and receive the same courtesy and probably greater attention than would the Prince of Wales.

On entering Williams College, Mr. Garfield was uncommitted in national politics ; perhaps his first lesson came from John Z. Goodrich, who at that time represented in Congress the western district of Massachusetts. In the fall of 1855 Mr. Goodrich delivered a political address in Williamstown on the history of the Kansas-Nebraska struggle, and the efforts of the handful of Re-publicans then in Congress to defeat the repeal of the Missouri Compromise. As Mr. Goodrich spoke, I sat at Garfield's side, and saw him drink in every word. He said as we passed out, " This subject is entirely new to me. I am go-ing to know all about it." He sent for documents, studied them till he became perfectly familiar with the history of the anti-slavery struggle, and from that hour has been the thorough Republican, the champion of right against injustice, that he is at this hour.   LAVALETTE WILSON.

LETTER FROM MR. ELIJAH CUTTER.

BOSTON, June 30, 1880.

He had a robust physique and an open countenance. There was no stint in his make-up, and no " style," no assumed gentility, but much of " nature's nobleman" about him.

He was a little in advance of the average class age, and had an exuberant growth of hair, while his maturity of thought and expression, not unmixed with " Westernisms," challenged our attention. Yet in all youthful feelings and im-pulses he was as truly *a boy* as any in the class. His unstudied and often unskil-ful handling of himself was always accompanied by real delicacy of feeling and mental adroitness and aptitudes. Garfield's greatness was to our young eyes enig-matical, but it was real. There was a *good deal of him*—body, soul and spirit. Nature had not defaulted in his make-up, and his talents were of the popular order.

That a serious purpose brought Garfield to college, and how bent he was on accomplishing it, none who knew him in daily life could doubt. He accomplished much and aspired to more, not alone in class studies, but in other and varied acquirements. He read much of history and poetry. He was passionately fond of Shakespeare, and gave to debates and other optional literary exercises much attention.

I think most if not all of our class will remember Garfield pleasantly for his companionable traits. Not in the ordinary sense a " hail fellow well met," he had that genial temperament which readily drew others about him. Who among the men of 1856 does not recall among the picturesque memories of East College, that of Garfield sitting on the fence or rolling at full length on the cam-pus, convulsed with some newly fledged joke, or apt nickname, or droll persona-tion, or college yarn ? There were a few fine specimens of nimble wits in the class, of which Garfield might not be reckoned one, but none more ready to appreciate and perpetuate the college humor than he, and in all that goes to maintain the recreative and sporting life among young men he was prominent.

I should like to speak of Garfield in his religious nature, and of those high moral convictions which rendered him conspicuous in college, not less than in his public career since, and of some deep struggles he went through while weighing the question of entering upon politics as a profession. Some of these experiences would exhibit Garfield in a true light, if the boy is but the father of the man. But I fear I should trespass both upon his confidence and your space.

I am, sir, yours very respectfully,

ELIJAH CUTTER.

LETTER FROM THE REV. E. N. MANLEY.

CAMDEN, N. Y., July 8, 1880.

Garfield played chess with interest and success. The game becoming fascinating, threatening study hours, and finally carrying him once or twice near to, if not over into, the small hours of night, he said, "This won't do," and stopped short off.

We used to have an annual holiday called "Mountain-Day." At the close of one, a Fourth of July evening, on the summit of old "Greylock," seven miles from college, there was a goodly gathering of students about their campfire, when Garfield, the recognized leader, taking a copy of the New Testament from his pocket, said, "Boys, I am accustomed to read a chapter with my absent mother every night; shall I read aloud?" All assenting, he read to us the chapter his mother in Ohio was then reading, and called on a classmate to pray.

I think it was at the breaking-up meeting of the class, at graduation, that, being called up for a speech, he said, " γαρ is a Greek proposition meaning for. Gar-field, for-the-field. That is what I suppose I am."

E. N. MANLEY, Pastor Presbyterian Church.

I have saved for the last a remarkable letter from the Rev. Edward Clarence Smith, of Philadelphia, a graduate of the Law as well as of the Divinity school, and an especial favorite with the class of 1856. As will be seen, it was written to Colonel Rockwell, and without the slightest notion that it would ever be wanted for publication.

LETTER FROM THE REV. EDWARD CLARENCE SMITH.

501 N. EIGHTEENTH ST., PHILADELPHIA, June 15, 1880.

To Colonel A. F. ROCKWELL, U. S. Army, Washington, D. C.

My Dear Old Friend and Classmate: I thank you for your kind letter of the 10th inst. I joy and rejoice with you. I am glad to hear from one who so thoroughly appreciates the great power and worth of our honored and beloved Garfield. What you say of his mental growth and maturing powers I fully endorse. In sheer force and reach of faculty, in breadth of thought and culture, I believe he is the peer of the best man in America to-day. But what seems grander to me is his unswerving loyalty to conscience, to truth, and to his country's good ; in a word, his magnificent manliness.

I sincerely believe that there are times in the history of such countries as ours when God makes special use of such men. In this scientific age, persons do not like to hear the word *Providence*. But there seem to be certain super-human arrangements and adjustments that philosophy cannot explain, and that work out righteous results. Human ingenuity does not devise them ; human wisdom does not foresee them. I call it the insertion of a Divine factor in history. It does not compel the human will ; it does not destroy personal freedom, but it does achieve its results with resistless might, and with infallible certainty. What think you of a *theologico-philosophico-mathematical* formula like this ? a × b = c, in which "a" is man's freedom, intact, but finite; "b" a divinely inserted factor, unlimited ; "c" the providential plan of God in the issue of things. Thus freedom is saved, and the ends of eternal rightness achieved. But, mathematics and metaphysics aside, it seems to me that our friend has often come near that holy place, where Providence touches the machinery which weaves out the plans of history, and, doubtless often, without being personally conscious of it.

There are but few sincere souls that are deemed worthy of such honor : "*Pauci quos aequus amavit Jupiter, aut ardens evexit ad aethera virtus.*" They are never self-seekers. They work where they are placed. Like Æneas, in the fable, they are often covered with a cloud woven by divine fingers, and the mass do not see them. But, when they are needed, the cloud breaks away ; they are known of men, and are summoned to do God's work, sometimes against their will. Washington was such a man, Lincoln was another, and I sincerely believe Garfield is a third. Such men can be known by their utter unselfishness, their inherent nobility of character, and always by their unconsciousness of themselves. Such men invariably impress their generation with a sense of their *personality*. To how many millions is Lincoln thoroughly known, though few have ever seen him ? The great heart of humanity recognizes such men, when they pass, by a kind of divinely implanted instinct.

I have long felt that Gen. Garfield was divinely intended to supply important links in the chain of our country's history. I have therefore anticipated, with you, his election to the Presidency. One of my friends reminded me to-day that just one year ago I showed him the photograph of Gen. Garfield as that of the next President. I have little doubt of his success. You have seen a storm-cloud move over the earth, and gather all the electric forces along its course into affinity with it so that the lightning of the earth runs to meet the lightning of the cloud : so in case of a divinely chosen man ; he carries in his great heart all the instincts, hopes and aspirations of an age. When he appears and comes near to men, the love and acclaim of a nation run to meet him. There is in my opinion no doubt of our honored friend's success. He cannot appear, but the people will know him. Did you observe this at Chicago ? The machinery was well forged, riveted, and clamped, air-tight and fire-proof. But the popular will burst the bonds, as though withes of straw. To change the figure, it seemed to be a case of spontaneous combustion. The party engines played, but the fires *would* burst through chink and crevice. Finally the galleries caught fire, and everything went.

Wasn't it grand to see our friend stand by Sherman, with heroic loyalty, to the last, protesting against the use of his name, and fearing nothing so much as disloyalty to manliness and friendship? A few words of prophecy: The galleries at Chicago caught fire, as we know. I foresee that the flames will sweep like a prairie fire over the continent; burning to the very edge of the St. Lawrence; to the surges that break upon Plymouth Rock; and even to the melancholy murmurs of the great western sea.

. . . God bless you, my dear fellow. Remember me affectionately to our honored and loved friend, when you see him; and, though he may never hear from me again, inasmuch as he is now likely to swing out of my horizon, yet tell him I glory in his achievements for good, and shall ever wish him *God-speed!*

Cordially and affectionately yours,

EDWARD CLARENCE SMITH.

With all the cross-lights that are thrown on Garfield's character and career at Williams, by those men who knew him best under circumstances when character is most perfectly developed, it is needless to say much in addition. No college man needs to be told that his most critical judges are his classmates, who are the last to bow before any fictitious or unworthily won success in after life. Other letters from Garfield's classmates —not used because more or less repetitions of those already in type—show, as those printed above all show, an enthusiasm of admiration such as I never before even heard or read of being displayed by old classmates toward one of their number, no matter how high distinction or power he may have attained. The secret is to be found in the perfect integrity, warm-heartedness, great-heartedness, and magnetic power of the man, which has made all the sons of Williams, older and younger, proud of him, jealous of his honor, and indignantly impatient of the scandals that he frankly met, manfully exposed, and fully answered, to the satisfaction of every fair-minded and intelligent man who has read his answers. If such stanch Democrats among the alumni of Williams—who have known Garfield long and well—as Justice Field, late Democratic candidate for the Presidency, and as the Hon. David Dudley Field, will give the slightest countenance to these exploded scandals, I shall feel that there is some sort of provocation for attempting the not difficult task of satisfying any reasonable and unprejudiced man that partisan malignity never pursued an eminent public man with less shadow of pretext than exists for ringing the variations on the scandals that have been perfectly answered by James A. Garfield.

(*Garfield to Col. A. F. Rockwell, U. S. A.*)

HIRAM, OHIO, August 13, 1866.

My Dear Jarvis: My visit to Williams has washed out the footprints of ten years and made me a boy again. Strolling on the shore of life it is with reluctance that I plunge back again into the noisy haunts of men. The noble reunion has wedded my heart more than ever to the class and to old Williams. Let us not hereafter cease to pay that reverence which is due to youth. I mean to go back to Williams as often as I can. The place and its associations shall be to me a fountain of perpetual youth. If wrinkles must be written upon our brows, let them not be written upon the heart. The spirit should not grow old.

(*Garfield to B. A. Hinsdale.*)

WASHINGTON, June 30, 1872.

After spending all the day Monday on the law case in Cleveland, I took the train for Williamstown, which I reached in the evening ; stayed throughout the examination and until Friday morning. The exercises were very solemn and impressive. The resignation of Dr. Hopkins was a noble act, and the final speech in which he delivered up the keys to his successor was one of the rarest grandeur and simplicity. His first paragraph was this : "Why do I resign? *First*, that I may not be asked why I do not resign. *Second*, because I believe in the law of averages, and the average man of seventy is not able to bear the burdens of this Presidency. And yet I can now bear it. Many of my friends think I should continue to bear it. I think it safer to test the law of averages."

I stayed with Dr. Hopkins as his guest, and it was very touching when the old President bade me good-by, saying, " You will observe that I reserved for the concluding and final act of my official life, before laying down the office, the conferring upon you the degree of LL.D. I was glad to have my work thus associated with your name."

CHAPTER VI.

On graduating from Williams with high honors, with the highest college popularity, and with the unreserved confidence and admiration of President Hopkins and all the faculty, Garfield naturally returned to Hiram for the beginning of his life-work as a trained and cultured man. There were his most intimate and enduring associations. There the roots of his vigorous nature had taken strong and deep hold in all directions. Above all, there lived Miss Lucretia Rudolph, whose family had removed to Hiram some years before, to enjoy its educational advantages. The acquaintance begun at Chester, many years previous, when both were students at the Geauga Seminary, had ripened into congenial companionship in the studies and reading pursued together at Hiram, where he found her living near the Institute. She became Garfield's pupil, some time afterward, and recited to him in Latin, Greek, and geometry, as well as in some other branches of study. She was a remarkably fine scholar, with keen perceptions, quick intuitions, and high ambitions. She sympathized with all of Garfield's strenuous struggles for a college education. She was his complement and better self. Their union was inevitable, and they were engaged in 1854, just as Garfield was about to set out for Williams. But with this sensible understanding, that the marriage should not occur until he was in such financial condition that he would run no risk. It was one of those deliberate purposes whose fulfilment the lovers put far enough ahead to be prepared for it. They were married on the 11th of November, 1858, by the Rev. Dr. Hitchcock, President of the Western Reserve College at Hudson, and a happier marriage, in all respects, was never consummated, or one more

calculated to keep the strong current of Garfield's forceful and
active life pure, sweet, uncontaminated, and within limits.

Garfield became Professor of Latin and Greek in 1856. The
institution was poor and his pay was small. But, as usual, his
activities burst out in all sorts of channels. He not only taught
with all his might, but delivered scientific lectures, learning
his science as he went along, and got considerable pecuniary
returns therefrom. It was a place and time for " plain living
and high thinking." He was used to both, and revelled in the
play of his manifold powers. He put new life into the " Institute," or " College," as it was successively called. He easily
rose to be its President. Between his college duties, lecturing,
reading of all sorts, occasional " preaching" for the " Disciples " around Hiram, and political speeches and orations, he
" threw" off, without fatigue or fretting, work enough to wear
down and out half a dozen ordinarily strong men. The im-
pulses set in motion by his enthusiastic and varied activities
were felt all over the Western Reserve. The people there
recognized a new moral and intellectual force in the young and
masterful College President, whose upward growth was the
rising subject of talk. With all, he was so frank, ingenuous,
communicative, manly, and unconscious of his own swift self-
promotion that all the " plain people" took him to their hearts.
He never " condescended to people of low estate." Conde-
scension was a manifestation of pride or vanity which was
utterly impossible to his nature. For every reason—and especially because Garfield had shown his equality to the new
and startling issues of slavery and freedom, of secession and the
Union, in public speeches of extraordinary intellectual grip,
clear perception of constitutional and of " the higher" law,
and oratorical power—it was inevitable that the people should
call him into the public service, at a period when so many of
the old leaders were faint, false, blind, or living in the Past.

He was elected, in 1859, by the people of Summit and Portage
Counties, as State Senator. His majority was large and attested
the strength of his popularity. Although only twenty-eight

years of age, and new to legislation, or any other official experience, he speedily took rank as one of the readiest and best informed debaters in a body containing many experienced and able men. Realizing the nature of the " irrepressible conflict" that was breaking up parties and confounding the wisdom of old leaders, he was not long in arraying himself alongside of Senator Jacob D. Cox—since General, Governor of Ohio, and Secretary of the Interior—and Senator Monroe, an Oberlin Professor, and the trio were recognized as the " Radical Senators."

The first report which Garfield made as a member of a committee in the State Senate, was on the revival and completion of the geological survey of the State. In such subjects as this his enthusiasms have always been easy to be moved, and it would be difficult for him even now to write a document of a dozen pages, which could more comprehensively and interestingly awaken the people of Ohio to the importance of a thorough geological survey of their State. His faculty for grouping statistics and making them eloquent and practical was well illustrated in this effective presentation of the vast resources of his State. A shorter report on the subject of the education of the neglected, destitute, and pauper children, was a fitting prelude to the large and more important efforts in the cause of education, as to which no one of our public men has developed such a combination of philosophical thinking, applied to a vast mass of statistics.

Another report, on the subject of weights and measures, is a brief but comprehensive presentation of the history of English and American systems, and of the progress that has been made in approximating scientific standards.

In the last part of Garfield's service as State Senator the foreshadowings of civil war found him ready in his place to take measures of precaution worthy of a great and a border State. His speech on the 24th of January, 1861, in behalf of a militia bill, for raising and equipping 6000 militia, is full of prevision of the coming struggle, and of the spirit which took him to the front when the storm burst. In reply to a reminder that at the preceding session he had opposed the bill as unnecessary, he frankly avowed that the change in the times had changed his attitude, and that the prevailing reason with him for the passage of the bill was the disturbing and threatening aspect of national affairs. And he met the issue with characteristic courage and frankness as to the protest against coercion, which, at that time, it will be remembered, was very prevalent at the North. He said : " If by coercion it is meant that the Federal Government shall declare and wage war against a State, then I have yet to see any man, Democrat or Republican, who is a coercionist. But, if by the term it is meant that the General Government shall enforce the laws, by whomsoever violated, shall protect the property and flag of the Union, shall punish traitors to the Constitution, be they ten men or ten thousand, then I am a coercionist. Every member of the Senate, by his vote on the eighth resolution, is a coercionist. Nine tenths of the people of Ohio are coercionists. Every man is a coercionist or a traitor."

In accordance with this speech was his report of a bill for the punishment of treason, which was a brief but lawyer-like presentation of the reasons for such a bill at such a time, with the frank avowal that " it is high time for Ohio to enact a law to meet treachery when it shall take the form of an overt act ; to provide that when her soldiers go forth to maintain the Union, there shall be no treacherous fire in the rear."

Doubtless his own instincts told him that he was sure to be in the front when the hour of conflict came, and like a good soldier, as well as a true patriot, his first act was to protect that rear.

It is perhaps impossible to give a better illustration of the manner in which Garfield's mind, from the period of his young manhood down to the present, has worked out in all directions in order to obtain its results, than is afforded by an incident of his service in the Ohio State Senate. He had heard from a distinguished and veteran lawyer that the true way to study the law, in his judgment, was for a student in any State to begin with a thorough reading of the statutes of the State. The beginner should familiarize himself with every effort to formulate the will of the State into law, and obtain his knowledge of legal principles from these individual illustrations of the attempt to apply principles of law to actual practice. This suggestion fell on Garfield's mind with great force; and as in his case there is seldom any long interval between receiving a decided impression and acting on it, he determined, not to study all the statutes of Ohio, but to go through the statutes in search of some definite information with regard to a particular subject, so that he could string his acquisitions on something and have some definite limitations of inquiry. It finally occurred to him that he would take up a single dollar and follow it on its travels through all the avenues of taxation into the treasury, and of expenditure out of it until it finally returned to the pocket of the taxpayer, from which it started. In the pursuit of the fortunes and adventures of this peculiar sort of a hero he found out just how the law of taxation was adjusted, through what officers it was attained, what were the powers of those officers with regard to taxation, what were their means of enforcing it, and how the money was expended, for what purposes, by what officers, exercising what authorities, and finally by virtue of what legislation, for what object, and through what means it returned to the source of its origin. In the course of this highly original method of studying law he came upon the startling discovery that, through the negligence of the framers of an amending act of legislation, the State for some few years preceding had been actually without any legal method of ascertaining legal weights and measures. So that the first result of his law studies in this direction was the necessity of repairing a very serious legislative blunder. The mental grasp and vigor and the comprehensive sweep of inquiry revealed in this single illustration shows one of the strongest and most peculiar characteristics of Garfield's intellectual methods, and reveals the secret of his constant preparedness for great emergencies, and of the athletic vigor and rich and abounding fulness of his mind.

But this is not all. Having thus, in the most unexpected manner, discovered the necessity for legislation to repair the results of legislative carelessness, he developed the same thoroughness in the discharge of his duty as legislator. He at once moved the appointment of a "select committee of one," which was the ordinary proceeding in such cases in the Ohio Legislature at that time, to examine and report on the whole system of weights and measures. The motion passed, and Garfield was appointed for that duty; and this report then submitted and published remains to this day the most exhaustive legislative report on the subject ever made in his State.

(Garfield to B. A. Hinsdale.)

HIRAM, May 3, 1858.

To B. A. HINSDALE, C. P. BOWLER, H. M. JAMES, ELIZABETH WOODWARD, CORDIE TILDEN, etc.

Dear Friends: Your very kind request that I should continue my lectures is received. I receive it as a pleasing testimonial of your confidence and respect, and would willingly accede to your request were it possible. For the present it is not possible, but I will endeavor to present a few more lectures on those topics before the close of the term, if circumstances will at all permit.

(Garfield to B. A. Hinsdale.)

HIRAM, January 10, 1859.

The Sunday after the debate I spoke in Solon on "Geology and Religion," and had an immense audience. Many Spiritualists were out. . . . The reports I hear from the debate are much more decisive than I expected to hear. I received a letter from Bro. Collins, of Chagrin, in which he says: "Since the smoke of the battle has partially cleared away, we begin to see more clearly the victory we have gained." I have yet to see the first man who claims that Denton explains his position; but they are jubilant over his attack on the Bible. What you suggest ought to be done I am about to undertake. I go there next Friday or Saturday evening and remain over Sunday. I am bound to carry the war into Carthage and pursue that miserable atheism to its hole.

Bro. Collins says that a few Christians are quite unsettled because Denton said, and I admitted, that the world had existed millions of years. I am astonished at the ignorance of the masses on these subjects. Hugh Miller has it right when he says that "the battle of the evidences must now be fought on the field of the natural sciences."

(Garfield to B. A. Hinsdale.)

COLUMBUS, January 15, 1861.

My heart and thoughts are full almost every moment with the terrible reality of our country's condition. We have learned so long to look upon the convulsions of European States as things wholly impossible here, that the people are slow in coming to the belief that there may be any breaking up of our institutions, but stern, awful certainty is fastening upon the hearts of men. I do not see any way, outside a miracle of God, which can avoid civil war with all its attendant horrors. Peaceable dissolution is utterly impossible. Indeed, I cannot say that I would wish it possible. To make the concessions demanded by the South would be hypocritical and sinful; they would neither be obeyed nor respected. I am inclined to believe that the sin of slavery is one of which it may be said that without the shedding of blood there is no remission. All that is left us as a State, or say as a company of Northern States, is to arm and prepare to defend ourselves and the Federal Government. I believe the doom of slavery is drawing near. Let war come, and the slaves will get the vague notion that it is waged for them, and a magazine will be lighted whose explosion will shake the whole fabric of slavery. Even if all this happen, I cannot yet abandon the belief that one government will rule this continent, and its people be one people.

Meantime, what will be the influence of the times on individuals? Your question is very interesting and suggestive. The doubt that hangs over the whole issue bears touching also. It may be the duty of our young men to join the army, or they may be drafted without their own consent. If neither of these things happen, there will be a period when old men and young will be electrified by the spirit of the times, and one result will be to make every individuality more marked and their opinions more decisive. I believe the times will be even more favorable than calm ones for the formation of strong and forcible characters.

Just at this time (have you observed the fact?) we have no man who has power to ride upon the storm and direct it. The hour has come, but not the man. The crisis will make many such. But I do not love to speculate on so painful a theme. . . . I am chosen to respond to a toast on the Union at the State Printers' Festival here next Thursday evening. It is a sad and difficult theme at this time.

(*Garfield to B. A. Hinsdale.*)

COLUMBUS, February 16, 1861.

Mr. Lincoln has come and gone. The rush of people to see him at every point on the route is astonishing. The reception here was plain and republican, but very impressive. He has been raising a respectable pair of dark-brown whiskers, which decidedly improve his looks, but no appendage can ever render him remarkable for beauty. On the whole, I am greatly pleased with him. He clearly shows his want of culture, and the marks of Western life; but there is no touch of affectation in him, and he has a peculiar power of impressing you that he is frank, direct, and thoroughly honest. His remarkable good sense, simple and condensed style of expression, and evident marks of indomitable will, give me great hopes for the country. And, after the long, dreary period of Buchanan's weakness and cowardly imbecility, the people will hail a strong and vigorous leader.

I have never brought my mind to consent to the dissolution peaceably. I know it may be asked, Is it not better to dissolve before war than after? But I ask, Is it not better to fight before dissolution than after? If the North and South cannot live in the Union without war, how can they live and expand as dissevered nations without it? May it not be an economy of bloodshed to tell the South that disunion is war, and that the United States Government will protect its property and execute its laws at all hazards?

I confess the great weight of the thought in your letter of the Plymouth and Jamestown ideas, and their vital and utter antagonism. This conflict may yet break the vase by the lustiness of its growth and strength, but the history of other nations gives me hope. Every government has periods when its strength and unity are tested. England has passed through the Wars of the Roses and the days of Cromwell. A monarchy is more easily overthrown than a republic, because its sovereignty is concentrated, and a single blow, if it be powerful enough, will crush it.

Burke, this is really a great time to live in, if any of us can only catch the cue of it. I am glad you write on these subjects, and you must blame yourself for having made me inflict on you the longest letter I have written to any one in more than a year.

(Garfield to B. A. Hinsdale.)
CLEVELAND, June 14, 1861.

The Lieutenant-Colonelcy of the Twenty-fourth Regiment has been tendered to me, and the Governor urges me to accept. I am greatly perplexed on the question of duty. I shall decide by Monday next.

(Garfield to B. A. Hinsdale.)
HIRAM, July 12, 1861.

I hardly knew myself, till the trial came, how much of a struggle it would cost me to give up going into the army. I found I had so fully interested myself in the War that I hardly felt it possible for me not to be a part of the movement. But the consideration that there were so many who could fill the office tendered to me and would covet the place, more than could do my work here perhaps, that I could not but feel it would be to some extent a reckless disregard of the good of others to accept. If there had been a scarcity of volunteers I should have accepted. The time may yet come when I shall feel it right and necessary to go; but I thought, on the whole, that time had not yet come.

CHAPTER VII.

GARFIELD, THE CITIZEN SOLDIER.

GENERAL GARFIELD's military record covers only a little over two years, but it was so full of peculiar incidents and achievements that it might well form the sole theme of a volume by some such accomplished military student and writer as General J. Watts DePeyster—"Anchor"—whose thorough appreciation of Thomas would qualify him largely for writing of a man who was after Thomas's own heart, as a soldier and as a man. But the plan and limits of this book forbid anything like a detailed account of Garfield, the soldier. The truth is, that there is so much of him that the faithful biographer is dismayed at the impossibility of even the most condensed review of his manifold and diverse achievements, in a single volume. For this reason I rejoice at the multiplicity of his biographers. There is material enough for each of them to work up into a valuable and interesting "Life."

But Garfield was only a soldier, as fifteen hundred thousand other patriotic citizens were soldiers. He was a living, and the ablest, representative of the class whom Quincy Ward has so nobly typified in enduring bronze, in the "Seventh Regiment" monument that adorns Central Park—the citizen soldier of ability, culture, enlightened patriotism, and readiness for any duty required by the State; who does not love nor follow fighting as a profession and for a livelihood, but who promptly adopts fighting as a duty, when the State can only be saved by the self-sacrifice of its citizens. Of this class Garfield was a great representative, in many respects. He was a splendid specimen of stalwart manhood; he had wonderful capacity to master any new science; he had won mastery over men and the art of commanding them, through purely intellectual and moral methods;

he had come to fill a large place of beneficent influence among his fellows, with widening opportunities daily opening before him in the parallel paths of duty and ambition, at home, and had much to sacrifice in seeking another field of action; his very success as a teacher and as a public man had so put him under bonds that he could not lightly accept even a field officer's commission, without that cool, deliberate, solemn sense of overpowering duty which ennobled and dignified the sacrifice he finally made, without a lingering qualm or compunction. At first he was inclined to refuse the commission offered him by Governor Dennison, who knew his powers and capacities, and had intrusted him with an important mission to the Governor of Indiana, from whom he obtained the loan of 5000 stand of arms for the swarming crowds of Ohio volunteers. But it was inevitable from the nature of the man that he should finally take the position where service involved the greatest danger and responsibility.

He set about raising recruits for the Forty-second Ohio Volunteers among the men who had been inspired by his patriotic appeals; among his students and constituents. It was mainly by his efforts that the regiment was filled up; to a good degree, by "Disciples," whose patriotism was consecrated by religious zeal. He was first commissioned, in August, 1861, as Lieutenant-Colonel, and soon promoted to be Colonel, to the universal satisfaction of his men. On the 17th of December, 1861, he took his well-drilled regiment from Camp Chase to the front. In the short time allowed him he had gained as much military knowledge as most of our volunteer colonels would have been able to acquire in years. Throwing the whole energy of his incomparable working powers into his new profession, he forgot everything but the one duty of transforming a mass of untrained patriots into a military machine. His success was as marvellous as it was natural. When he reported to General Buell, in Louisville, that able soldier and keen judge of men at once saw that his new reinforcement meant more than a fresh regiment of raw troops; it was the acquisition of a great brain, inspired with

COLONEL GARFIELD.

the highest moral courage and resolve, and sustained by the body of an athlete. The new colonel was not to be put on guard duty and subject to the drill and instructions of a West Point martinet ; he was to have free scope for his resources in an independent command, and to be given a task not laid down in the books, nor taught at West Point, that of clearing out of Eastern Kentucky a large force of rebels, who outnumbered his own command, from a vast tract of wild, difficult, and naturally defensible country. Nor did Buell tell him how to do this tremendous job. He asked Garfield to make his own plans, and when they were made and reported Buell saw at a glance that he had not mistaken Garfield's genius for fighting.

Let us take a brief glance at the big job which Buell intrusted to a fresh volunteer colonel, both in the planning and in the execution. Humphrey Marshall, obese but able, had invaded Eastern Kentucky with 5000 men ; had fortified a natural stronghold at Paintville, and was overrunning the whole region with small detachments, recruiting for the rebel forces, discouraging, persecuting, and robbing Union men. The area of his operations was larger than that of Massachusetts ; inhabited by about 100,000 poor and ignorant white men and a few thousand negroes. Marshall was acting more as a politician than as a soldier. His scattered but effective operations were part of a general plan to wrest Kentucky from the Union. To Garfield was assigned the formidable task of defeating a project that would have been well-nigh fatal to the Union cause, had it succeeded. To accomplish it he had only four regiments of infantry and 600 cavalry--in all about 2500 men—divided by large stretches of mountain country that was harried by guerillas and full of disloyal people. He had to send communications to his scattered forces, to insure a co-operative movement, and then run the risk of being defeated in detail before his troops could be massed ; and, after all that was safely accomplished, he had to attack twice his own force, strongly intrenched in commanding positions.

He succeeded in getting his dispatches carried to his separate forces, through his judgment in selecting a "native" scout, John Jordan, whose adventures, expedients, and hair-breadth escapes in getting through the guerilla bands have been the subject of a most romantic story. After a ride of a hundred miles, the fearless and keen-witted scout took to Colonel Cranor, at Paris, at midnight, an order to move his command, the 40th Ohio, 800 strong, to Prestonburg, and to transmit an order to Lieutenant-Colonel Woolford, at Stamford, to join him with three hundred cavalry. The scout encountered like perils on his return, but got safely to Garfield's tent, on the 6th of January, at midnight. So far all went well.

Garfield at once prepared to move his own column of 1400 men on Marshall's intrenched 5000—known to be that number from an intercepted letter which Garfield had in his pocket, and prudently kept secret. Before this Garfield had sent false scouts into Marshall's camp, who made him believe that the Union force was many times its actual size. There were three roads to Marshall's position. Garfield manœuvred so as to deceive the enemy as to his real line of attack, drove in Marshall's pickets along the river, and lured Marshall into detaching 1000 infantry and a battery to resist a supposed attack on Paintville. Then he is led to apprehend danger from another quarter, and transfers these troops to the western road. Two hours later the picket line on the centre is driven in, Marshall is confused, and Paintville abandoned.

On the 8th of January Marshall learns from a spy that Cranor, with 3300 men (!), is within half a day's march to the westward. On this the statesman-soldier gets utterly discouraged, breaks up his camp, abandons most of his supplies, and seeks safety in summary retreat. When Cranor's command arrives, it is utterly exhausted and unfit to move. But Garfield is full of fight, takes 1100 volunteers, 400 of them from Cranor's command, and on the 9th moves toward Prestonburg, sending his cavalry to harass the retreating enemy. Near Prestonburg he hears of Marshall three miles further up the stream, and sends back to Lieutenant-Colonel Sheldon, at Paintville, to bring up

all the available men, for a fight the next morning. All night
long he is getting full knowledge of Marshall's positions and
of the topography. Again he sends John Jordan into the
enemy's camp, to learn his exact position. Breaking camp at 4
A.M. he skirmishes aggressively and successfully till noon, when
he reaches the main line, and then fiercely charges 5000 men,
with twelve pieces of artillery, finely placed on a steep and
rocky hill, with his 1100 heroes, all animated by his own spirit,
but unprovided with a single cannon. It was a desperate hand-
to-hand fight for five hours, with charges and repulses, and
fresh charges, till at sunset the 5000 are about ready to swoop
down on, envelop, and destroy the heroic 1100, or what was
left of them. It was a straining crisis for Garfield, who was
praying for Cranor and Sheldon, as Wellington prayed for
" night or Blucher." At the same time a rebel major, from a
high elevation, saw the advancing blue-coats, and turned rapidly and gave the word. In a moment Marshall's demoralized
force was whirling away, in full retreat, and Garfield was the
victor in the most important small engagement of the war.
Pursuit of the flying foe was instant, and the cheers of the
" Boys in Blue" made the valley ring. Soon the reports of
the brief and brilliant campaign cheered loyal hearts that had
not felt the solace of victory since the disaster at Big Bethel.

Within ten days Thomas had routed Zollikoffer, and Kentucky
was saved to the Union.

Buell had virtually made Garfield a Brigadier, by giving him
a brigade to command, and had given him an independence of
planning and execution such as many corps commanders never
enjoyed. Lincoln gave him a Brigadier's commission, dated
on the day of the fight I have briefly sketched. But the fighting was the smallest part of his achievement. (See note.)

NOTE.—General Buell recognized both the brilliancy and importance of Garfield's operations in a general order, which contained the following :

" They have overcome formidable difficulties in the character of the country,
the condition of the roads, and the inclemency of the season ; and, without artillery, have in several engagements, terminating in the battle of Middle Creek
on the 10th inst. (January), driven the enemy from his intrenched positions and

Having cleared out Humphrey Marshall's forces, Garfield moved his command to Piketon, one hundred and twenty miles above the mouth of the Big Sandy, from which place he covered the whole region about with expeditions, breaking up rebel camps and perfecting his work. Finally, in that poor and wretched country, his supplies gave out, and, as usual, taking care of the most important matter himself, he went to the Ohio River for supplies, got them, seized a steamer, and loaded it. But there was an unprecedented freshet, navigation was very perilous, and no captain or pilot could be induced to take charge of the boat. Garfield at once availed himself of his canal-boat experience, took charge of the boat, stood at the helm for forty out of forty-eight hours, piloted the steamer through an untried channel full of dangerous eddies and wild currents, and saved his command from starvation.

In the middle of March he made the famous Pound Gap expedition, which deserves a separate chapter. Briefly, Marshall had retired to this narrow pass in the Cumberland Mountains, easily made impregnable, and a most admirable position from which to swoop down, with plundering parties, into Kentucky. No direct attack could have dislodged the 500 rebels left constantly on guard in the Gap, defended by breastworks and quartered in log huts. So Garfield made a sudden forced march of two days, reached the foot of the Gap at night, and the next morning made the rebels believe that he meant a direct attack, while he marched the most of his command through a narrow and tortuous mountain path, led by a faithful guide in a blinding snow storm, and suddenly pounced down on the astonished rebels in the rear of their fortifications. The surprise and the victory were complete ; the nest and stronghold of the plunderers was captured, a large number of them were killed, wounded, or taken prisoners, and Marshall's campaign was

forced him back into the mountains with the loss of a large amount of baggage and stores, and many of his men killed and captured. These services have called into action the highest qualities of a soldier—fortitude, perseverance, and courage."

brought to a ridiculous close, whereupon Garfield marched back
his command to Piketon, which he reached in four days from
his departure, having taken his command about a hundred miles
over a rough and difficult country. On his return he was ordered
to report to Buell in person. The latter was moving to join
Grant at Savannah, but Garfield overtook the army, was assigned to the command of a brigade, and took part in the second
day's fight at Shiloh. He was in all the operations in front
of Corinth, rebuilt and guarded the bridges on the Memphis
and Charleston Railroad, and did his share in erecting fortifications. He fell a victim to the malariousness of that region and
was prostrated during the months of July and August. When
he became convalescent he was ordered to Washington, where
his then recognized ability was needed on the Fitz John Porter
court-martial, the most impartially constituted, ablest, and
fairest court of the sort ever organized in this country. On its
adjournment, in January, 1863, he was sent to Rosecrans, who
was at first somewhat prejudiced against Garfield, regarding
him as a " political preacher." But a few days of intercourse
revealed the absurdity of this apprehension ; Rosecrans saw the
prodigious resources and frank manliness of Garfield, and made
him " Chief of Staff," in the full European sense of the word,
the first appointment of that sort made in our army. It was a
high, responsible, difficult position, only second to that of the
commander of the Army of the Cumberland. Such rapid promotion, won without pressure or influence, proceeding from
the recognition of demonstrated qualities by two such able soldiers as Buell and Rosecrans, the very opposites in temperament
and natural predilections, shows that Garfield only needed time
and opportunity to have become one of the great commanders
of the Union Army.

Acting as the counsellor, adviser and executive officer of
Rosecrans, Garfield's vigorous nature found active employment
in all the operations in Middle Tennessee. He was everywhere
felt. He grew daily in the confidence of Rosecrans. The crowning epoch of his service as Chief of Staff came with the great

battle of Chickamauga. The test of his moral courage and individuality had come before. Rosecrans, with his passion for completing all details, had delayed the advance which Stanton was impatiently urging. Finally Rosecrans asked the written opinions of his seventeen generals as to the advisability of an advance. Every one was opposed to it. But Garfield prepared a masterly paper, reviewing all the written opinions, analyzing their objections and answering them. His argument was irresistible. With such a paper on file Rosecrans could no longer delay, and the army moved, but it was commanded, for the most part, by officers who felt mortified over the powerlessness of their protests. One of them, General Crittenden, said to Garfield, as the army began to move :

"It is understood, sir, by the general officers of this army, that this movement is your work. I wish you to understand that it is a rash and fatal move, for which you will be held responsible."

Garfield resolutely took the responsibility that was thrown on him. Then followed the fight for the objective point of the advance, Chickamauga. That the battle was not a great and decisive Union victory, the best military critics now agree, was due to the misunderstanding of a hastily written order to General Wood, commanding the right wing. All the other orders were written by Garfield. This was written by Rosecrans himself. Obeying this fatal order too literally, Wood opened a gap in our line which the rebels quickly saw and entered, breaking the right from the centre and sweeping Rosecrans and his chief of staff with a mass of demoralized troops toward Chattanooga. Rosecrans thought that all was lost. Brave to desperation, so far as his own life was concerned, he was easily " stampeded " when his command seemed broken. But Garfield's resources rose with the emergency. He implored Rosecrans to let him seek the centre and make it a rallying point from which to prevent utter rout, by well-directed fighting. His instinct told him that Thomas, commanding the centre, was holding his own with stubborn sturdiness. With the help of " The Rock of

Chickamauga," the proud name won by Thomas on that trying day, he could prevent defeat from becoming utter rout and destruction. Rosecrans bid Garfield God-speed and hastened back to the river, to prepare for throwing up works at Chattanooga, behind which to save the swarming fugitives from the front.

Garfield, with a few orderlies, set out on the perilous ride, which was far more momentous and trying than Phil. Sheridan's famous "Ride to Winchester." Through the forest and over hills ; not knowing where the rebels picket lines might be ; an orderly wounded near him and his own horse shot under him ; with chaos in his rear and the unknown in front—rode Garfield, carrying in his head all the plans of battle and the latest news from the doubled-up right. His arrival at Thomas's headquarters was like the reinforcement of a corps. He aided Thomas by his intelligence and advice, and supplemented the old veteran's stanchness by a fresh and aggressive enthusiasm. He won nobly that day a Major-General's commission, and, what he valued far more, the heart of "Old Pap Thomas."

After Chickamauga, Garfield was sent to Washington, to reconcile the differences between Rosecrans and Stanton, and to state to Mr. Lincoln the condition and needs of the Army of the Cumberland, which he did with such clearness and vigor that Mr. Lincoln told him he had never before understood so perfectly the actual situation of any army in the field. In December, 1863, Garfield, very reluctantly, resigned his commission, in order to perform the duties to which his constituents had called him, nearly fifteen months before.

During all of his phenomenally active military career he had constantly kept up his literary culture. He took with him several small volumes of Harper's edition of the classics, and read them whenever he could steal a few moments of leisure. He read a little Latin every day. He rather settled down on Horace as his favorite, regarding him as "the most philosophic of the pagans." He also kept up his interest in all home matters, wrote often to his wife and to his friend Hinsdale, and in

all ways did what he could to nourish his affections, to retain
his culture, and to keep up a realizing sense of his citizenship, in
the broadest and highest sense of that noble word.

In his official report of operations in Middle Tennessee, General Rosecrans
pays Garfield the following high but deserved tribute :

"*All my staff merited my warm approbation for ability, zeal, and devotion
to duty : but I am sure they will not consider it invidious if I especially mention
Brigadier-General Garfield, ever active, prudent and sagacious. I feel much
indebted to him for both counsel and assistance in the administration of this
army. He possesses the energy and the instinct of a great commander.*"

General Rosecrans has lately given his opinion of General Garfield to a
California reporter. He said : "Garfield was a member of my military family
during the early part of the war. When he came to my headquarters I must
confess that I had a prejudice against him, as I understood he was a preacher
who had gone into politics, and a man of that cast I was naturally opposed to.
The more I saw of him the better I liked him, and finally I gave him his choice
of a brigade, or to become my chief of staff. He chose the latter. His views
were large, and he was possessed of a thoroughly comprehensive mind. Late in
the summer of 1863 he came to me one day, and said that he had been asked to
accept the Republican nomination for Congress from the Ashtabula (O.) district,
*and asked my advice as to whether he ought to accept it, and whether he could
do so honorably. I replied that I not only thought he could accept it with honor,
but that I deemed it to be his duty to do so.* 'The war is not yet over,' I said,
'nor will it be for some time to come. There will be many questions arising in
Congress which require not alone statesmanlike treatment, but the advice of
men having an acquaintance with military affairs will be needful ; and for that
and several other reasons, you would, I believe, do equally as good service to
this country in Congress as in the field.' I consider Garfield head and shoulders
above any of the men named before the convention, and far superior to any of
the political managers upon the floor."

(*Garfield to B. A. Hinsdale.*)

MURFREESBOROUGH, Tenn., Feb. 16, 1863.

My horses and part of my staff were delayed on the Cumberland by the
attack on Fort Donelson, and did not reach here until a few days ago. I have
been the guest of Gen. Rosecrans since my arrival, and I have never been more
acquainted with the interior life of any man in the same length of time in my
life. He wants me to stay with him as chief of staff instead of taking command of a division. I am greatly in doubt which to choose. He is one of the
few men in this war who enters upon all his duties with a deeply devout religious
feeling, and looks to God as the disposer of the victory. His very able report of
the late battle here ends with this fine sentence from the Catholic Church service, which he does not quote with any cant or affectation : "N——————
ne, non nobis, sed tuo nomine da gloriam."

(*Garfield to B. A. Hinsdale.*)

HEADQUARTERS, DEPARTMENT OF THE CUMBERLAND,
MURFREESBOROUGH, May 26, 1863.

Tell all those copperhead students for me that, were I there in charge of the school, I would not only dishonorably dismiss them from the school, but, if they remained in the place and persisted in their cowardly treason, I would apply to Gen. Burnside to enforceGeneral Order No. 38 in their cases. . . .

If these young traitors are in earnest they should go to the Southern Confederacy, where they can receive full sympathy. Tell them all that I will furnish them passes through our lines, where they can join Vallandigham and their other friends till such time as they can destroy us and come back home as conquerors of their own people, or can learn wisdom and obedience.

I know this apparently is a small matter, but it is only apparently small. We do not know what the developments of a month may bring forth, and, if such things be permitted at Hiram, they may anywhere. The Rebels catch up all such facts as sweet morsels of comfort, and every such influence lengthens the war and adds to the bloodshed.

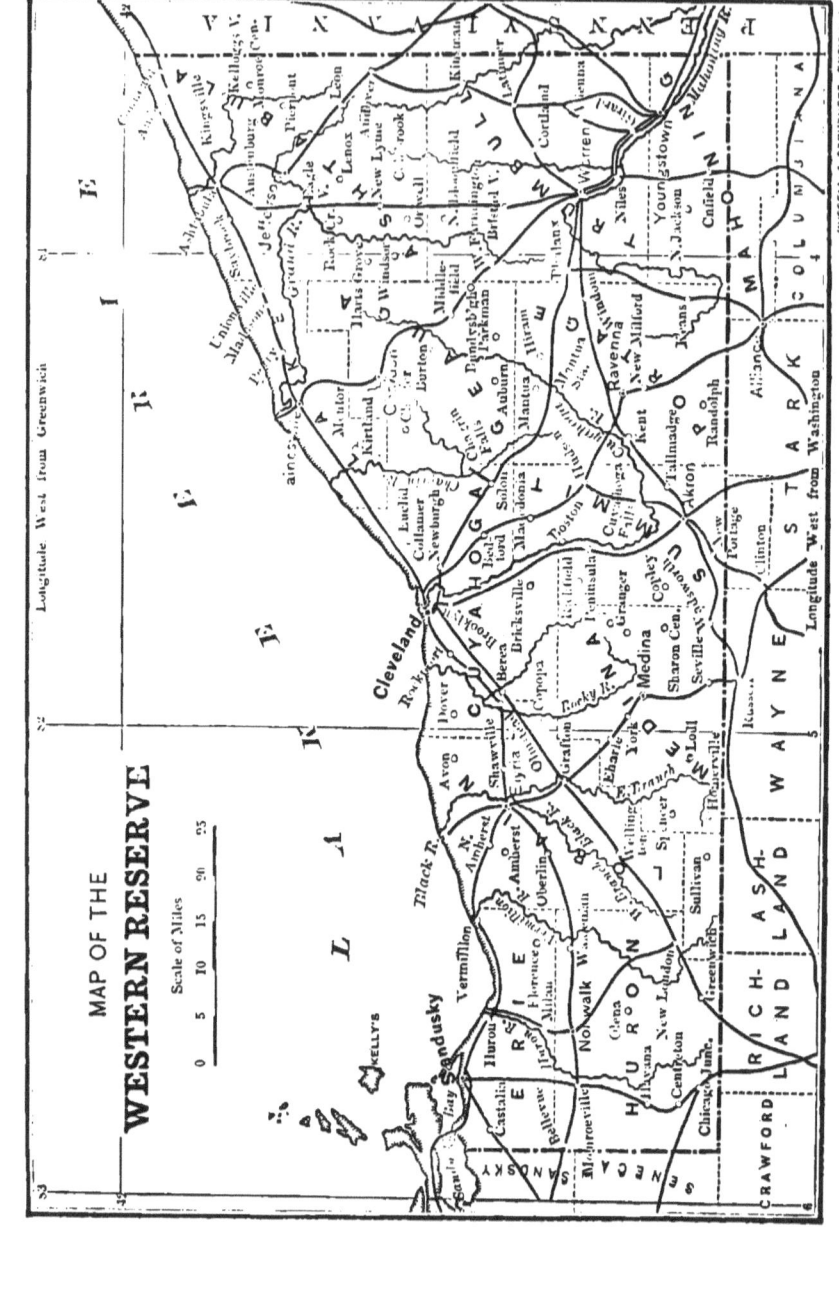

MAP OF THE
WESTERN RESERVE

Scale of Miles

0   5   10   15   20   25

HUSSEL & STRUTHERS, ENG'S Pub.

CHAPTER VIII.

WHILE it was clear to himself and to his military superiors that he had probably before him a brilliant military career, the Union men of the Nineteenth Congressional District of Ohio, without the slightest solicitation, effort, or co-operation on his part, nominated him to represent them in Congress. Such a nomination, from such a source, was the highest honor which any man, under the circumstances, could have received. It would have been a high compliment for any man, however long in the public service, to represent the constituency which had kept Joshua R. Giddings continuously in Congress for nearly a quarter of a century, while he was in the forefront of the fight against human slavery. To Garfield, then less than thirty-one years of age, it was an especially distinguished tribute. It came from those who knew him from the beginning—all his hardships, privations, struggles, conquests and characteristics. The "old Nineteenth"—hardest of all districts to please—took him to its heart, draped him with the mantle of Giddings, and adopted him as its leader.

NOTE.—In considering Garfield's Congressional career, amid the comparatively few home struggles it brought him, it is all important to realize what sort of constituency it has been that has nine times successively placed him in the seat of Joshua R. Giddings. To represent the tenement-house districts of New York for seventeen years is one thing. To represent a keenly intelligent, moral, and independent rural constituency in New England or New York for a long series of years, is quite another thing. Such a constituency as the latter has honored Garfield with its continuous verdicts of "Well done, good and faithful servant," with these essential differences, viz.: First, the "Western Reserve," in Northern Ohio, was settled by the manliest, most enterprising, vigorous and independent sons of New England and New York. They were the "picked men of peoples," as were the original settlers of the Eastern States. Bluff old "Ben" Wade once talked about a characteristic "Western Reserve" constituent, who,

And yet the acceptance of this proud position cost him many severe struggles between contending convictions of duty. He would not have left the army under any consideration, had he not, like most of our soldiers and statesmen at that time, firmly believed that the rebellion would be virtually subdued within the fifteen months that would elapse between that time and the opening of the Thirty-eighth Congress, for which he was nominated.

Even after he went into Congress, as the war was still doubtful, his impulse to resign and go back into the army was very strong. After the removal of Rosecrans, his former commander, General Thomas, who was a dear friend of Garfield, was very anxious to have him come back into the army, and tendered him in a private letter the command of an army corps if he would go there. Thomas had become the head of the whole Army of the Cumberland, and with such an invitation

"after he had thought and prayed over a political question for twenty-four hours, was pretty sure to be right, and could not be moved." It is needless to say that this old supporter of Wade is equally true and faithful to Garfield. All that sort of men in "the Reserve" are, so far as heard from. Then the "Western Reserve" has been the nursery of more free and independent political thinking and action than any other equal section of the Union. Political leaders are nowhere else held to such strict accountability. Even Giddings, when he grew careless, lost his grip and was supplanted. The average "Western Reserve" Republican makes his official representatives feel that the term "public servants" is full of meaning. He "keeps the run" of all they do and say. If they are scandalized he wants the object of scandal to clear his skirts completely. He has no use for tainted men. They must purge themselves wholly, or go back to private life. On the whole, the "Western Reserve" is a section by itself, and seems to deserve to be more generally understood, as to its geographical limits. For this reason I have had the accompanying map prepared. In that region of universal intelligence, high morality, intense political activity and searching inquiry, James A. Garfield was born, and has always had his residence. In the most critical part of that region is his Congressional district, which completely and thoroughly overhauled all the scandals that now survive on the lips of the intelligently malicious and in the darkened brains of the ignorant. His constituents tried him and pronounced the verdict, "Not guilty." That verdict has been repeated again and again, with increasing emphasis, and there is hardly an intelligent and honest boy in the whole "Reserve" who would not resent the slightest imputation on the man whom the "Reserve" almost idolizes and trusts to the uttermost, James A. Garfield.

Garfield's impulse to go back was almost irresistible. But on going to Mr. Lincoln with the matter, the President made a personal point with him. "In the first place," said he, "the Republican majority in Congress is very small, and there is great doubt whether or not we can carry our measures ; and in the next place, we are greatly lacking in men of military experience in the House to regulate the legislation about the army."

Fresh from active service in the army, whose duties, dangers, excitements and friendships he left with many pangs of sincerest and manliest regret, General Garfield began what proved to be a long career of honorable, industrious, and patriotic service of his country in Congress, at the opening of the Winter session, in 1863.

In looking over the debates and proceedings in the *Congressional Globe* for that important session we seem to be reading ancient history, so many men, then prominent and powerful in one or the other branch of Congress, have gone to join the silent majority. If we measure time by great national developments, changes, and revolutions, more than two ordinary generations have passed while General Garfield, in the House, has been gaining the few frosted hairs that tell the story of constant work, amid great and trying energies.

In order that younger readers may bring to mind the surroundings of the young and brilliant Major-General, as he first undertook the duties of statesmanship in the national councils, it may be well to revive, by the mention of their names, some at least of the strong men who left their impress on the legislation of the country.

Beginning with the Senate, and in the north-eastern corner of the Republic, Maine was strongly represented by William Pitt Fessenden and Lot M. Morrill—the former preternaturally acute and dialectically vigorous ; the latter sound, broad, strong, and sometimes eloquent. The humorist of the Senate, John P. Hale, of New Hampshire, was somewhat in his decadence. Vermont, fortunate, because judicious and faithful, in her choice of Senators, was represented by Solomon Foot and Jacob Collamer, both veterans, but both vigorous and formidable, especially on questions of law and of the Constitution. Charles Sumner and Henry Wilson were great powers, but in different ways, the former in debate, the latter in upholding the army as chairman of the Committee on Military Affairs. Anthony was even then Rhode Island's elegant and scholarly representative in the Senate, as he has been ever since. James Dixon and La Fayette S. Foster worthily upheld the influence of Connecticut. The ablest Southern Senator was Reverdy Johnson, of Maryland, who under Mr. Seward's instructions afterward laid the foundations for the Treaty of Washington, and never got due credit therefor. New York was represented by two non-speech-making Senators—War Governor E. D. Morgan, who did more to sustain the war in the Senate than many more talkative members, and the amiable and learned Judge Ira D. Harris. Cowan and Buckalew, of Pennsylvania, were great powers in their day, but are forgotten. Ohio was strongly represented by the intense and combative individuality of " Ben" Wade, and by John Sherman, already a veteran in the succession of honors won in the House and added to in the Senate ; as courageous as his great soldier brother and almost as ready in debate as Fessenden. From the West were such strong Senators as the venerable but fearless Henry S. Lane, of Indiana ; Zachariah Chandler, of Michigan ; Trumbull, of Illinois ; Howe and Doolittle, of Wisconsin ; Ramsey, of Minnesota, and Grimes, of Iowa. Many of these men belonged to the past, and did not know it. Some were the predestined victims of party divisions, and did not dream of their fate.

The House had in it, naturally, far more of the Present and the Future. Its then most fortunate and promising member was Schuyler Colfax, the universally popular Speaker. But there were three young members who were destined to a more lasting prominence. The senior of these, who had enjoyed previous service in the House, was Roscoe Conkling, already recognized by Congress and the country as a magnificent and convincing speaker. The other two of the triumvirate that was never formed were James G. Blaine and James A. Garfield. Only a year the senior of Garfield, Blaine was about to begin a career as brilliant as that of Henry Clay and the acquisition of a popularity unique in our political history. But in this Congress there were many members whose power was far greater than that of either of the trio, who may yet be as much compared as Clay, Webster, and Calhoun were in former days. In the first place there was Elihu B. Washburne, "the watch-dog of the treasury," the "father of the House"—courageous, practical, direct, and aggressive. Then there was Thaddeus Stevens, who was one of the very few men capable of driving his party associates—a character as unique as and far stronger than John Randolph; General Robert C. Schenck, fresh from the army, but a veteran in Congress, one of the ablest of practical statesmen; ex-Governor Boutwell, of Massachusetts; ex-Governor Fenton, of New York, a very influential member, especially on financial questions; Henry Winter Davis, the brilliant orator, of Maryland; Wm. B. Allison, since one of the soundest and most useful of Iowa's Senators; Henry L. Dawes, who fairly earned his promotion to the Senate, but who accomplished so much in the House that his best friends regret the transfer; John A. Bingham, one of the most famous speakers of his time; James E. English, of Connecticut, who did valiant and patriotic service as a War Democrat; George H. Pendleton, now Senator from Ohio and a most accomplished statesman, even in his early service in the House; Henry G. Stebbins, who was to make a speech sustaining Mr. Chase's financial policy that was unequalled for its salutary effect on public opinion; Samuel J. Randall, now Speaker; John A. Griswold, who was cheated out of the Governorship of New York by Tammany frauds; William Windom, one of the silent members who has grown steadily in power; James F. Wilson, who was destined to decline three successive offers of Cabinet positions by President Grant; Daniel W. Voorhees, of Indiana, now Senator; John A. Kasson, of Iowa, long our minister to Austria; Theodore M.

Pomeroy, of New York, afterward acting Speaker for a brief period ; Wm. R. Morrison, of Illinois, since a Democratic candidate for the Presidency ; Wm. S. Holman and George W. Julian, of Indiana, both able men, and Fernando Wood—these were all prominent members of the House. It will be seen that the House was a more trying arena for a young member like Garfield than the Senate would have been ; for the contests of the former—unsubdued and unmitigated by " the courtesy of the Senate"—were conducted by as ready and able a corps of debaters as ever sat in that body.

In looking over the debates of the opening session of this Congress the subjects of discussion and the arguments seem as remote from the present as the reports of the House of Commons in the days preceding the repeal of the Corn Laws would appear to the Englishman of the present. It is interesting to see in what spirit the representative of " the boys at the front," as Garfield was regarded by his associates, met the various and exciting questions which were growing out of the rebellion and of the war for its suppression. Naturally enough, we find that the first motion made by General Garfield in the House, on the 13th of January, 1864, was one asking unanimous consent for a resolution authorizing the printing of ten thousand extra copies of the official reports of his former chief, Major-General Rosecrans. On the next day, for the first time he took part in the debates, although his experience as State Senator in Ohio had been a sufficient preparation for the ordinary exigencies of debate and parliamentary discussion in the House. But neither at the beginning nor at any period during the whole of his career in Congress has he ever shown the slightest disposition to create artificial occasions for the display of speech-making in the *Globe* and *Record* reports. This particular debate, which took place on the 14th of January, was on a subject which naturally interested a man who, in the midst of active service in the field, had been revolving the great problems of dealing with the rebellion and rebels. His antagonist was one of the most formidable and readiest in the House, no less than Mr.

Samuel S. Cox, then hailing from Ohio, and inclined to mitigate the pains and penalties of rebellion as much as possible. The discussion was on a joint resolution in regard to the seizure and confiscation of the property of rebels. After considerable sparring, Mr. Cox asked General Garfield if he would break the Constitution to aggravate the punishment of the traitor, or to punish the innocent children of the rebels, to which artful question Garfield replied with his usual frank and manly ingenuousness and sincerity. Said he : " I would not break the Constitution at all, unless it should become necessary to overleap its barriers to save the Government and the Union." " But," added he, " I do not see that in this bill we do break the Constitution ;" and then said, in language which gives the key-note of his whole Congressional career up to the close of the last session, " If the gentleman can show me that it overleaps the Constitution I will vote against it with him, even though every member of my party votes for it ; that makes no difference to me."

General Garfield was not in haste to make what is called a " set speech." It required an actual occasion to call him out, as was the case when he spoke at some length, on the 31st of March, 1864.

The practical nature of his mind, his constitutional antagonism to corporate monopolies that neither serve the public nor allow that service to be performed by others, and his ability in the handling of financial questions, are well shown in this maiden speech. The very subject of the speech precluded the idea of a display of the peculiar sort of sentimentality, or patriotic verbiage, which is the staple of most speeches made " for Buncombe." It was directed against the impudence, insolence, and inefficiency of a corporation which, in its time, known as the Camden and Amboy monopoly, was the occasion of more well-directed imprecations than any other corporation of its size that ever existed. It was then proposed to establish a postal railroad route across the State of New Jersey, which was at that time generally known as the " State of Camden and

Amboy." About that time Governor Joel Parker had issued an astounding proclamation affirming the right of New Jersey as a "sovereign State" to protect and defend her "sovereignty," which, in this connection, meant the sovereignty of Camden and Amboy, as superior to that of the United States, so far as any efforts on the part of the United States to facilitate and cheapen the transmission of the mails, the troops and the military supplies of the Government, were concerned. In reply to Governor Parker's queer application of the phrase, "sovereign State," General Garfield remarked that, "Mr. Coleridge somewhere says that abstract definitions have done more harm in the world than plague and famine and war. I believe it! I believe that no man will ever be able to chronicle all the evils that have resulted to this nation from the abuse of the words 'sovereign' and 'sovereignty.'" Then he went on specifying the attributes of sovereignty, and said, among other things, " Sovereignty has the right to put ships on the ocean and the high seas. Should a ship set sail under the authority of New Jersey : it would be seized as a smuggler, forfeited and sold. Sovereignty has a flag, but, thank God, New Jersey has no flag ; Ohio has no flag. No loyal State fights under the 'Lone Star,' the 'Rattlesnake,' or the 'Palmetto Tree ;' no loyal State of this Union has any flag but the banner of beauty and glory, the flag of the Union. These are the indispensable elements of sovereignty. New Jersey has not one of them." In reply to the remark that New Jersey was a loyal State, and had sent her citizens into the army, he said : " They are not fighting for New Jersey, but for the Union, and when it is once restored, I don't believe these men will fight for the Camden and Amboy monopoly. Their hearts have been enlarged, and there are patriotic men of New Jersey, in the army and at home, who are groaning under this tyrannical monopoly, and they come here and ask us to strike off the shackles that bind them, and I hold it to be the high right and duty of this body to strike off their fetters and let them go free."

On the 26th of April, after the passage of several bills making large railroad grants, Mr. Washburne moved an adjournment, but General Garfield, in a very suggestive speech of three lines, contributed materially to the discussion by remarking that, " As there must be very little public land left after what we have done to-night, I hope gentlemen will be allowed to go through with it."

The great and almost appalling difficulty in attempting to give even a fair notion of the scope and nature of Garfield's work in the Thirty-eighth as in all the succeeding Congresses, arises from the wonderful versatility, activity, industry, and ability of the man. The more I have attempted to grasp and group the salient features of his immense work, the more the work has grown on me. It is impossible, within the limits of even half a dozen volumes to reproduce with any fulness his Congressional achievements. Take, for instance, a bare catalogue of his speeches or remarks from the index of the *Congressional Globe* for the first session of the Thirty-eighth Congress—1863 to 1865—viz. : " Deficiency bill," " Bill to continue bounties," " Revenue bill," " Confiscation," " Conscription bill," " Bill to revive grade of Lieutenant-General," " Resolution of thanks to General Thomas," " Sale of surplus gold," " Relating to enlistments in the Southern States," " Bill to drop unemployed general officers," " New Jersey railroad bill," " Currency bill," " The state of the Union, in reply to Mr. Long," " The expulsion of Mr. Long," " A correspondence with the Rebels," " Revenue bill (No. 405)," " The inquiry in relation to the Treasury Department," " The Army appropriation bill," " Pennsylvania war claims," " The bankrupt bill," " Repeal of fugitive slave law," " Bill to provide for claims for rebellion losses."

In subsequent Congresses the list of important subjects and bills discussed by Garfield grew much larger. It will be seen that it is only practicable to make anything like a fair presentation of what he did and said by selecting a few of the great subjects of debate, and grouping under separate heads the facts and the utterances which show the continuous development of his thinking and policy. And as it is Garfield's peculiar distinction that, although he came from the army into Congress, and easily obtained prominence and leadership in discussing military questions and those growing out of the war, he early began to give his best energies to the much more difficult and less sensational financial questions, I shall give the main part of the limited space allowed for reviewing his Congressional activities to the development of his views on the Currency question and the Tariff question. It will be seen that for over half a generation he has been fitting himself to be a wise leader of the American people, as regards two of the great and difficult problems which are now of all-commanding importance.

(*Garfield to B. A. Hinsdale.*)

WASHINGTON, December 11, 1865.

We have begun, as you have seen, and currents are beginning to develop their direction and strength only feebly as yet. We appear to have a very robust House, and indications thus far show it to be a very sound one. The message is much better than we expected, and I have hoped that we shall be able to work with the President. He sent for me day before yesterday, and we had a free conversation. I gave him the views of the earnest men North as I understand them, and we tried to look over the whole field of the difficulties before us.

They are indeed many and formidable. Sumner and Boutwell and some more of that class are full of alarm ; less, however, than when they first came. Some foolish men among us are all the while bristling up for fight, and seem to be anxious to make a rupture with Johnson. I think we should assume that he is with us, treat him kindly, without suspicion, and go on in a firm, calmly considered course, leaving him to make the breach with the party if any is made. I doubt if he would do it under such circumstances. The caucus resolution of Thad. Stevens was bad in some of its features. It was rushed through before the caucus was fully assembled, and, while it expresses the sentiment of the House in its main propositions, there are some points designed to antagonize with the President. It still lies over in the Senate, where it will be modified, if it passes at all.

(*Garfield to B. A. Hinsdale.*)

WASHINGTON, January 11, 1868.

This lengthy statement shows you why I passed over a day without writing you the usual letter. Having passed the time, I concluded to wait for your letter and write in response.

I hope we shall not allow ourselves to get in the habit of omitting or postponing these New Year's letters ; for they not only keep us advised of the progress, fortune, or misfortune of each other, but they link us to our best selves, and help us measure our own tendencies better than we can do in almost any other way. . . .

The longer I continue in Congress, the more numerous and difficult are the duties that press upon me. These increase in proportion to the increase of my circle of acquaintance, and, I suppose, increase my influence. I have sometimes almost despaired of keeping up with the work. The result is I get but little time for careful study ; still, I am doing some reading, and am making general advance in some studies.

I have accepted an invitation from the Social Science Association of Boston to prepare a paper on some financial theme at its next annual meeting in February at Albany, though I am beginning to fear shall not get the time to do all I desire in the way of preparation. I must do something to keep my thoughts fresh and growing. I dread nothing so much as falling into a rut and feeling myself becoming a fossil. . . .

We are boarding this winter, and, for that reason, not so pleasantly situated as we have been hitherto. We have rooms in one house and board in another.

(Garfield to A. B. Hinsdale.)

WASHINGTON, D. C., January 1, 1867.

I am less satisfied with the present aspect of public affairs than I have been for a long time. I find that many of the points and doctrines, both in general politics and finance, which I believe in and desire to see prevail are meeting with more opposition than heretofore, and are in imminent danger of being overborne by popular clamor and political passion.

In reference to reconstruction I feel that if the Southern States should adopt the Constitutional Amendments within a reasonable time, we are literally bound to admit them to representation ; if they reject it, then I am in favor of striking for impartial suffrage, though I see that such a course is beset with grave dangers.

Now Congress seems determined to rush forward without waiting even for the action of the Southern States, thus giving the South the impression, and our political enemies at home a pretext for saying that we were not in good faith when we offered the Constitutional Amendments. . . .

Really there seems to be a fear on the part of many of our friends that they may do some absurdly extravagant thing to prove their radicalism. I am trying to do two things : dare to be a radical and not be a fool. which, if I may judge by the exhibitions around me, is a matter of no small difficulty.

I wish the South would adopt the Constitutional Amendments soon and in good temper. Perhaps they will. . . .

Next, the Supreme Court has decided the case I argued last winter, and the papers are insanely calling for the abolition of the court. . . .

In reference to finance, I believe that the great remedy for our ills is an early return to specie payments, which can only be effected by the contraction of our paper currency. There is a huge clamor against both and in favor of expansion.

You know my views on the tariff. I am equally assaulted by the free traders and by the extreme tariff men. There is passion enough in the country to run a steam-engine in every village, and a spirit of proscription which keeps pace with the passion. My own course is chosen and it is quite probable it will throw me out of public life.

CHAPTER IX

THERE can be no better illustration of Garfield's character, nor of his peculiar ability to deal with great and difficult practical questions, than is afforded by his speeches on the various phases of the currency question. In this respect his record in many important features, is absolutely unique. He had no special instructions from his constituents to adopt the bold line of policy which he assumed so early in his Congressional career, while there were many members whose constituencies held such decided opinions, on one side or the other of the financial issues, that their election to Congress was a sufficient instruction and guide, for they were merely the mouthpieces of their constituents. But General Garfield, who rapidly came to be regarded as the representative, not merely of his own district, but of his State, was not elected originally on any such issue, and, as its proportions developed growing importance and gave rise to more exciting agitations, his own State was, at first, inclined to yield to the specious doctrines that, at one time or another, have prevailed in every civilized country. He could easily have evaded this issue, at the outset at least, if it had been in his nature to dodge any responsibility or duty. Instead of this, with a perfect intuition of the surpassing magnitude of the currency question, he began to prepare himself for its intelligent comprehension and discussion, by a course of study and investigation which very few of our statesmen have given to it. He exhausted all the histories of the various experiments of dealing with public debts and of furnishing paper currency that had been made in this country ; he followed the investigation back into English history, studying all the text-books ; he mastered the French language, so as to be able to read the untranslated French treatises on political economy and the currency, and sought in all directions, from the experience of all countries, whatever light or information could aid him in dealing with the financial situation in which we were left at the close of the war. Thus thoroughly grounded in knowledge, armed with authorities in defence of sound principles and practices, and inspired with an abiding horror of the countless evils brought on all classes of society by false systems of finance, he was ready to take the side of the currency question which, with such knowledge and such equipment, a man whose whole nature revolted at time-serving and cowardly expedients, and from dishonesty and injustice in every form, would naturally take. Through whatever mutations of public sentiment on these questions convulsed the people of his State ; through the darkest eras in our financial history ; under whatever pressure, and amid whatever suggestions of immediate party expediency, Garfield maintained a course so ingenuous, courageous and consistent in principle, that his most malign enemy might be safely challenged to explore his record at every point.

The speech which he made on the 16th of March, 1866, on the public debt and specie payments, covers substantially the whole ground of the great argument that was only concluded— if it is concluded—by the grand success of the Secretary of the Treasury in safely and easily accomplishing specie payments, after a protracted and ceaseless struggle, in which his sagacity, his tact, and his persistence have earned for him the right to be named and honored alongside of Washington's immortal Secretary, Alexander Hamilton. The speech was not a long one, but it was one that reached down to the foundations of a wise and honest system of finance. It was a good beginning for the series of arguments with which, from time to time, in Congress and out of Congress, General Garfield was always ready to meet every species, phase, and form of false systems of finance. The time of the delivery of this speech is important to be considered. It was long before the Republican Party had been brought—largely through the heroic firmness of two successive Presidents—Grant and Hayes—into substantial unity on the main features of the currency question. It is easy enough now for Republican statesmen to advocate what Garfield so courageously advocated fourteen years ago in time, and a generation ago in events. His speech was a strong plea for conferring upon the Secretary of the Treasury the advantage of that large discretion in funding the debt which subsequent experience has proved to be absolutely essential to the restoration of a sound financial system. It was, also, not only a courageous demand for an immediate adoption of a settled policy of return to specie payments, but a bold arraignment of the folly of continuing the stimulus of inflation, and a bold argument for contracting an irredeemable currency, so as to prepare the way for practical resumption. It was a plain, business-like, earnest speech, based on the highest financial authorities, illustrated by the financial disorders of the country, and abounding in epigrammatic exposure of the fallacies that were destined to yield a terrible fruitage of evil, because there were not more Garfields in Congress.

The House was not ready to support the judicious bill which Garfield advocated, and it was lost by a small majority, when he changed his vote so as to enable him to move to reconsider, which motion was sustained by the House, on the 19th, by a vote of 81 to 67, but before moving the previous question he made a few brief remarks, in which he took and returned the shots of such experienced and able debaters as Thaddeus Stevens, Judge Kelley and others, and strenuously maintained that the honest and heroic policy was the only safe, and would be the only successful, one to pursue. In reply to Judge Kelley, Garfield said, and he knew what he was saying : " There is no leading financier, no statesman now living, or one who has lived within the last half century, in whose opinions the gentleman can find any support. They all declare, as the Secretary of the Treasury declares, that the only honest basis of value is a currency redeemable in specie at the will of the holder. I am an advocate of paper money, but that paper

money must represent what it professes on its face.   I do not
wish to hold in my hands the printed lies of the Government ;
I want its promise to pay, signed by the high officers of the
Government, sacredly kept in the exact meaning of the words
of the promise.   Let us not continue to practise this conjuror's
art, by which sixty cents shall discharge a debt of one hundred
cents.   I do not want industry to be everywhere thus crippled
and wounded, and its wounds plastered over with legally-
authorized lies."

In concluding, he spoke with impassioned and prophetic
earnestness, and what he said may well go into his record, for
the circumstances under which, and the time in which, he
spoke, are essential elements in considering the character and
statesmanship of the speaker.   Said he :

" We leave it to the House to decide which alternative it will
choose.   Choose the one, and you float away into an unknown
sea of paper money that shall know no decrease until you take
just such a measure as is now proposed to bring us back to
solid values.   Delay the measure, and it will cost the country
dear.   Adopt it now, and with a little depression in business
and a little stringency in the money market, the worst will be
over, and we shall have reached the solid earth.   Sooner or
later such a measure must be adopted.   Go on as you are now
going on, and a financial crisis worse than that of 1837 will
bring us to the bottom.   I for one am not willing that my name
shall be linked to the fate of a paper currency.   I believe that
any party which commits itself to paper money will go down
amid the general disaster, covered with the curses of a ruined
people.

" Mr. Speaker, I remember that on the monument of Queen
Elizabeth, where her glories were recited and her honors
summed up, among the last and the highest, recorded as the
climax of her honors, was this—that she had restored the money
of her kingdom to its just value.   And when this House shall
have done its work, when it shall have brought back values to
their proper standard, it will deserve a monument."

A careful examination of Garfield's entire record on the
financial issues, and of the speeches made thereon both in and
out of Congress, will be found interesting to that large class of

practical business men who believe that it is of the utmost importance to have in the White House for the next four years an Executive as sound and judicious and immovable by clamors as we have had there for nearly four years.

Garfield did not wait for the development of public opinion, or even Republican opinion, in favor of the financial principles which have been found to be wise and essential, by the experience of all civilized countries. As we have seen, he took early ground on these questions, a ground broad enough on which to meet all the changing phases of discussion which have agitated the country. Faithful, conscientious, well-directed study had fortified his vigorous mind for the long struggle in which he was to take so conspicuous a part. The breadth of his views, his courageous enunciation of them, and his clear perception of the situation, are illustrated in more speeches than can even be referred to within the limits of this volume ; but a cursory view of a few of these speeches will sufficiently develop the results of Garfield's stalwart thinking on these subjects. In a speech which he delivered in the House on the 15th of May, 1868, he showed, to begin with, his appreciation of the fact that war times had gone, and that the more difficult problems of finance were looming up as the tests of the wisdom and patriotism of Congress and the people. No man realized these difficulties earlier or more thoroughly than he did, or how they should be met. Said he, at the outset of this speech :

" All the questions which spring out of the public debt, such as loans, bonds, tariffs, internal taxation, banking and currency, present greater difficulties than usually come within the scope of American politics. They cannot be settled by force of numbers nor carried by assault, as an army storms the works of an enemy. Patient examination of facts, careful study of principles which do not always appear on the surface, and which involve the most difficult problems of political economy, are the weapons of this warfare. No sentiment of national pride should make us unmindful of the fact that we have less experience in this direction than any other civilized nation. If this fact is not creditable to our intellectual reputation, it at least affords a proof that our people have not hitherto been crushed

under the burdens of taxation. We must consent to be instructed by the experience of other nations, and be willing to
approach these questions, not with the dogmatism of teachers,
but as seekers after truth.''

Whereupon he went into a review of the financial troubles
that were causing such distress in Great Britain and throughout
pretty much the whole Continent of Europe, as well as in the
United States. These difficulties he did not attribute to chance ;
that was not the nature or training of his naturally inductive
and logical mind He showed why and how the industrial
revolution caused by the return of two million of able-bodied
men, discharged from the Army and Navy to active production,
and the enormous inflation of currency and prices, had produced
widespread distress, discontent and disaster.   As usual, in discussing such questions, he availed himself of thorough previous
preparation, and made a startling exhibit from a table prepared
at his request, a year before, by Mr. Edward Young, in the revenue service, exhibiting a comparison of wholesale prices at New
York in December, 1865, and December 1866. The average
decline in this period in the prices of all commodities was at
least 10 per cent, and the distress which followed was inevitable. He then proceeded to illustrate the functions of currency, and the unavoidable dangers and disturbances caused by
an irredeemable paper currency, showed the relation of currency
to prices, and demonstrated that an inflated currency was the
sorest sort of taxation, whose chief burden fell on laboring
men. He went over the history of every panic in the country,
and showed the direct relation between the increase or decrease
of the currency and the financial condition of the country. His
illustrations of the nature and effect of the currency not regulated in its volume by supply and demand, and by constant
convertibility into coin, were such as could be easily understood
by any ordinary laborer. Said he. '' The dollar is the gauge
that measures every blow of the axe, every swing of the scythe,
every stroke of the hammer, every fagot that blazes on the
poor man's hearth, every fabric that clothes his children, every

mouthful that feeds their hunger. The word dollar is a sub-
stantive word, the fundamental condition of every contract, of
every sale, of every payment, whether from the national treasury
or from the stand of the apple-woman in the street. Now,
what is our situation ? There has been no day since the 25th
of February, 1862, when any man could tell what would be the
value of our legal currency dollar the next month or the next
day. Since that day we have substituted for a dollar the
printed promise of the Government to pay a dollar ; that
promise we have broken. We have suspended payment, and
have, by law, compelled the citizen to receive dishonored paper
instead of money."

He did not attempt to disguise or mitigate the stern fact that
the transition from irredeemable paper to a currency worth its
face in coin would be very trying and hard to bear. Consider
the fact that at the time this speech was delivered the most
promising and popular Democratic statesman from Ohio, and
who had been the candidate of his party for the office of Vice-
President, Mr. George H. Pendleton, was moving his own
party, and thousands of discontented Republicans who wanted
Congress to " make money easy," with his seductive proposition to cancel with greenbacks $1,500,000,000 of five-twenty
bonds. This was the measure, under the stress of whose probable popularity Mr. Pendleton was expecting the Presidential
nomination by his party. At this very time Garfield had the
courage, in his place in Congress, to utter these wholesome
words, which had nothing in them of immediate promise of
relief to the business troubles of his constituents. Said he :

" The simple fact in the case is that Congress went resolutely
and almost unanimously forward in the policy of gradual resumption of specie payments and a return to the old standard
of values, until the pressure of falling prices and hard times
began to be felt ; and now many are shrinking from the good
work they have undertaken, are turning back from the path
they so worthily resolved to pursue, and are asking Congress to
plunge the nation deeper than ever into the abyss from which
it has been struggling so earnestly to escape. Did any reflect-

ing man suppose it possible for the country to return from the high prices, the enormous expansion of business, debt, and speculation occasioned by the war, without much depression and temporary distress ? The wit of man has never devised a method by which the vast commercial and industrial interests of a nation can suffer the change from peace to war, and from war back to peace, without hardship and loss. The homely old maxim, ' What goes up must come down,' applies to our situation with peculiar force. The ' coming down ' is inevitable. Congress can only break the fall and mitigate its evils by adjusting the taxation, the expenditures, and the currency of the country, to the changed conditions of affairs. This it is our duty to do with a firm and steady hand.''

Going through the successive experiments of the country in paper money, and censuring strongly the error of Congress in 1866 in preventing a further contraction of the currency, he then submitted his own plan for restoring the paper dollar as the honest representative of its face value. His process was a very simple one : it was to direct and authorize the Secretary of the Treasury, on and after the first day of December, 1868, to pay gold coin for any legal-tender note that might be presented at the office of the Assistant Treasurer in New York, at the rate of one dollar in gold for $1.30 in legal-tender notes. On and after the first day of January, 1869, the rate should be one dollar in gold for $1.29 in legal-tender notes, and during each successive month the amount of legal-tender notes required for exchange for one dollar in gold should be one cent less than was required for the preceding month, until the exchange should be one dollar in gold for one dollar in legal-tender notes—dollar for dollar. But there was a proviso that nothing in the act should be so construed as to authorize the retirement or cancellation of any legal-tender notes of the United States. There were one hundred million dollars of gold in the Treasury at that time, which would have been sufficient, with the half million a day received from customs, to carry out the provisions of this bill. This was not in the nature of a new experiment, for it was tried in England under an act passed, in 1819, under the leadership of Robert Peel, which reached resumption in the same gradual manner. The English act at once gave a fixed value to paper money, and business so readily adjusted itself in anticipation, that specie payments were resumed two years before the time fixed by the law.

Garfield, with his sublime confidence in the intelligence, integrity and courage of the American people, believed that if Congress would do something definite to restore an honest currency, the people would soon adjust themselves to the evils of the transition, and reminded Congress that after the first defeat at Bull Run many officers of the Government thought it not safe to let the people know at once the whole extent of the disaster, but that the news should be broken gently, that the nation might be better able to bear it ; but " long before the close of the war it was found that the Cabinet and Congress and all the officers of the United States needed for themselves to draw hope and courage from the great heart of the people. It was only necessary for the nation to know the extent of the danger, the depth of the need, and its courage, faith, and endurance were always equal to the necessity."

On the 15th of July, following the speech on the currency, Garfield made a reply to General Butler and Mr. Frederick A. Pike, who had been ventilating some rather specious fallacies with regard to the taxation of United States bonds, a theme which, from its very nature, has been the favorite subject of demagogues who pay the American people the poor compliment of believing that they can be induced to sacrifice the national credit, which is the foundation of all credit and prosperity, and the common interest of the people in order to strike, or to appear to strike, at the class known as the " bloated bondholders," which designation is as false and deceptive as the arguments that have been called out by a supposed prejudice. Garfield first riddled the argument made by Mr. Pike on the basis of misconceptions and perversions of English legislation on the subject, and, of course, was ready with the facts and authorities that rendered his exposure scathing and effectual. There was a running debate between Mr. Pike and Mr. Butler, on one

side, and Garfield, on the other, in which Garfield met his antagonists at every point, showed superior knowledge of facts,
dates, statutes and events, and strengthened his argument by
an exposure of the fallacies of his opponents, and by showing
his own superior mastery of the whole subject.   This was a debate in which mere cramming on an unprepared mind, however
vigorous and ready, would have been of no avail.   It required
thorough, extensive and well-digested knowledge and thinking,
as the condition of success in such an encounter.   After resisting successfuly every onset of his antagonists, he showed the
immediate evil effects of taxing the bonds in a merely financial
point of view, illustrating it by the fact, which was peculiarly
effective in Butler's case, that while the Massachusetts five per
cent gold bonds were quoted in London at 89 and 90, the ten-
forty gold-bearing 5 per cent United States bonds were at 68¼,
merely because Massachusetts had not only kept faith through all
the vicissitudes of the war, but had not sought technical
grounds of escape from her obligations.   But rising from the immediately pecuniary point of view, he honored his party by expressing his pride in it, because, '' having saved the life of the
nation by its policy, it now declares its unalterable purpose to
save by its truth and devotion, what is still more precious, the
faith and honor of the nation.''   He quoted the declaration
made by the old English gentleman in the days of Charles
II., as one that does honor to human nature.   '' He said he
was willing at any time to give his life for the good of his
country, but he would not do a mean thing to save his country
from ruin.''   '' So sir,'' said Garfield, '' ought a citizen to feel
in regard to our financial affairs.   The people of the United
States can afford to make any sacrifice for their country, and
the history of the last war is proof of their willingness ; but the
humblest citizen cannot afford to do a mean or a dishonorable
thing, to save even this glorious Republic.''

Two of Garfield's speeches on the currency question are sufficiently representative of his latest views to afford the material for illustrating the continuous and consistent workings of his mind on this vitally important subject.

The first of these speeches was delivered in the House on the 16th of November, 1877, on the House bill for the repeal of the third section of the act entitled "An Act for the Resumption of Specie Payments." At the very outset of this, he reiterated the assertion he had made frequently before, that the contest for a sound currency was not a new one, nor the arguments for a vicious currency peculiar American inventions. Said he : "Hardly a proposition has been heard on either side which was not made one hundred and eighty years ago in England, and almost a hundred years ago in the United States." With his usual intellectual habit of combating partial truths or passing errors of popular judgment by larger inductions from facts and from history, he urged that it "was only when long spaces of time are considered that we find at last that level of public opinion which we call the general judgment of mankind ; and from the turbulent ebb and flow of the public opinion of to-day he appealed to that settled judgment of mankind on the sub-ject-matter of debate." Going back to the period of universal prosperity which prevailed just before the war, he recalled the fact that :

"If any one thing was settled above all other questions of financial policy in the American mind at that time, it was this : that the only sound, safe, trustworthy standard of value was coin of standard weight and fineness or a paper currency con-vertible into coin at the will of the holder. That was and had been for several generations the almost unanimous opinion of the American people. It was true there was here and there a theorist dreaming of the philosopher's stone, dreaming of a time when paper money, which he worshipped as a kind of fetich, would be crowned as a god, but those dreamers were so few in number that they made no ripple on the current of public thought, and their theories formed no part of public opinion. The opinion of 1860 to 1861 was the aggregated result of the opinions of all the foremost Americans who have left their record upon this subject.

"No man," said he, "ever sat in the seat of Washington as President of the United States who has left on record any word that favors inconvertible paper money as a safe standard of value. Every President who has left a record on the subject has spoken without qualification in favor of the doctrine I have announced. No man ever sat in the chair of the Secretary of the Treasury of the United States who, if he has spoken at all on the subject, has not left on record an opinion equally strong, from Hamilton down to the days of the distinguished father of my colleague [Mr. Ewing], and to the present moment. The general judgment of all men who deserve to be called the leaders of American thought, ought to be considered worth something in an American House of Representatives on the discussion of a great topic like this."

Then he briefly developed the reasons for the great convulsions of public opinion on this before-settled subject, which were occasioned by the peculiar circumstances of the war, and reminded the House that

" Only twelve years have passed—(for as late as 1865 this House, with but six dissenting votes, resolved again to stand by the old ways and bring the country to sound money)—only twelve years have passed, and what do we find ? We find a group of theorists and doctrinaires who look upon the wisdom of the fathers as foolishness. We find some who advocate what they call ' absolute money ' ; who declare that a piece of paper stamped a ' dollar ' is a dollar ; that gold and silver are a part of the barbarism of the past, which ought to be forever abandoned. We hear them declaring that resumption is a delusion and a snare. We hear them declaring that the eras of prosperity are the eras of paper money. They point us to all times of inflation as periods of blessing to the people and prosperity to business ; and they ask us no more to vex their ears with any allusion to the old standard, the money of the Constitution. Let the wild swarm of financial literature that has sprung into life within the last twelve years witness how widely and how far we have drifted. We have lost our old moorings, have thrown overboard our old compass ; we sail by alien stars, looking not for the haven, but are afloat on a harborless sea."

In combating the financial fallacies of Mr. Buckner, Mr. Harrison, Judge Kelley and others, he showed his thorough familiarity with the financial experiments in the way of resumption in France, England, and Germany, and defended as a blessing the resumption act of 1819 in England, showing that the distresses suffered by that country from 1821 to 1826 did not arise from the resumption of specie payments, but from other causes, the two especial causes being the corn laws and over speculation. Then he riddled the fallacies of those who assume that legislation in favor of the immediate interests of the debtor class is for the benefit of laboring men. His argument on this theme is one so well adapted to popularize sound doctrine of finance that it is entitled to be quoted from at some length, to wit:

" As a matter of fact, the poor man, the laboring man, cannot get heavily in debt. He has not the security to offer. Men lend their money on security ; and, in the very nature of the case, poor men can borrow but little. What, then, do poor men do with their small earnings ? When a man has earned, out of his hard work, a hundred dollars more than he needs for current expenses, he reasons thus : ' I cannot go into business with a hundred dollars ; I cannot embark in trade ; but, as I work, I want my money to work.' And so he puts his small gains where they will earn something. He lends his money to a wealthier neighbor, or puts it into a savings bank. There were in the United States, on the first of November, 1876, forty-four hundred and seventy-five savings banks and private banks of deposit ; and their deposits amounted to $1,377,-000,000, almost three fourths the amount of our national debt. Over two and a half millions of the citizens of the United States were depositors. In some States the deposits did not average more than $250 each. The great mass of the depositors are men and women of small means—laborers, widows, and orphans. They are the lenders of this enormous aggregate. The savings banks, as their agents, lend it—to whom ? Not to the laboring poor, but to the business men who wish to enlarge their business beyond their capital. Speculators sometimes borrow it. But in the main, well-to-do business men borrow these hoardings. Thus the poor lend to the rich.

" Gentlemen assail the bondholders of the country as the rich men who oppress the poor. Do they know how vast an amount of the public securities are held by the poor people ? I took occasion, a few years since, to ask the officers of a bank in one of the counties of my district, a rural district, to show me the number of holders and amounts held of United States bonds on which they collected the interest.   The total amount was $416,000.   And how many people held them ?   One hundred and ninety-six.   Of these, just eight men held from $15,000 to $20,000 each ; the other one hundred and eighty-eight ranged from $50 up to $2500.   I found in that list, fifteen orphan children and sixty widows, who had a little left them from their fathers' or husbands' estates, and had made the nation their guardian.   And I found one hundred and twenty-one laborers, mechanics, ministers, men of slender means, who had saved their earnings and put them in the hands of the United States, that they might be safe.   And they were the ' bloated bond-holders,' against whom so much eloquence is fulminated in this House.

" There is another way in which poor men dispose of their money.   A man says, I can keep my wife and babies from starving while I live and have my health ; but if I die they may be compelled to go over the hill to the poor-house ; and, agonized by that thought, he saves of his hard earnings enough to take out and keep alive a small life-insurance policy, so that, if he dies, there may be something left, provided the insurance company to which he intrusts his money is honest enough to keep its pledges.   And how many men do you think have done that in the United States ?   I do not know the number for the whole country ; but I do know this, that from a late report of the insurance commissioners of the State of New York, it appears that the companies doing business in that State had 774,625 policies in force, and the face value of these policies was $1,922,000,000.   I find, by looking over the returns, that in my State there are 55,000 policies outstanding ; in Pennsylvania, 74,000 ; in Maine 17,000 ; in Maryland, 25,000, and in the State of New York, 160,090.   There are, of course, some rich men insured in these companies : but the majority are poor people ; for the policies do not average more than $2,200 each. What is done with the assets of these companies, which amount to $445,000,000 ?   They are loaned out.   Here again the creditor class is the poor, and the insurance companies are the agents of the poor to lend their money for them.   It would be dishonorable for Congress to legislate either for the debtor class or for the creditor class alone.   We ought to legislate for the whole country.   But when gentlemen attempt to manufacture sentiment against the resumption act, by saying it will help the rich and hurt the poor, they are overwhelmingly answered by the facts.

" Suppose you undo the work that Congress has attempted—

to resume specie payment—what will result? You will depreciate the value of the greenback. Suppose it falls ten cents on the dollar. You will have destroyed ten per cent of the value of every deposit in the savings banks, ten per cent of every life-insurance policy and fire-insurance policy, of every pension to the soldier, and of every day's wages of every laborer in the nation.

" In the census of 1870 it was estimated that on any given day there were $120,000,000 due to the laborers for their unpaid wages. That is a small estimate. Let the greenback dollar come down 10 per cent and you take $12,000,000 from the men who have already earned it. In the name of every interest connected with the poor man, I denounce this effort to prevent resumption. Daniel Webster never uttered a greater truth in finance than when he said that of all contrivances to cheat the laboring classes of mankind none was so effective as that which deluded them with irredeemable paper money. The rich can take care of themselves ; but the dead-weight of all the fluctuation and loss falls ultimately on the poor man who has only his day's work to sell.

" I admit that in the passage from peace to war there was a great loss to one class of the community, to the creditors ; and in the return to the basis of peace some loss to debtors was inevitable. This injustice was unavoidable. The loss and gain did not fall upon the same people. The evil could not be balanced nor adjusted. The debtors of 1862–65 are not the debtors of 1877. The most competent judges declare that the average life of private debts in the United States is not more than two years. Of course, obligations may be renewed, but the average life of private debts in this country is not more than two years. Now, we have already gone two years on the road to resumption, and the country has been adjusting itself to the new condition of things. The people have expected resumption, and have already discounted most of the hardships and sufferings incident to the change. The agony is almost over ; and if we now embark again upon the open sea, we lose all that has been gained and plunge the country into the necessity of trying once more the same boisterous ocean, with all its perils and uncertainties. I speak the deepest convictions of my mind and heart when I say that, should this resumption act be repealed and no effectual substitute be put in its place, the day is not far distant when all of us, looking back on this time from the depth of the evils which are sure to result, will regret, with all our power to regret, the day when we again let loose the dangers of inflation upon the country."

His own position on the subject of greenbacks is perfectly delineated in this paragraph of the same speech :

" We who defend the resumption act propose not to destroy the greenback but to dignify it, to glorify it. The law that we defend does not destroy it, but preserves its volume at $300,000 000, makes it equal to and convertible into coin. I admit that the law is not entirely free from ambiguity. But the Secretary of the Treasury, who has the execution of the law, declares that section 3579 of the Revised Statutes is in full force, namely :

" ' When any United States notes are returned to the Treasury, they may be reissued, from time to time, as the exigencies of the public interest may require.'

" Although I do not believe in keeping greenbacks as a permanent currency in the United States, although I do not myself believe in the Government becoming a permanent banker, yet I am willing for one, that, in order to prevent the shock to business which gentlemen fear, the $300,000,000 of greenbacks shall be allowed to remain in circulation at par, as long as the wants of trade show manifestly that they are needed."

In 1878 he was invited to make a speech in behalf of honest money in Faneuil Hall. This argument was so admirably adapted to meet the ingenious fallacies with which General Butler at that time was agitating the laboring classes in Massachusetts that it was printed in a neat pamphlet, together with a refutation of some of General Butler's recent misstatements on the currency question, by Mr. William Endicott, Jr., a document of extraordinary incisiveness and vigor ; and the speech and the letter together were universally circulated in Massachusetts, and produced a powerful effect on the then pending campaign. The introduction of this speech stated a general truth, which is just as applicable to the present campaign as it was to that of 1878 in Massachusetts. Said he :

" Real political issues cannot be manufactured by the leaders of political parties, and real ones cannot be evaded by political parties. [Applause.] The real political issues of the day declare themselves and come out of the depths of that deep which we call public opinion. The nation has a life of its own as distinctly defined as the life of an individual. The signs of

its growth and the periods of its development make the issues
declare themselves ; and the man or the political party that
does not discover them, has not learned that character of the
nation's life. Now, as heretofore, attempts are being made to
create political issues. They will all fail. [Applause.] One
group of politicians is seeking to find in the reminiscences of
the Presidential Election of 1876 the political issues of this
year. They cannot raise the dead. [Applause.] Others believe they can make State issues the chief topic of this year.
But you are about to create the Forty-sixth Congress, and give
it the impulse of your aspirations and opinions. The issues are
too large for the boundaries of any State. They declare themselves and challenge you to meet them."

Then, reviewing the successive dominant issues that had controlled the politics of the country since the firing on Sumter, he
was brought to that which he regarded as the fourth and the
last, and this issue still remains. It is that of the finances, as to
which he began by recalling the heroic period of the war, when
the exigencies of the Government were met by voluntary loans
and cheerfully-paid taxes by the people. Then he recurred to the
forced loan required by the exigencies of the war, in the shape
of the issue of irredeemable greenbacks. Referring to Lincoln's recommendation of the organization of national banks,
the final step in broadening our financial ability to meet extraordinary emergencies, he said that, great as were the tasks
undertaken by him and his associates, they did not claim wisdom enough "to regulate the inexorable laws of value and of
trade ; and that brought him face to face with the most popular of all the financial fallacies that have afflicted the country—
that of a currency issued by the Government to meet "the
wants of trade," as to which there is no better definition of
what is practicable and impracticable than Garfield gave in the
following passage :

"Is there any man in America wise enough to measure the
wants of trade and tell just how much currency is needed ?
Who forgets the infinite difficulty to find a man with brain
enough and resource enough to feed an army and to clothe it
and to house it ? Its house is of the rudest—only a piece of

cloth ; its clothing is of the simplest, and its food is a definitely-prescribed ration. But it is considered worthy of the glory of one glorious life to be able to feed and clothe and house an army of a hundred thousand men. [Applause.] Now, fellow-citizens, suppose somebody should offer to take the contract of feeding, clothing, and housing Boston and its suburbs, including half a million of men. Remember that all nations are placed under contribution to supply the city of Boston : every clime sends its supplies ; every portion of our own land, all our roads of transportation are looked to to supply the tables, houses, and the clothing of this community. Do you suppose any man in the world is wise enough, is skilful enough to supply the wants of this population, in a circle of twenty miles around Boston ? Now multiply that by a hundred, and get the population of the United States. Is there any man in this world wise enough, is there any congress in the world wise enough, to measure the wants of 45,000,000 of people and tell just what is needed for their supplies ? [Applause.] No, fellow-citizens ; but there is something behind legislation that does—does all so quietly and so perfectly. Every man seeking his own interest, millions of men acting for themselves, acting under the great law of supply and demand, the laws of trade, feed Boston, feed the United States, clothe, house, and transport the nation and carry on all its mighty works in perfect harmony and with ease, because the higher law above legislation—the law of demand and supply—pervading and covering all, settles that great question, far above the wisdom of one man, or a thousand men to determine it.

"And now, one of the great means by which all these mighty transactions are carried on is the currency that circulates and exchanges values among all these people. Every transaction, abroad or at home, of the eleven hundred million dollars' worth of trade we have with Europe and Asia, of the ten times greater value of our home trade, is carried on and regulated by that great pervading law, higher than legislation and wiser than the wisdom of men. To that law we must conform our currency system, or it will perish. Any congress or any party that tells you they are going to vote a sufficient supply of currency for the wants of trade, tells you they are going to do an impossibility. [Applause.] It cannot be. [Applause.] And it was for that reason that the men of 1862 and 1864 established a system of banking to be diffused throughout the Republic, which was held to the strictest accountability for the character of its securities to the depositors and bill-holders ;

but the volume of its circulation was to depend, not upon the uncertain will and more uncertain wisdom of Congress, but upon the law of demand and supply. Bound always to redeem their notes in greenbacks or coin, their own interests and safety would lead them to enlarge or contract that volume, as the tide of business should ebb or flow.

"Such was the origin, and such the character of the financial system established by the men who guided the war for the Union." [Applause.]

He then proceeded to show what the Government had done to relieve the people of the terrible burdens of debt that were necessarily incurred in the salvation of the Union. He showed that in exact proportion as the nation had observed good faith to its creditors had prosperity come in and grown, and had the burdens of taxation been diminished.

"All the finance of the period," said he, "is summed up in the present overmastering duty to resume specie payments and keep the promise. And here," he added, "I meet the chief debate on the issues of this year. This proposition is met throughout America by a storm of indignant opposition, and we stand to-day in the very teeth of a storm that we must either meet in honor or be swept away by. On that ground we meet our antagonists, and challenge them to the combat."

Then he tackled squarely the fiat money delusion in all its phases ; riddled completely General Butler's scheme of a non-exportable and inconvertible fiat money ; brought to view the purposes of the Fathers of the Constitution in limiting the powers of Congress as to fixing the standards of value ; defined the nature and use of paper money, and ridiculed the idea that Congress could increase the wealth or the comforts of the nation by any amount of issues of irredeemable paper.

Some of his illustrations were peculiarly applicable to the most ordinary understanding. Said he :

"Suppose the farmers in your agricultural districts should say, We are in distress ; our great need is more land ; if we had more land we would get on better with our affairs ; and now let us get a law through the General Court that every man may

surrender up his deed and have a new one written, with two
acres for every one. [Laughter and applause.] When you can
enlarge your farm by changing the figures in your deeds [laugh-
ter] ; when your dairymaid can make more butter and cheese
by watering her milk [applause] ; when you can have more
cloth by decreasing your yardstick one half [laughter] ; when
you can sell more tons of merchandise by shortening your pound
one half—then, and not until then, you can increase the value
of your property or labor by decreasing your standard of
values." [Applause].

In the same line of illustration was what he said of the effect
of an inflated currency of uncertain value :

"An uncertain currency that goes up and down, hits the
laborer, and hits him hard. [Prolonged applause.] It helps
him last, and hurts him first. [Applause.] Therefore, of all
men in America, the man who should demand the resumption
of specie payment, and the fixing and making certain the
standard of value, is the laboring man, who can only suffer
when that standard is departed from. [Applause.] The capitalist can take advantage of the market ; if he has anything to
buy, he is not compelled to buy it all to-day; he can wait until
the market price is low, and buy at advantage. If he has anything to sell, he is not compelled to sell it to-day, but can wait
until the price is up, and sell it at the best. Not so with the
laboring man, who goes to market with just one thing to sell,
and that is his day's work. He must sell it to-day, at the
price to-day, or it will be wholly lost. [Applause.] What he
needs to buy he must buy now, when necessity compels him.
He cannot, like the capitalist, dodge the call of inflation or
contraction, but pays the day's standard of value ; and so it
strikes him both ways, and strikes him hard. [Applause.]
What, therefore, the laboring man needs, is this, that when he
has earned his money, he shall get it in a currency that will
keep over night." [Prolonged applause and cheers.]

Quoting in a subsequent part of this speech the prediction of
Macaulay made in 1857, that the conflicts between capital and
labor would ultimately destroy our institutions, he said that
with all his soul he repelled that prophecy as false ; and the
reasons which he gave for his faith were admirably calculated
to lead discontented men who were clutching at specious and

temporary measures for relief from business misfortunes to broader views of the nature and blessedness of our institutions. Said he :

"My first answer is this : No man who has not lived among us can understand one thing about our institutions ; no man who has been born and reared under monarchical governments can understand the vast difference between theirs and ours. How is it in monarchical governments? Their society is one series of caste upon caste. Down at the bottom, like the granite rocks in the crust of the earth, lie the great body of laboring men.   An Englishman told me not long ago that in twenty-five years of careful study of the agricultural class of England, he had never known one who was born and reared in the ranks of farm laborers that rose above his class and became a well-to-do citizen.   That is a most terrible sentence, that three millions of people should lie at the bottom of society, with no power to rise.   Above them the gentry, the hereditary capitalist ; above them, the nobility ; above them, the royalty ; and, crowning all, the sovereign—all impassable barriers of caste.

"No man born under such institutions can understand the mighty difference between them and us in this country.   Thank God, and thank the fathers of the Republic who made, and the men who carried out the promises of the Declaration, that in this country there are no classes, fixed and impassable.   Here society is not fixed in horizontal layers, like the crust of the earth, but, as a great New England man said, years ago, it is rather like the ocean, broad, deep, grand, open, and so free in all its parts that every drop that mingles with the yellow sand at the bottom may rise through all the waters, till it gleams in the sunshine on the crest of the highest waves.   So it is here in our free society, permeated with the light of American freedom. There is no American boy, however poor, however humble, orphan though he may be, that, if he have a clear head, a true heart, a strong arm, he may not rise through all the grades of society, and become the crown, the glory, the pillar of the State.

"Here, there is no need for the old-world war between capital and labor.   Here is no need of the explosion of social order predicted by Macaulay.   All we need is the protection of just and equal laws—just alike to labor and to capital.   Every poor man hopes to lay by something for a rainy day—hopes to become a capitalist, for capital is only accumulated labor. Whenever a laborer has earned one hundred dollars more than he needs for daily expenses, he becomes to that extent a capitalist, and needs to be safe in its enjoyment. [Applause.]

" There is another answer to Macaulay. He could not understand—no man could understand until he had seen it—the almost omnipotent power of our system of education, that teaches our people how to be free by teaching them to be intelligent.   But fellow-citizens, who has read the letter of Macaulay that did not remember it a year ago last July, when in ten great States of the Union millions of American citizens and millions of American property were in peril of destruction ? when the spirit of mob ran riot ? when Pittsburg flamed in ruin and smoked in blood, and many of our great cities were in peril of destruction—who did not remember the doctrine of Macaulay then, and did not anew resolve that the bloody track of the Commune should have no pathway on our shore ? [Great applause.]

" I have introduced all this for the purpose of saying that behind the element that now attacks the public faith ; behind the misguided honest men who have adopted the greenback theory ; behind them, and preparing the movement, is communism, coming from its dens in Europe and this country."

This speech made a deep and profound impression in Massachusetts at the time, and gave him a rank in the opinions of the Republican leaders in that State which accounts largely for the universal gratification with which his nomination at Chicago was received.

(*Garfield to B. A. Hinsdale.*)

WASHINGTON, D. C., January 20, 1867.

Your letters are, and have always been, a source of great pleasure to me ; for I feel that we have much less need than most people of those commonplace platitudes and guarded utterances which so abound in correspondence. I hope our New Year's custom will never be abandoned till one of us is removed beyond the necessity of earthly communications. I am preparing for the financial legislation which will develop all the mania of the paper age. I expect to be overborne by the brute force of votes ; but I expect to be vindicated before long, when the people look back from the gulf of financial ruin into which they are hastening, and see that I was the true friend of their industrial interests. The appeal from Philip drunk to Philip sober is not a pleasant one to make ; it is not complimentary to Philip. . . .

(*Garfield to B. A. Hinsdale.*)

WASHINGTON, D. C., December 5, 1867.

The appointment took the House completely by surprise. Schenck had no such expectations, and was in favor of my appointment as chairman of Ways and

Means. Next to the pleasure of having that place by the consent of the House is the satisfaction I have of knowing that the regret is very general that I was not appointed. Of course, the place I am in is important, but out of the chosen line of my studies. I don't intend to be thrown out of financial work, and, already, a few of us who have ideas on the subject are talking of forming a sort of volunteer outside committee to consider these subjects together and debate them in the House. . . . I have examined the testimony and reports of the Judiciary Committee in reference to impeachment, and have been compelled to conclude that they have not made out a case. I shall, therefore, vote against the measure. It may, and probably will, cost me my political life. I see all this, and, after having studied the question of impeachment carefully, I see my duty most clearly, and I am glad to tell you that my heart and will have not hesitated for a moment in deciding my course.

You and I are trying experiments—you to see whether a man can think and speak his convictions and stay in the Disciple ministry ; I, whether I can do the same and represent a Western Reserve constituency. We shall know before long whether the experiment can succeed ; if it fails, the world is wide, and we are free.

(*Garfield to B. A. Hinsdale.*)

WASHINGTON, D. C., December 15, 1867.

I appreciate what you say in reference to the currency question. My convictions on some points of that subject are so clear that I have a very plain duty to do, from which I dare not flinch, were I coward enough to desire to.

The Phillipses are quite mistaken in supposing that theirs is a case without precedent. On the contrary, there are an abundance of precedents, both in our own and other countries, and they all teach the same lesson. Financial subjects are nuts and clover for demagogues. Men's first opinions are almost always wrong in regard to them, as they are in regard to astronomy, and he who reads the truths that lie deepest is in imminent danger of being tabooed for a madman. . . . It may be that before very long that the only escape out of the Butler-Pendleton bond repudiation scheme on the one hand, and the contraction and inflation fight on the other, is by the shortest road to specie payments, when the contractionists will be willing to let the inflationists have their fill of paper money so long as they redeem it, and when the cry that the soldier or his widow is paid in poorer money than the bondholder would be ended. The early return to specie payments would settle more difficult and dangerous questions than any one such act has done in history, so far as I know. I am glad to have the opportunity of standing up against a rabble of men who hasten to make weather-cocks of themselves.

Think of this : December 8th, 1865, the House passed the following resolution by ayes 144, noes 6 : " *Resolved,* That this House cordially concurs in the views of the Secretary of the Treasury in relation to the necessity of a contraction of the currency, with a view to as early resumption to specie payments as the business interests of the country will permit, and we hereby pledge coöperation to this end as speedily as possible."

Ten years ago but thirty-two men were found to vote against a bill to stop contraction altogether.　There are near a hundred of the same men who voted on the two measures.

(*Garfield to B. A. Hinsdale.*)
HIRAM, OHIO, New Year's Eve, 1867–1868.

I fear I am not able to write you anything that will be more than an apology for my usual New Year's letter.　I have just returned from a tedious trip to Ashtabula, where I made a two hours' speech on finance, and, when I came home, came through a storm of paper-money denunciation in Cleveland, only to find on my arrival here a sixteen-page letter full of alarm and prophecy of my political ruin for my opinions on the currency.

(*Garfield to B. A. Hinsdale.*)
WASHINGTON, April 10, 1874.

I have no doubt the speech will do me great injury in the district, and add new fuel to the hostility against me ; but I would not on any account flinch from my conviction on this subject.　I have probably never received higher encomiums for anything I have done in Congress than for this liberal speech ; but, of course, the praise comes mainly from those who are not of the West.

(*Garfield to B. A. Hinsdale.*)
WASHINGTON, April 23, 1874

Who will deny that Grant is one of the luckiest men that ever sat in the Presidential chair.　For twenty years no President has had an opportunity to do the country so much service by a veto message as Grant has, and he has met the issue manfully.　You will read the veto message before this, and see how valid a blow he struck the inflation iniquity.

CHAPTER X.

THE difficult and complicated questions involved in the discussion of the antagonistic systems of "Protection" and "Free Trade" have been gradually assuming more and more prominence in the public mind, since the issues growing out of the war have been either settled or reduced into secondary rank. It is quite likely that, as the nation becomes more consolidated and sectional animosities die out, the Tariff question will again rise to the proportions which it occupied during the long period when our ablest statesmen gave their best energies to its discussion, and when Presidents were elected or defeated largely on account of the popularity or unpopularity of their views on the subject of Protection. It might have been expected that Garfield, whose interest in, and knowledge of, political matters was like that of most men of his age at the time preceding the war and for years afterward, would have given little thought to the principles which underlie the great controversies made memorable in our history by such discussions as those of Clay, Calhoun, Webster, Benton, and other great statesmen. To a certain extent this was true. When, at the age of 17, he had fixed the whole purpose of his resolute nature on the acquisition of a college education, and when that involved not only hard study but hard work and great privations in the attainment of the means for getting an education, he determined to interest himself in nothing that would divert his mind or energies from the manly path he had laid out for himself to pursue. It is possible that he might have been confirmed in this purpose by the influence of a fellow-pupil of great strength of character and individuality, who was imbued with the views of the class then known as the "Come-outers." These people, enthused by the extreme

anti-slavery views of Garrison, had come to the religious conviction that it was wrong to have any connection with or interest in the politics of the age, on the ground that both political
parties were so far complicated with the maintenance of the
institution of slavery that to sustain either party would be to
help preserve what they regarded as the sum of all villainies
and wrongs. His schoolmate's earnest talk in this vein made
such an impression on Garfield that it might have been damaging
in its results, but for the publication, about that time, of a series of
articles by Alexander Campbell, the great founder of the " Disciples," or the " Campbellite" sect, as they have been wrongly termed, which took the bold ground that there was Biblical and Christian authority for the maintenance of the relation of master and
slave. But with this qualification, that whoever adopted this
theory was bound to apply the Christian law of love to the
neighbor in his relations with the slave—a qualification which,
it is needless to say, would have been pretty nearly impracticable to maintain in fact. The great power of Campbell over
young Garfield's mind, and the clearness of Campbell's demon-
stration, rescued him from the ultra-fanaticism of his schoolmate. But from that time till he completed his college course
he gave as little thought and time to the study and discussion
of any other political questions than those growing out of the
institution of slavery, as it was possible for so vigorous and
active a mind to refrain from bestowing.

In the senior year in college his attention was first directed,
in the usual course of study in Wayland's " Political Economy,"
to the question of Protection and Free Trade, to which it was
his destiny to give a much more thorough study than has been
pursued by any of our statesmen whose political reputations
have been made since the war. Wayland's text-book is that of
a moderate, conservative, and philosophical writer, whose tendencies were toward Free Trade, but who recognized and admitted the practical difficulties in the way of realizing it. Garfield gave himself to the study of this text-book with all the
vigor and independent habit of thinking which have character-

ized him from the beginning. * He did his own thinking. His mind was open to the reception of the conflicting views that were presented in his text-book, and upheld by that broad-minded and statesman-like teacher, President Mark Hopkins. His immediate teacher, Professor Perry, was more inclined to radical Free Trade doctrines, but had not then developed into the *doctrinaire* which he has since become. At the close of the chapters in Wayland on the subject of Protection and Free Trade, Professor Perry asked Garfield what were the impressions that he had received, and the views he entertained. His reply at that time was remarkable, not only for its terseness and comprehensiveness, but as showing the keen intuitions of his nature and his readiness to accept practical limitations ; in fact, his whole life had been such a strenuous struggle against practical limitations that he was in little danger of becoming a mere theorist. His reply to Professor Perry was this :

"*As an abstract theory, the doctrine of Free Trade seems to be universally true, but as a question of practicability, under a government like ours, the protective system seems to be indispensable.*"

On this broad basis Garfield has firmly stood, and built up a national reputation as a statesman, in the handling of the question of Protection.

For ten years after this definition of his views, the state of the country—the absorbing and exciting nature of the slavery question, of the war, and of the legislation growing out of the war—prevented him from giving much attention to subjects involving merely financial considerations. But in 1866, in a speech which he made in the House, he showed that integrity, consistency, and development of intellectual conviction which is so greatly characteristic of his mind.

In his speech in Congress he simply enlarged the definition which he gave to Professor Perry. He said :

" We have seen that one extreme school of economists would place the price of all manufactured articles in the hands of foreign producers by rendering it impossible for our manufacturers to compete with them ; while the other extreme school, by making it impossible for the foreigner to sell his competing wares in our market, would give the people no immediate check upon the prices which our manufacturers might fix for their products. I disagree with both these extremes. I hold that a properly adjusted competition between home and foreign products is the best gauge by which to regulate international trade. Duties should be so high that our manufacturers can fairly compete with the foreign product, but not so high as to enable them to drive out the foreign article, enjoy a monopoly of the trade, and regulate the price as they please. This is my doctrine of protection. If Congress pursues this line of policy steadily we shall, year by year, approach more nearly to the basis of free trade, because we shall be more nearly able to compete with other nations on equal terms. I am for a protection which leads to ultimate free trade. I am for that free trade which can only be achieved through a reasonable protection."

From the platform which he laid down for himself then he has never been driven by clamor, by misrepresentation, or by fear of being misunderstood. Every speech he has made since then on the Tariff has been in rigid consistency with the principles laid down in the above comprehensive paragraph. On the 1st of April, 1870, he made another speech on the Tariff question, which shows the progress of his study of the historical illustrations of the practical workings of Protection. He was perfectly ready to admit, at the outset, that, as an abstract theory of political economy, Free Trade has an attractive aspect, and that much can be said in its favor ; nor did he deny that the scholarship of modern times is largely on that side, or that the great majority of thinkers of the present day are leaning in the direction of what is called Free Trade ; but while making these concessions, with his customary liberality, he held that it was equally undeniable that the principle of Protection has always been recognized and admitted, in some form or other, by all nations, and is to-day, to a greater or less extent, the policy of every civilized government. Going through with the history of the planting of colonies in the New World, and of the policy pursued by England, particularly, toward her colonies, he summarized the methods by which England sought to make the colonists the mere dependent customers of the mother country, for every article which it was to the interest of England to export.

By this record of continuous and more and more oppressive tyranny over the colonists he illustrated the evil effects of such a system, and accounted for the subsequent reaction in England and in European nations toward Free Trade. The sentiment of Free Trade, as a protest against the old system of oppression and prohibition, he believed to be a sound one, but he held and proved that, underlying all theories, there had been a strong and deep conviction in the minds of the great majority of our people in favor of protecting American industry. And in the use of this phrase, "American industry," he was particular to avoid any misapprehension as to his meaning. He objected to any theory that treats the industries of the country as they were treated in the preceding census, where we had one schedule for "agriculture" and another for "industry," as though agriculture were not an industry, as though commerce and art and transportation were not industries. Said he :

"American industry is labor in any form which gives value to the raw materials or elements of nature, either by extracting them from the earth, the air, or the sea, or by modifying their forms or transporting them through the channels of trade to the markets of the world, or in any way rendering them better fitted for the use of man. All these are parts of American industry, and deserve the careful and earnest attention of the legislature of the nation. Wherever a ship ploughs the sea, or a plough furrows the field ; wherever a mine yields its treasure ; wherever a ship or a railroad train carries freight to market ; wherever the smoke of the furnace rises or the clang of the loom resounds ; even in the lonely garret where the seamstress plies her busy needle, there is industry."

Then, as ever since, he was willing to modify the Tariff wherever a change would give most relief to industry, and he advised those who wanted to undertake this difficult task to study the key to our financial problems, or at least the chief factor in every such problem, the "doctrine of prices," and suggested that, if he was to direct any student of finance where to begin his studies he would refer him to the great work of Thomas Tooke on the "History of Prices," as the foundation upon which to build the superstructure of his knowledge.

Going through the then recent history of prices in connection with the increase of duties, and the annual expenditures of the government, as well as the condition of our foreign trade, he pointed out the fact, which was ignored by "high tariff" men, that the markets of neighboring countries were not buying our products in the same proportion as before the war, and that one of the most efficient methods of encouraging home industry was to secure extensive markets, which could only be brought about by adjusting our prices so as to open our trade to more of the markets of the New World.

When it came to the question of adjusting taxation, he held, first, that we should tax the "vices" of the people, "if that term may be properly applied to some of their social habits." He admitted, and was one of the first to do so, that the income tax was "vexatious and inquisitorial," and hoped that our revenues would soon allow its abolition. Discussing what is known as the "Morrill Tariff" that was adopted, in 1861, in a most extraordinary and exceptional state of affairs, and which required extensive adjustments to conditions that existed in 1866, he said that he had "refused to be the advocate of any special interest as against the general interest of the whole country." "Whatever," said he, "may be the personal or political consequences to myself, I shall try to act first for the good of all, and, within that limitation, for the industrial interests of the district which I represent." That he was sincere in this expression was proved by the position which he took in regard to a provision of the "Schenck Tariff Bill" which most concerned the only great manufacturing interest in his own district —that is, the duty on pig-iron. There were at that time nineteen iron-furnaces in blast in his district, nine more in the district of his colleague, Judge Ambler, and several more in the adjoining district, represented by another colleague, Mr. Upton. The bill reduced the duty on pig-iron $2, which was 22¼ per cent less than the existing duty. Nevertheless, with a full knowledge of the certain results in his own district, and on a most influential body of men, of his declaration, he frankly said : "If the House of Representatives thinks that this ought to be done, and if I shall be convinced that the public requires it, I shall not resist it."

It is unnecessary to refer to many of Garfield's speeches on the Tariff question. He has been so consistent throughout that it is only needed that extracts be given from a few of the more important of those speeches, delivered at considerable intervals from one another. In 1878 an exceedingly able, ingenious, and eloquent plea for a Tariff adjusted to the old Southern doctrines was made by that distinguished Virginian, Mr. J. Randolph Tucker. Mr. Tucker's presentation of the subject to a Democratic House was so able that Garfield felt called upon to make a somewhat elaborate reply, and, as it showed the results of twelve years of study and reflection, since the making of the speech to which reference has been made above, it is worth while to give a tolerably full conception of its drift and powerful points. Having read and re-read it carefully, and having read all the great speeches made in Congress for forty years before the war on this difficult question, it is my deliberate conviction that the sound American doctrine of Protection has never been stated with equal clearness, breadth, and practicality. At the very outset he demolished the foundations of Mr. Tucker's argument, which were based on the construction of the Constitution which was, before the war, and still is, recognized by most Southern statesmen. Mr. Tucker thought that if we were to adopt a proper construction of the Constitution we should find that the regulation of commerce does not permit the protection of manufactures, nor can the power to tax be applied directly or indirectly to that object.

Without entering into an elaborate discussion of that ques-

tion, Garfield said : " I cannot refrain from expressing my admiration of the courage of the gentleman from Virginia, who in
that part of his speech brought himself into point-blank range
of the terrible artillery of James Madison, one of the Fathers
of the Constitution, and Virginia's great expounder of its provisions.   More than one hundred pages of the collected works
of James Madison are devoted to an elaborate and exhaustive
discussion of the very objection which the gentleman (Mr.
Tucker) has urged."

And he made his statement good, by full quotations from the
great Virginia expounder.   Having thus cleared away the Virginia and South Carolina doctrines of the Constitution, he proceeded to build up his own doctrine, from the language of the
Constitution itself and from the practice of the Fathers of the
Government, quoting the language of the Constitution which
says that " Congress shall have power to lay and collect taxes,
duties, imposts, and excises, to pay the debts and provide for
the common defence and general welfare of the United States."
He held that the power to tax was the great motive power of
the Government, and that " its regulation impels, retards, re-
strains, or limits all the functions of the Government."   With
a broad comprehension of the creative ideas of the Fathers of
the Government, he said :

" The men who created this Constitution also set it in operation, and developed their own idea of its character.   That idea
was unlike any other that then prevailed upon the earth.   They
made the general welfare of the people the great source and
foundation of the common defence.   In all the nations of the
Old World the public defense was provided for by great standing armies, navies, and fortified posts, so that the nation might
every moment be fully armed against danger from without or
turbulence within.   Our fathers said : ' Though we will use the
taxing power to maintain a small army and navy sufficient to
keep alive the knowledge of war, yet the main reliance for our
defence shall be the intelligence, culture, and skill of our people ;
a development of our own intellectual and material resources,
which will enable us to do everything that may be necessary to
equip, clothe, and feed ourselves in time of war, and make ourselves intelligent, happy, and prosperous in peace.' "

On this broad historic and philosophic basis he erected his theory of carrying out the intention of the Fathers, and of making this country really independent, as to all the essentials, both of existence and of self-defence, against any foreign enemy. He showed that the purpose of the Fathers to make their emancipation complete by adding to agriculture all the mechanical arts, inspired the legislation of all the earlier Congresses, and that our legislation was continuously shaped with this view, until, under the lead of John C. Calhoun, the Protective Tariff of 1816 was enacted. After going through a discussion of the practical operation of the "Morrill Tariff" as compared with those of the Revenue Tariff for fifteen years preceding the war, he boldly confronted the glittering generalities of Mr. Tucker, as expressed in these beautiful sentences :

"Commerce, Mr. Chairman, links all mankind in one common brotherhood of mutual dependence and interests, and thus creates that unity of our race which makes the resources of all the property of each and every member. We cannot if we would, and should not if we could, remain isolated and alone. Men under the benign influence of Christianity yearn for intercourse, for the interchange of thought and the products of thought as a means of a common progress toward a nobler civilization.

*   *   *   *   *   *   *   *

"Mr. Chairman, I cannot believe this is according to the Divine plan. Christianity bids us seek, in communion with our brethren of every race and clime, the blessings they can afford us, and to bestow in return upon them those with which our new continent is destined to fill the world."

This he admitted was "a grand conception, a beautiful vision of the time when all the nations should dwell in peace." . . . "If," said he, "all the kingdoms of the world should become the kingdom of the Prince of Peace, then I admit that universal Free Trade ought to prevail. But that blessed era is yet too remote to be made the basis of the practical legislation of to-day. We are not yet members of 'the parliament of man, the federation of the world.' For the present the world is divided into separate nationalities ; and that other divine command still applies to our situation : 'He that provideth not for his own household has denied the faith, and is worse than an infidel,' and until that latter era arrives patriotism must supply the place of universal brotherhood." But he was careful to isolate himself from that class of Congressmen whose support of the Tariff has been due to the special interests of their localities, and from those whose opposition to Protection has been due to the same influences, and it may be safely said that no instances can be found in his Congressional career when he has done or refused to do anything in the way of Tariff legislation not in consistency with these broad declarations.

" Too much of our tariff discussion has been warped by narrow and sectional considerations. But when we base our action upon the conceded national importance of the great industries I have referred to, when we recognize the fact that artisans and their products are essential to the well-being of our country, it follows that there is no dweller in the humblest cottage on our remotest frontier who has not a deep personal interest in the legislation that shall promote these great national industries. Those arts that enable our nation to rise in the scale of civilization bring their blessings to all, and patriotic citizens will cheerfully bear a fair share of the burden necessary to make their country great and self-sustaining. I will defend a tariff that is national in its aims, that protects and sustains those interests without which the nation cannot become great and self-sustaining."

Then recurring to the fundamental doctrine of national development, as essential to national safety and independence, he added :

" So important, in my view, is the ability of the nation to manufacture all these articles necessary to arm, equip, and clothe our people, that if it could not be secured in any other way I would vote to pay money out of the Federal Treasury to maintain Government iron and steel, woollen and cotton mills, at whatever cost. Were we to neglect these great interests and depend upon other nations, in what a condition of helplessness would we find ourselves when we should be again involved in war with the very nations on whom we were depending to furnish us these supplies ? The system adopted by our fathers is wiser, for it so encourages the great national industries as to make it possible at all times for our people to equip themselves for war, and at the same time increase their intelligence and skill so as to make them better fitted for all the duties of citizenship both in war and in peace. *We provide for the common defence by a system which promotes the general welfare.*"

The last sentence of which is the most epigrammatic statement of the American system of Protection, as understood by Garfield, which has ever been made in Congress ; and a still more particular and definite statement of Garfield's general attitude on the question of Protection is found in the same speech, and seems to be about as comprehensive a platform and as practical a statement of this question as has ever been proposed by any of our public men :

"My view of the danger of extreme positions on the questions of tariff rates may be illustrated by a remark made by Horace Greeley in the last conversation I ever had with that distinguished man. Said he,

"'My criticism of you is that you are not sufficiently high protective in your views.'

"I replied,

"'What would you advise ?'

"He said,

"'If I had my way—if I were king of this country—I would put a duty of $100 a ton on pig-iron and a proportionate duty on everything else that can be produced in America. The result would be that our people would be obliged to supply their own wants ; manufactures would spring up, competition would finally reduce prices, and we should live wholly within ourselves.'

"I replied that the fatal objection to his theory was that no man is king of this country, with power to make his policy permanent. But as all our policies depend upon popular support, the extreme measure proposed would beget an opposite extreme, and our industries would suffer from violent reactions. For this reason I believe that we ought to seek that point of stable equilibrium somewhere between a prohibitory tariff on the one hand and a tariff that gives no protection on the other. What is that point of stable equilibrium ? In my judgment it is this : a rate so high that foreign producers cannot flood our markets and break down our home manufacturers, but not so high as to

keep them altogether out, enabling our manufacturers to com-
bine and raise the prices, nor so high as to stimulate an un-
natural and unhealthy growth of manufactures.

"In other words, I would have the duty so adjusted that
every great American industry can fairly live and make fair
profits, and yet so low that if our manufacturers attempted to
put up prices unreasonably, the competition from abroad would
come in and bring down prices to a fair rate. Such a tariff I
believe will be supported by the great majority of Americans.
We are not far from having such a tariff in our present law. In
some respects we have departed from that standard. Wherever
it does, we should amend it, and by so doing we shall secure
stability and prosperity."

The latest exposition of General Garfield's views on the Tariff
is found in a report by the minority of the Committee on Ways
and Means, submitted to the House on the 24th of May last.
The report, which was his production, contains several interesting exhibits showing the operations of the Tariff, especially in
developing the wool-growing interests, and the operation of the
proposed tariff on wool manufacturers, as well as interesting
statements in regard to the growth of the manufacture of
earthenware in the United States and its remarkable development. The report itself is a brief and thoroughly practical
document, reviewing some of the inconsistencies and injustices
of the tariff proposed by the majority of the Committee. Some
of the illustrations of the evils that might grow out of the proposed tariff changes are entirely in the line of Garfield's consistent policy of developing into a state of reasonable independence
and security those manufactures which are most essential to the
practical independence of the country, as to every article which
might become indispensable in case of foreign war. He noted
the growth, under the favoring protection of the existing tariff,
of such manufactures as that of steel files, which had within a
few years become fully established, so as to reduce the cost of
these articles to a point far lower than was ever before known
in the country. The minority report states Garfield's views in
regard to amending our tariff system in this very succinct and
practical manner, to wit :

" The undersigned agree that in many respects the tariff system should be amended. Where rates are exorbitant they should be reduced as rapidly and as far as the wants of the revenue and the prosperity of our great national industries will permit.   There are articles in the tariff on wools and woollens that may be reduced ; and perhaps the whole group can safely bear some reduction.   But on the whole, no part of our tariff system has been more amply vindicated by experience than that which relates to wools and woollens.   The foundations of these provisions were laid in 1861 ; but in 1867 the existing rates were established, after a long and exhaustive investigation, and with the concurrence of the two interests which had theretofore been in opposition.

" The basis of that legislation was this : that upon the several grades of imported wool a duty should be imposed sufficient to promote the growth of sheep husbandry in the United States. A specific duty was then imposed on woollen goods, as near as possible equal to the duty put upon the wool which entered into the manufacture.   This was not protection, but simply an equivalent duty, which placed the woollen manufacturer on the free-trade level.   To this specific duty was then added a duty of 35 per centum ad valorem on woollen goods, as a protection to the manufacturer against foreign competition.   This adjustment of the law has remained substantially unchanged for thirteen years ; and during the six years preceding the adjustment the law contained similar though less complete provisions.

" With this preliminary statement the undersigned invite attention to the results of this legislation.

" In 1836 the wool product of the United States was estimated at 42 millions of pounds per annum ; in 1860, according to the census, it had risen to 60 million pounds per annum ; under the operations of the Morrill Tariff the product had risen in 1867 to 147 millions of pounds per annum ; in 1877 it had risen to 208 million pounds per annum ; and it is now estimated to be 250 million pounds per annum.   In the twenty-four years preceding the war the wool product of this country had increased but 40 per cent ; while the present annual product of wool is 400 per cent greater than that of twenty years ago.

" The development of our sheep husbandry has been most remarkable in the West and South.   In 1862 Messrs. Hollister & Dibbles introduced 400 merino ewes into California, where sheep husbandry at that time was almost unknown.   Now California takes the lead of all the States of the Union, and produces not less than fifty million pounds of wool per annum, an amount nearly equal to the total wool product of the United States in 1860. The growth of the wool interest has been hardly less rapid in Texas, which now occupies the second rank as a wool-growing State.

" With this vast increase in the quantity, the improvement in quality has been equally marked. While the farmers of the United States have been thus enabled to increase their food supply and increase the raw material for the clothing of our people, the effect of the tariff on woollens has been correspondingly beneficent. In 1860 we were largely dependent for our clothing upon foreign wool-growers and foreign manufacturers, at such prices as they were able to dictate. Now the woollen fabrics used by our people are mainly manufactured by the skill and labor of our own artisans from the product of our own flocks.

" No attentive observer who visited the Centennial Exposition failed to notice the astonishment with which the French and English manufacturers examined the fine cloths produced by American looms ; and no feature of that great exhibition reflected more credit upon American enterprise and skill. As a revenue measure the Tariff of 1867 on wools and woollens has been very effective, having produced $360,000,000 of revenue in the last thirteen years—an average of $28,000,000 per annum.

" The bill of the committee destroys the adjustments of the existing tariff on wool and woollens, and wholly disregards the relations which these two branches of industry sustain to each other. Should it become a law, it will be impossible for our farmers to compete in the market with the mestiza wools of South America ; and it will be equally impossible for our manufacturers to compete with those of France and England. Of course any legislation that destroys the woollen manufactures is equally destructive to sheep husbandry, for the farmer would no longer have a market for his wool. That nation can hardly be called independent which does not possess the materials and the skill to clothe its own people.

" For a more detailed statement of the effects of this bill upon our wool and woollen industries, we refer to the very able an instructive letter, hereto appended (marked A), of Mr. John L. Hayes, secretary of the National Association of Wool Manufacturers. To this letter is also appended a letter (marked B) of Mr. William Whitman, a leading manufacturer of Boston, Mass.

" In reference to the provisions of the committee's bill which reduce the duties upon stoneware and crockeryware—an interesting and important industry of recent origin in this country—attention is invited to the accompanying letter (marked C) of Mr. Homer Laughlin, of East Liverpool, Ohio, chairman of the executive committee of the United States Potters' Association, and also the letter of Hon. I. D. Blake, of New Jersey (marked D).

"Other features of the committee's bill are equally open to just criticism ; but enough has been said to indicate the spirit of hostility to our national industries which pervades it, and the partial and unjust treatment of the various subjects which it embraces."

It would be far easier to fill a whole volume with interesting extracts from the speeches of General Garfield on the Tariff than it is to select from the numerous illustrations of the statesmanship he has displayed on this question those which it is consistent with the limits of this book to use ; but if all of his public utterances were published together in chronological order they would only enhance, by the multiplicity of illustrations, the impression that must be made on any fair-minded and intelligent man by the few extracts which have been given ; and the most complete collection would only the more effectually and variously prove the consistency of his policy on this subject. From the beginning of his public life he has favored the Protection that would lead to liberating the protected articles to Free Trade. He has always been opposed to merely prohibitory protection, and has been in favor of a tariff which would enable our people to fairly compete with the world and to keep our national industries alive. He has opposed a tariff on any article so high as to encourage manufacturers to form monopolizing combinations, in the absence of foreign competition. In the maintenance of this middle ground he has been exposed to the attacks of two extreme classes. The first class is that of Free Traders, who want Free Trade at once, and who forget that, even if it were practicable, Congress is not merely a debating society, but the representative of vast numbers of distinct local interests, all of which have to be considered and harmonized by any leader who attempts to accomplish actual re-

formatory legislation.   On the other hand, he has had to stand
the fire of extreme Protectionists, because they wanted their own
private interests furthered by legislation, without regard to the
general interests.   He says, himself, of his attitude, that the position he has held on the Tariff question is exceptional in his
career, in this respect : that it has been a middle between two
extremes.   He says : "I have usually been at one pole or the
other ; there I stood on the equator, and there insisted that the
true doctrine was the point of stable equilibrium, where we
could hold a tariff that would not be knocked down every time
the Free Traders got into power, and boosted up every time the
Protectionists got into power, but to give the country a stable
policy where the tendency would be toward amelioration all the
while.   I have held that equitable ground throughout, and held
it against the assaults, now from one side and now from the
other, and I estimate it one of the greatest of my achievements
in public life to have held that equipoise."

In spite of the well-known consistency of his record on the
Tariff, it has been his fortune, as it has been that of other great
statesmen, to be the victim of gross misapprehensions as to particular declarations of his views, or as to his acts in Congress.
For instance, at a time when Secretary Boutwell regarded it
as of the utmost importance to our credit abroad that the English
statesmen and people should understand the nature of the fight
which our soundest statesmen were making in behalf of an
honest currency, he sent to Mr. Gladstone and to Mr. Bright a
copy of Garfield's then recent speech on the currency question,
which the Secretary regarded as highly creditable to American
statesmanship.   In recognition of the ability and soundness of
this argument, Mr. Gladstone and Mr. Bright had General Garfield elected an honorary member of the Cobden Club, an honor
rarely conferred except in recognition of distinguished statesmanship or ability in treating economic subjects.   From this
simple fact it was hastily assumed that General Garfield had
won the favor of a Club identified with the propagandism of
Free Trade by his position on the Tariff, while, in fact, the

thing which obtained for him this unexpected compliment was a speech in which there was not the least reference to the Tariff question.

A still more annoying misapprehension grew out of the discussions, during the last session of Congress, on the question of removing the duty from wood-pulp. As the newspaper interest was generally and naturally in favor of this reduction, it is not at all strange that considerable criticism was called out by a misapprehension of Garfield's position. This misapprehension was due to the circulation, among all the newspapers of the country, of a misstatement as to what his position was, and of a charge that he was responsible for maintaining an odious monopoly in the manufacture of paper. If Garfield had been at all disposed to cringe and curry favor with the greatest, and sometimes the most dangerous, power in this country, that of the Press, he would have avoided taking the stand which he did in regard to this matter ; but he treated the paper manufacture in the same broad spirit in which he treated the iron manufacture, as to which his course at one time exposed him to a good many "shrieks of locality." He was determined not to budge an inch under the concentrated fire of ever so many newspapers that had not taken the trouble to learn the facts before pronouncing judgment. In regard to the duty on wood-pulp, there were, of course, some newspapers that favored protection on other articles and did not want any tariff on the materials used in paper manufacture. These papers were willing to support Protection as a system, but thought it was quite consistent and reasonable for them to be exempted from its operation, as regards their own business. To such a philosophy as that he could not give his assent. He was willing to reduce the duty on wood-pulp as low as it could be reduced without destroying an industry which in a few years had assumed formidable proportions, and had largely aided in reducing the price of paper from twenty-seven cents a pound to five and one half cents a pound. The discovery of the German inventor who conceived the idea of supplying the growing demand for paper material by the

simple process of grinding soft wood into pulp had given such a
sudden and vast accession to the stock of paper material that the
effect of its introduction was a steady and rapid reduction of
prices of the manufactured article.   In fact, without this discovery, it is difficult to imagine how the demand for paper could have
been supplied or prices kept within any reasonable limits.   For
nearly a century there had been a growing competition in the
world between reading and rags.   The readers had multiplied
their demands much faster than the supply of rags had been kept
up.   It had finally reached the point that Germany and other
foreign countries discouraged the exportation of rags, and American paper manufacturers had been obliged to establish branch
mills in Egypt for the reduction of rags to pulp.   It was not until
the discovery of the availability of soft wood to supply this important demand of civilization that there seemed to be any possi-
bility of keeping up the cheap manufacture of one of the most
essential elements of our progress.   There was great distrust of
the new discovery at first, and it was not until the owners of
the wood-pulp patents established paper-mills of their own that
the utility of the new discovery was vindicated, and from that
time the growth of this branch of industry was remarkably
rapid, so that fifty-seven wood-pulp-mills were put in operation,
and have turned out such a mass of cheap material for paper that
the whole industry has assumed a new phase.   The duty on
paper pulp was twenty per cent.   General Garfield proposed to
reduce this duty to ten per cent, which he thought would about
reach the lowest point consistent with preventing our own home
production from being overslaughed by importations of wood-
pulp from Canada, where no royalty was paid to the owners of
the patent.

This is the whole story of his connection with the wood-pulp
duty.   It was a simple matter in itself, but he probably had to
encounter more newspaper criticism, a great deal of it from
some of his most sincere admirers and supporters, than for
any other act of his Congressional life.   He appreciated this
from the first, understood it, disliked it, but did not fear it, and

did not vary his policy a hair's-breadth from the strict line which he has pursued from the beginning of his Congressional career, in deciding as to the details of Protection. On the whole, it is probable that most of the newspaper editors who favored him with indignant execrations think all the more of him at present because he was so steady and unmoved, even by the clamor of the Press. He had no selfish motive whatever to stand by this particular duty on wood-pulp. There was not a paper-mill in his district. Among the most earnest advocates of the abolition of the duty were editors who were his warmest personal friends. It was easy for him to have evaded any contest of this sort, or to have yielded. He did neither. He performed his duty, took all the attacks on himself good-naturedly, and was very little disturbed by them.

(Garfield to B. A. Hinsdale.)

WASHINGTON, October 14, 1865.

I have read the history and philosophy of the Tariff question very thoroughly, though I have not yet finished it. When I see you I want to give you the salient points in the history of British commercial policy ; it is very curious and interesting. . . .

In the literary way I have fallen upon one of the finest things I have ever met. It is Walter Savage Landor's " Pericles and Aspasia," which gives in the most vivid and beautiful style the best summary I have ever seen of the spirit and character of Greek history, politics, philosophy and literature. It has been a very rich treat to us all. We are yet in the midst of it.

(Garfield to B. A. Hinsdale.)

WASHINGTON, December 20, 1879.

I have noticed the insincere and absurd talk of the politicians about high tariff bills. Put these two things together : "Garfield is too valuable a man in the House to be spared," " Garfield is unsound on the tariff, and ought not to be elected to the Senate." Yet these arguments are used by the same men. If I were to consult my own preference entirely, apart from public opinion, and if I could be sure of continued robust health, I would prefer to remain in the House ; but the bone-breaking work that position has brought upon me for the last few years admonishes me that my final break-down of health must soon come if I continue where I am. The Senate is a smaller body, and I shall there probably escape the responsibilities and labors of leadership. Then it would seem churlish to stand in the way of the reasonable ambition of my friends in the Nineteenth District, and so, if the Senatorship comes to me, I shall take it ; but with some sadness and regret. The talk of the newspapers about the successorship has been premature and embarrassing to all of us.

CHAPTER XI.

So far as the national reputation of members of Congress is concerned, it is mostly founded on their more important speeches and measures. So far as their reputation among Congressmen is concerned, the ability, fidelity, and judgment with which committee work is performed is a much more decisive test of relative standing. There always have been in Congress a few members who seldom made speeches of any length, and yet commanded unusual respect from their fellow-members, and wielded a very large influence, from their familiarity with the details which are only learned in committees.

Garfield has fairly won a distinguished reputation in both ways. In his speeches, which are familiar to all our people, he has vindicated the right to the leadership of his party in the House, which was accorded to him by common consent when Mr. Blaine left the House. In the arduous duties devolving upon him as a member of most important committees he has won the high respect of his fellow-members of successive Congresses, without regard to their party predilections.

His first assignment, when he entered Congress, to committee work, was a very natural one. Coming fresh from the army, and from a position requiring as much knowledge of army organization, needs and other details as was required of the commanding general whose chief of staff he was, his services were at once sought for the Committee on Military Affairs, then by far the most important in the House. No member of that committee contributed so much to its knowledge of the actual condition and needs of the army. His reports were models of fulness and accuracy, in dealing with the various questions that came before the committee.

The constitution of the Committee on Military Affairs in the 38th Congress was as follows, the names being given in the order of precedence :

> ROBERT C. SCHENCK, of Ohio.
> JOHN F. FARNSWORTH, of Illinois.
> GEORGE H. YEAMAN, of Kentucky.
> JAMES A. GARFIELD, of Ohio.
> BENJAMIN LOAN, of Missouri.
> MOSES F. ODELL, of New York.
> HENRY C. DEMING, of Connecticut.
> F. W. KELLOGG, of Michigan.
> ARCHIBALD McALLISTER, of Pennsylvania.

It was somewhat of a surprise to the Speaker of the House when the 39th Congress assembled in 1865, and Garfield was asked by the Speaker if he had any request to make about the composition of committees, to hear Garfield say that he had but one request, and that was that he should be left off from the Military Committee and assigned to that of Ways and Means ; and yet the former committee had before it the great work of reorganizing the army, and other difficult and important questions, involving the exercise of a great deal of power and wisdom. But Garfield's vigorous and prescient mind was quick to anticipate and leap into the new emergencies that were beginning to be foreshadowed, and he wanted to put himself in the place where the line of his duty would put him most completely in the way of preparation. It was his theory that the great coming question was that of finance, and he was determined to be prepared for its discussion. From that early period in his Congressional career dates the beginning of that wonderful growth in the mastery of all the questions of detail about tariff, taxation, currency, and the public debt, which has marked all his public utterances.

The Committee on Ways and Means in the 39th Congress consisted of the following able statesmen :

> JUSTIN S. MORRILL, of Vermont.
> SAMUEL HOOPER, of Massachusetts.

JAMES BROOKS, of New York.
JAMES A. GARFIELD, of Ohio.
JOHN WENTWORTH, of Illinois.
ROSCOE CONKLING, of New York.
JAMES R. MOORHEAD, of Pennsylvania.
WILLIAM B. ALLISON, of Iowa.
JOHN HOGAN, of Missouri.

In the 40th Congress there was a just recognition of his services as a member of the Committee on Military Affairs in the 38th Congress, by his appointment as chairman of that committee by the Speaker. The committee was constituted as follows :

JAMES A. GARFIELD, of Ohio.
WILLIAM A. PILE, of Missouri.
JOHN H. KETCHAM, of New York.
HENRY D. WASHBURN, of Indiana.
GRENVILLE M. DODGE, of Iowa.
GREEN B. RAUM, of Illinois.
ISAAC R. HAWKINS, of Tennessee.
CHARLES SITGREAVES, of New Jersey.
BENJAMIN R. POWER, of Pennsylvania.

In the 41st Congress the Speaker made recognition both of the acknowledged ability and research of Garfield in regard to all the financial questions, and of the newly acquired importance of the Committee on Banking and Currency, by making him its chairman. The committee consisted of the following members :

JAMES A. GARFIELD, of Ohio.
JOHN LYNCH, of Maine.
NORMAN B. JUDD, of Illinois.
JOHN COBURN, of Indiana.
WORTHINGTON C. SMITH, of Vermont.
JOHN B. PACKER, of Pennsylvania.
ISRAEL G. LASH, of North Carolina.
SAMUEL S. COX, of New York.
THOMAS S. JONES, of Kentucky.
HORATIO C. BURCHARD, of Illinois.

He was also appointed on the Select Committee on the Ninth Census, in which he occupied the second place, although the

great burden of shaping the work of the committee fell upon
him, at the request of the Speaker, who desired him to yield the
place out of courtesy to William B. Stokes, of Tennessee. The
labors devolved on this committee were very arduous, and the
results of their work, and especially of General Garfield's direct-
ing share in it, can be seen in the official reports. No preceding committee on this subject had ever made such an exhaustive
and scientific presentation of the ends to be achieved by a national census, or of the means by which they could most readily
and certainly be effected. The committee was composed as
follows :

> WILLIAM B. STOKES, of Tennessee.
> JAMES A. GARFIELD, of Ohio.
> NATHANIEL P. BANKS, of Massachusetts.
> WILLIAM B. ALLISON, of Iowa.
> ADDISON J. LAFLIN, of New York.
> SHELBY M. CULLOM, of Illinois.
> MARTIN W. WILKINSON, of Minnesota.
> RICHARD J. HALDEMAN, of Pennsylvania.
> JOHN G. SCHUMACHER, of New York.

He was also appointed a member of the Committee on Rules,
which is always made up with especial reference to the parliamentary knowledge of its members. The committee was constituted as follows :

> The Speaker (JAMES G. BLAINE).
> NATHANIEL P. BANKS, of Massachusetts.
> THOMAS W. FERRY, of Michigan.
> JAMES A. GARFIELD, of Ohio.
> JAMES BROOKS, of New York.

In the 42d Congress Garfield was made chairman of the Committee on Appropriations, on which had been devolved the
most responsible duties and the greatest powers previously assigned to the Committee of Ways and Means. The committee
was constituted as follows :

> JAMES A. GARFIELD, of Ohio.
> AARON A. SARGENT, of California.

OLIVER J. DICKEY, of Pennsylvania.
FREEMAN CLARKE, of New York.
FRANK W. PALMER, of Iowa.
EUGENE HALE, of Maine.
WILLIAM E. NIBLACK, of Indiana.
SAMUEL S. MARSHALL, of Illinois.
THOMAS SWANN, of Maryland.

Garfield was continued on the Committee on Rules, which consisted of

The Speaker (JAMES G. BLAINE).
NATHANIEL P. BANKS, of Massachusetts.
JAMES A. GARFIELD, of Ohio.
SAMUEL S. COX, of New York.
SAMUEL J. RANDALL, of Pennsylvania.

In the 43d Congress Garfield was reappointed chairman of the Committee on Appropriations, which consisted of the following members :

JAMES A. GARFIELD, of Ohio.
EUGENE HALE, of Maine.
WILLIAM A. WHEELER, of New York.
CHARLES O'NEILL, of Pennsylvania.
HENRY H. STARKWEATHER, of Connecticut.
WILLIAM LOUGHRIDGE, of Iowa.
JAMES N. TYNER, of Indiana.
ISAAC C. PARKER, of Missouri.
SAMUEL S. MARSHALL, of Illinois.
THOMAS SWANN, of Maryland.
JOHN HANCOCK, of Texas.

As during two previous Congresses, he was appointed on the Committee on Rules, which consisted of

The Speaker (JAMES G. BLAINE).
HORACE MAYNARD, of Tennessee.
JAMES A. GARFIELD, of Ohio.
SAMUEL S. COX, of New York.
SAMUEL J. RANDALL, of Pennsylvania.

In the 44th Congress Garfield was placed on the Committee

on Ways and Means. As the House was Democratic, he was
naturally placed below all the Democrats on the committee,
and below William D. Kelley, who was much his senior in Congressional service. The committee was constituted as follows :

WILLIAM R. MORRISON, of Illinois.
FERNANDO WOOD, of New York.
JOHN HANCOCK, of Texas.
PHILIP L. THOMAS, of Maryland.
BENJAMIN H. HILL, of Georgia.
CHESTER W. CHAPIN, of Massachusetts.
J. RANDOLPH TUCKER, of Virginia.
WILLIAM D. KELLEY, of Pennsylvania.
JAMES A. GARFIELD, of Ohio.
HORATIO C. BURCHARD, of Illinois.
HENRY WATTERSON, of Kentucky.

The last-named only filled a vacancy toward the end of this
Congress, and his position on the committee was probably due to
his own request.

In the 45th Congress the Committee on Ways and Means consisted of the following members :

FERNANDO WOOD, of New York.
J. RANDOLPH TUCKER, of Virginia.
MILTON SAYLER, of Ohio.
WILLIAM M. ROBBINS, of North Carolina.
HENRY R. HARRIS, of Georgia.
RANDALL L. GIBSON, of Louisiana.
JAMES PHILLIPS, of Connecticut.
WILLIAM D. KELLEY, of Pennsylvania.
JAMES A. GARFIELD, of Ohio.
HORATIO C. BURCHARD, of Illinois.
NATHANIEL P. BANKS, of Massachusetts.

The Committee on Rules in this Congress consisted of

The Speaker (SAMUEL J. RANDALL).
ALEXANDER H. STEPHENS, of Georgia.
MILTON SAYLER, of Ohio.
NATHANIEL P. BANKS, of Massachusetts.
JAMES A. GARFIELD, of Ohio.

In the 46th Congress the Committee on Ways and Means consisted of

FERNANDO WOOD, of New York.
J. RANDOLPH TUCKER, of Virginia.
RANDALL L. GIBSON, of Louisiana.
JAMES PHILLIPS, of Connecticut.
WILLIAM R. MORRISON, of Illinois.
R. Q. MILLS, of Texas.
JOHN S. CARLISLE, of Kentucky.
WILLIAM H. FELTON, of Georgia.
JAMES A. GARFIELD, of Ohio.
WILLIAM D. KELLEY, of Pennsylvania.
OMAR D. CONGER, of Michigan.
WILLIAM P. FRYE, of Maine.
MARTIN H. DWINNELL, of Minnesota.

The Committee on Rules consisted of :

The Speaker (SAMUEL J. RANDALL).
ALEXANDER H. STEPHENS, of Georgia.
JOSEPH C. BLACKBURN, of Kentucky.
JAMES A. GARFIELD, of Ohio.
WILLIAM P. FRYE, of Maine.

A good conception of the thoroughness with which Garfield discharged his onerous duties as chairman of the Committee on Appropriations may be formed from reading the speech which he made on "Revenues and Expenditures," on the 5th of March, 1874. With a pretty thorough knowledge of all the important speeches that have been made in Congress since the foundation of the Government, I do not believe that there was ever before made in that body a presentation of the philosophy and methods of adjusting the revenues and appropriations of the Government which covered so much ground in so brief a space, or which disclosed so clearly the principles on which appropriations should be made.

At the outset he announced his disagreement with the assumption implied in the common maxim that we should "cut our garment according to our cloth," which he admitted was correct as applied to private affairs, but not at all applicable to the wants of nations. "Our national expenditures," said he, "should be measured by the real interests and the proper needs of the Government. We should cut our garment so as to fit the person to be clothed. If he be a giant, we must provide cloth sufficient for a fitting garment."

"It was the effort of the Committee on Appropriations," he said, "to find what are the real and vital necessities of the Government; to find what amount of money will suffice to meet all its honorable obligations, to carry on all its necessary and essential functions, and to keep alive those public enterprises which the country desires its Government to undertake and accomplish."

He regarded it as unfortunate that the work of appropriations was not connected directly with the work of taxation, in which case "the necessity of taxation would be a constant check upon extravagance, and the practice of economy would promise as its immediate result the pleasure of reducing taxation."

As to the effect of taxation on the people, he said that "they willingly bear the burdens of taxation when they see that their contributions are honestly and wisely expended to maintain the government of their choice, and to accomplish those objects which they consider necessary for the public welfare. So far as the Government is concerned, the soundness of its financial affairs depends upon the annual surplus of its revenues over expenditures. A steady and constant revenue, drawn from sources that represent the prosperity of the nation, a revenue that grows with the growth of national wealth, and is so adjusted to the expenditures that a constant and considerable surplus is annually left in the treasury above all the necessary current demands—a surplus that keeps the treasury strong, that holds it above the fear of sudden panic, that makes it impregnable against all private combinations, that makes it a terror to stock-jobbing and gold-gambling—this is financial health."

Reviewing the financial history of the Government, he called attention to the history and causes of deficits and of surpluses, and then passed to the wonderful history of the reduction of taxes since the war, and the effects of the reduction of revenue on this surplus.

One of the most interesting portions of this thorough examination into the workings of our system of appropriations and expenditures was an analysis of expenditures for the preceding fiscal year, from which at a glance any intelligent reader could ascertain precisely the amounts expended for every department of the Government—for the maintenance or construction of public works, for interest on our funded debt, and for all the various other objects of Government outlay. These expenditures he grouped in different classifications, with the usual analytic ability of his discussions of such questions, and took up in detail the objects in whose support retrenchment was practicable and advisable. Three classes of expenditures called for his special attention, and his policy toward each of these illustrates his views of wise economy and expenditure. As to the expenditures on rivers and harbors, he called attention to the fact "that in fifteen of the last thirty-four years not a dollar was appropriated for rivers and harbors in the United States. Our friends on the other side of the House, when they were in power, believed in the doctrine that Congress had no right to make internal improvements, and in fifteen of their years of power our docks and piers were rotting and our harbors were filling up, because the theory of non-improvement left them to perish. More than seventy-five per cent of all that has ever been appropriated to open our rivers and clear out 'our harbors and make a highway for commerce on our coasts and upon our inland lakes and rivers has been appropriated since the war by the party now in power."

These works, he said, he named only to praise them. "They are carried on under the War Department, and no man, I believe, has ever charged corruption in the expenditure of the in money. But it is one of that class of expenditures that can in part be postponed, that need not be done in a year. It is well that enough has been done to make it possible for us to open our internal avenues of commerce as the growth of trade requires."

As to the expenditures for the maintenance of our light-house system he was equally liberal. Said he: "I look upon it as one of the wonders of our early history that during the first three months of the life of the first Congress our fathers struck out on a new line, unknown in the history of legislation, when they declared in one simple act that the light that gleamed from every Pharos on our shores should be free to the ships and sailors of all nations. Until recently the United States has stood absolutely alone in allowing the nations of the world to have the benefit of lights without charge. I always feel a keen sense of satisfaction when I am permitted to aid in making appropriations to keep these lights burning on our shores. The life-saving stations which have been added are expenses of the same character. I would do nothing to cripple these great interests."

But as to another branch of public works, that of the construction of public buildings, he was as free in his condemnation of haste and extravagance as he had been of praise in regard to the two preceding classes.

A late illustration of the grasp of Garfield's study of the revenues and expenditures of the Government which was prosecuted in the course of his service on the Committee on Appropriations may be found in an article of his in the *North American Review* for June, 1879. In that exceedingly clear and readable article he quoted a passage from a speech which he made on revenues and expenditures in the House in 1872, which, for the interest and attractiveness with which he succeeded in investing a subject that is generally regarded as forbidding by reason of its dryness and technicalities, may well be compared with that brilliant budget of Gladstone's earlier parliamentary career, which has been so famous. In this speech he gave his philosophy of expenditures and appropriations, and prophesied, among other things, at what time in our history we could probably reach a peace level of expendi-

tures after the war—at what time we could get down so low
that we could not get any lower, and that the natural growth
of the country would require a revival of trade and rise of
prices ; and in forecasting the time he took a very large risk in
saying that " at a certain period so far ahead it will be found
that we shall touch bottom on the scale of reduction, and at
that time we shall probably get our interest down to such
a figure, and our annual expenditures down to such a figure,
and thereupon and thereafter the growth of the country will
make the peace increase starting up again necessary." The
period he had fixed on was about the end of 1876. In his
North American article he showed that his only mistake was
that this revival came about a year later than the time which he
predicted in 1872, and the figures were almost identical. This
prediction was not a mere speculative theory, but was on the
basis of an immense induction of historical facts, which convinced him that the expenditures of a war could not be reduced
so as to strike a peace level short of a period twice the length
of the war itself after it. He showed that this was the case in
England's wars, and that it was so in all our wars from the beginning ; that the expenditures reached their height, of course,
at the close of the war, then they began to drop gradually down
an inclined plane until they struck the new level of peace,
where the rise began again gradually, and this was arrived at in
a period twice as long after a war as the length of the war itself. Our war was substantially five years long, ending finan-
cially in 1866. Add ten years, and the period of decline fixed
on the basis of this calculation would extend to 1876 ; and he
said in his speech in 1872, " We shall reach our peace level
then." He made an analysis, showing what were our war expenditures and those resulting from the war, and what the
peace expenses were, proving that the peace expenses would
increase all the time, growing with the growth of the country,
and that the war expenses would decrease. There were two
processes ; but the war expenditures were so great that their
decrease would be more rapid than the peace increase ; and after

a while those two lines would meet, and the sloping incline of peace would come.

Besides the work devolved upon him in the regular and special committees to which I have referred, Garfield has been called on from time to time to serve on special committees requiring an unusual amount of labor, care, and judgment; and special occasions of great magnitude have given to the work of the regular committees to which he belonged unusual responsibilities and labors.   For instance, the investigation into the causes of the gold panic, which was ordered by the House in December, 1869, was devolved on the Committee on Banking and Currency, of which he was chairman.   It is probable that no special subject of investigation by a Congressional committee attracted more universal attention at the time than did this, and for very obvious reasons.   Charges had been made calculated to create the impression that there had been some sort of connection between the gigantic and reckless operations of New York gamblers in gold and the action of the President of the United States in regard to the selling of gold.   There were few intelligent people who gave to these charges any sort of credence ; but there was a sufficient array of circumstances to give a basis for a swarm of calumnies likely to affect seriously the reputation of the President, and of course to impair the respect in which our Government and institutions were held abroad.   It was deemed advisable, therefore, that the transactions which had occasioned so much comment and scandal should be rigorously investigated and the bottom facts brought to the surface.   The conduct of this investigation by General Garfield was the subject of universal admiration at the time, and of most complimentary comments by the press of New York, particularly the tact and adroitness and firmness with which he managed and drew out that most remarkable and irrepressible of witnesses, Mr. James Fisk, Jr.   The results of the most thorough inquiry were embodied in the report of the committee, and its statements of all of the essential facts developed by their inquiry were so clear and satisfactory that no question has arisen since as to the accuracy of the committee's findings. The reputation of the Executive was vindicated, while the nefariousness and recklessness of the conspiracy were exposed in the most striking manner.

(Garfield to Col. A. F. Rockwell.)

HIRAM, OHIO, August 30, 1869.

It seems as though each year added more to the work that falls to my share. This season I have the main weight of the census bill and the report to carry, and the share of the Ohio campaign that falls to me, and in addition to all this I am running in debt and building a house in Washington. On looking over I found I had paid out over $5,000, since I first went to Congress, for rent alone, and all this is a dead loss ; so, finding an old staff-officer (Maj. D. G. Swaim), I negotiated enough to enable me to get a lot on the corner of Thirteenth and I Streets, north, opposite to Franklin Square, and I have got a house three quarters done. It may be a losing business, but I hope I shall be able to sell it when I am done with it, so as to save myself and the rent.

(Garfield to Col. A. F. Rockwell.)

HIRAM, OHIO, August 6, 1870.

I have at last reached home in the green fields and pure air of the country, and for the first time in many months have a few days of comparative rest now before the opening of the fall campaign.

My work during the last Congressional year has been harder than ever before. I gave eighty days' hard work last summer and fall to the census, and, though I carried my bill successfully through the House, it failed in the Senate. Then I spent forty days' on the Gold Panic Investigation and Report, nearly all the work of which I did. Then I gave three or four weeks' hard work to the Tariff Bill, and more than that amount to the Currency Bill, which I had charge of and which created a long and strong combat. Add to this all the usual outside work and two cases in the Supreme Court, one of which I argued and won, and you will see that it filled my days and many of my nights with about as close grubbing as I was capable of performing. On the whole, I have done as much as I had any reason to hope I should.

I was very much obliged for your discussion of the Indian affairs. You can see how nearly impossible it is for a member of Congress, nearly a thousand miles away from the scene of Indian events, and knowing nothing but what he learns from vague and contradictory reports, to understand the real situation, and to provide wise and efficient means for managing a subject so difficult and so impossible to handle by general laws or regulations. I have from the first been in favor of the transfer of the Indian Bureau to the War Department ; but the Piegan massacre and the personal quarrel of which you speak prevented the transfer. I twice got the bill through the House. I shall take the liberty to write to Secretary Cox and quote some passages from your letter.

(Garfield to Col. A. F. Rockwell.)

WASHINGTON, December 13, 1871.

I am now up to my eyes in the work of the Committee on Appropriations, of which I am Chairman, though I do manage to steal a little time from work and sleep, almost every day to read over carefully a few lines from Horace, to keep the breath of classical life in my body.

(Garfield to Col. A. F. Rockwell.)

WASHINGTON, March 5, 1875.

At last the long, hard struggle is over, and I lie stranded, like a ship ashore, water-logged and shattered by the battle of wind and waves.

'You will perhaps think I am always saying the same thing at the end of a session ; but, I am sure, no other five days of my Congressional life have been so crowded with heavy work as those just ended. Forty-eight hours ago six of my appropriation bills were in peril. Two of them had not passed the House the first time, and the others were in the Senate or in Conference Committees. They were all passed in good shape at half-past eleven A.M. yesterday.

The amount of intellectual work I have done, and the physical strain which has accompanied it, is something more than everything I have ever done before

(Garfield to Col. A. F. Rockwell.)

WASHINGTON, December 4, 1875.

The committees have not yet been announced, but you will probably see them before this reaches you. I have followed rather austerely the rule of self-respect, and have kept aloof from all combinations. I have asked nothing, nor have I permitted my friends to ask anything for me. I was gratified and surprised when the Republican members of the Ohio delegation united in a unanimous expression of their desire that I should be appointed Chairman of the Committee on Appropriations, but I asked them not to make any requests for me.

CHAPTER XII.

No Republican leader of the House ever had devolved upon him a responsibility so great or a duty so arduous as were thrown upon Garfield by the extra session of Congress, in 1879, called within three weeks after the adjournment of the regular session, on the 4th of March, which left the Executive and Legislative branches of the Government in a deadlock of unyielding antagonism, and all the branches of the Government without the supplies essential to their maintenance. In fact, it may be said that no such exigency was ever before presented to any leader of the House. Before that time Congress had never undertaken to condition the performance of its duty to support the Government on the acquiescence of the Executive in the demands of the former. Legislation, it is true, had been incorporated in appropriation bills, which practically left the President little discretion. But these legislative " riders" did not amount to a formal and formidable declaration of the intention of Congress to coerce the Executive. And this was precisely the appalling situation which was presented when the winter session of 1878-9 came to its unsatisfactory close. In the stormy debates which preceded this deadlock, Garfield, as the responsible leader of the Republican minority, had fairly offered to the majority not so much a compromise of the principles involved in the legislation which the majority attempted to force the Executive to accept, as a Conservative Republican revision, adapted to the times, of the legislation which had been put upon the statute-books in periods of essentially different character. The very fairness of his proposition and the broad statesmanship which he displayed in the closing debates of that session had alienated from him, to a greater or less extent, many

Republican members of Congress with whom he had been in most cordial co-operation, and who afterward heartily rallied under his leadership.

From this fact, and from the lack of intimate relations between several Republican leaders in Congress and the President, the duties imposed on Garfield in the extra session were such as demanded in their performance the most sagacious judgment, and frequently the highest degree of moral courage. No leader of the party in either branch of Congress at any period was ever before placed in such a peculiar and delicate position. But he did not shrink from the straightforward performance of his duty, and its difficulty not only nerved him to greater efforts to maintain what he regarded as the only tenable position on which his party could stand, but what was far more important than this, to maintain the constitutional balance of power between the three departments of the Government, whose continuance is absolutely essential to the preservation of our institutions. His speech in the House on the 29th of March shows the solemnity of his impression of the magnitude and perils of the crisis through which he was to pilot the way to safety with honor. He did not shrink at the outset from stating what was really the most terrible indictment of the policy of the majority in Congress. Said he :

" MR. CHAIRMAN : I have no hope of being able to convey to the members of this House my own conviction of the very great gravity and solemnity of the crisis which this decision of the Chair and of the Committee of the Whole has brought upon this country. I wish I could be proved a false prophet in reference to the result of this action. I wish I could be overwhelmed with the proof that I am utterly mistaken in my views. But no view I have ever taken has entered more deeply and more seriously into my convictions than this : that this House has to-day resolved to enter upon a revolution against the Constitution and Government of the United States. I do not know that that intention exists in the minds of half the Representatives who occupy the other side of this hall. I hope it does not. I am ready to believe it does not exist to any large extent. But I mean to say the consequence of the programme

just adopted, if persisted in, is nothing less than the total sub-
version of this Government."

Then he reviewed the history of the struggle in the preceding
session, and gave the history of the formation of the issue between the two parties—the demands on the one side, and the
resistance on the other—and placed the grounds of his resistance on the broad principles of the Constitution. He pointed
out several ways in which our Government could be destroyed
without armed revolution. For example, by a refusal on the
part of the people to elect Representatives to Congress ; or a
majority of one branch or the other of Congress might, on the
first day of the session, vote to adjourn on the hour of meeting,
and continue to vote so at every session during the two years of
the existence of that Congress ; or a majority of either body
might vote down every bill to support the Government by appropriations. All these methods of destroying the Government
are permitted by the Constitution, because the people "being
themselves the creators of all the agencies and forces to execute
their own will, and choosing from themselves their Representatives to express that will in the forms of law, it would have been
like a suggestion of suicide to assume that any of these great
voluntary powers would be turned against the life of the Government. Public opinion—that great ocean of thought from
whose height all heights and all depths are measured—was
trusted as a power amply able, and always willing, to guard all
the approaches on that side of the Constitution from any assault on the life of the nation."

"Up to this hour," he continued, "our sovereign has never
failed us. There has never been such a refusal to exercise those
primary functions of sovereignty as either to endanger or cripple the Government ; nor have the majority of the representatives of that sovereign in either house of Congress ever before
announced their purpose to use their voluntary powers for its
destruction. And now, for the first time in our history, and I
will add for the first time for at least two centuries in the history of any English-speaking nation, it is proposed and insisted

upon that these voluntary powers shall be used for the destruction of the Government. I want it distinctly understood that
the proposition which I read at the beginning of my remarks,
and which is the programme announced to the American people
to-day, is this : that if this House cannot have its own way in
certain matters, not connected with appropriations, it will so
use, or refrain from using, its voluntary powers as to destroy
the Government.''

Going deep down to the foundations of the philosophy of our
Government, he bottomed his whole argument on these comprehensive propositions, which were ample to sustain the superstructure of illustration with which he strengthened and adorned
it. Said he :

'' Our theory of law is free consent. That is the granite
foundation of our whole superstructure. Nothing in the Republic can be law without consent—the free consent of the
House ; the free consent of the Senate ; the free consent of the
Executive, or, if he refuse it, the free consent of two thirds of
these bodies. Will any man deny that ? Will any man challenge a line of the statement that free consent is the foundation
rock of all our institutions ? And yet the programme announced
two weeks ago was that if the Senate refused to consent to the
demand of the House, the Government should stop. And the
proposition was then, and the programme is now, that, although
there is not a Senate to be coerced, there is still a third independent branch in the legislative power of the Government,
whose consent is to be coerced at the peril of the destruction of
this Government ; that is, if the President, in the discharge of
his duty, shall exercise his plain constitutional right to refuse
his consent to this proposed legislation, the Congress will so
use its voluntary powers as to destroy the Government. This
is the proposition which we confront ; and we denounce it as
revolution.''

Although he was willing, at the regular session, to make
reasonable amendments to the laws which it was proposed to
carry on the backs of appropriation bills, he took the broad
principle that, however inoffensive the proposition, if it was
demanded '' that as a matter of coercion it shall be adopted,
against the free consent prescribed in the Constitution, every

fair-minded man in America is bound to resist you, as much as
though his own life depended upon the resistance." And he
then challenged all comers to show a single instance in our
history when this consent was coerced. "This," said he, "is
the great, the paramount issue, which dwarfs all others into
insignificance."

Then, showing that the election law, which was denounced
as so great an offence as to justify the destruction of the Government rather than let it remain on the statute-books, was
passed with the active co-operation of prominent Democratic
members of both houses, and thus aggravating the criminality
of their changed position, he intensified the point he made
by stating that "the proposition now is that, after fourteen
years have passed and not one petition from one American
citizen has come to us asking that this law be repealed, while
not one memorial has found its way to our desks complaining
of the law, so far as I have heard, the Democratic House of
Representatives now hold that if they are not permitted to force
upon another house and upon the Executive against their consent the repeal of a law that Democrats made, this refusal shall
be considered a sufficient ground for starving this Government
to death."

This phrase, "starving the Government to death," was one
of those inspirational condensations of argument and truth
which only occur to statesmen of creative and original minds.
It covered the whole ground, reached to the vitals of the controversy, and exposed to the people the nature and the deadli-
ness of the conspiracy that had tried to ambush itself under
English precedents of redressing grievances that were totally
inapplicable to our system of three independent, free, and equal
branches of the Government.

Without undertaking to review or to revive the special points
of argument with which this speech and a following speech on
the same subject on the 4th of April, fairly bristled, it is sufficient to quote one passage which stands a fair chance of going
down to posterity and of taking its place alongside of Web-

ster's defences of the Constitution against attacks prompted by the same spirit and originated in the same quarter.   Said he :

"Touching this question of Executive action, I remind the gentleman that in 1856 the National Democratic Convention, in session at Cincinnati, and, still later, the National Democratic Convention of 1860, affirmed the right of the veto as one of the sacred rights guaranteed by our Government.   Here is the resolution :

"'That we are decidedly opposed to taking from the President the qualified veto power by which he is enabled, under restrictions and responsibilities amply sufficient to guard the public interests, to suspend the passage of a bill whose merits cannot secure the approval of two thirds of the Senate and House of Representatives until the judgment of the people can be obtained thereon.'

"The doctrine is that any measure which cannot be passed over a veto by a two thirds vote, has no right to become a law ; and the only mode of redress is an appeal to the people at the next election.   That has been the Democratic doctrine from the earliest days—notably so from Jackson's time—until now.

"In leaving this topic, let me ask what you would have said if, in 1861, the Democratic members of the Senate, being then a majority of that body, instead of taking the heroic course and going out to battle, had simply said, 'We will put on an appropriation bill an amendment declaring the right of any State to secede from the Union at pleasure, and forbidding the President or any officer of the Army or Navy of the United States from interfering with any State in its work of secession.'   Suppose they had said to the President, 'Unless you consent to the incorporation of this provision in an appropriation bill, we will refuse supplies to the Government.'   Perhaps they could then have killed the Government by starvation ; but even in the madness of that hour, the leaders of rebellion did not think it worthy their manhood to put their fight on that dishonorable ground.   They planted themselves on the higher plane of battle and fought it out to defeat.

"Now, by a method which the wildest secessionist scorned to adopt, it is proposed to make this new assault upon the life of the Republic.

"Gentlemen, we have calmly surveyed this new field of conflict ; we have tried to count the cost of the struggle, as we did that of 1861, before we took up your gage of battle. Though no human foresight could forecast the awful loss of blood and treasure, yet in the name of liberty and union we accepted the issue and fought it out to the end. We made the appeal to our august sovereign, to the omnipotent public opinion of America, to determine whether the Union should perish at your hands. You know the result. And now lawfully, in the exercise of our right as Representatives, we take up the gage you have this day thrown down, and appeal again to our common sovereign to determine whether you shall be permitted to destroy the principle of free consent in legislation under the threat of starving the Government to death.

"We are ready to pass these bills for the support of the Government at any hour when you will offer them in the ordinary way, by the methods prescribed by the Constitution. If you offer those other propositions of legislation as separate measures, we will meet you in the fraternal spirit of fair debate and will discuss their merits. Some of your measures many of us will vote for in separate bills. But you shall not coerce any independent branch of this Government, even by the threat of starvation, to surrender its voluntary powers until the question has been appealed to the sovereign and decided in your favor. On this ground we plant ourselves, and here we will stand to the end."

In his speech on the 4th of April he reminded the Democratic members that they had only to wait two years, when they could have the three consents to all the legislation they wanted which are required by the letter and spirit of the Constitution, to wit, the free consent of the House, the free consent of the Senate and the free consent of the Executive, provided by that time they had convinced the people that the legislation they desired was needed and just. Until then he asked them to restrain their rage until they had the lawful power to strike down these statutes. But, lest he should be misunderstood, he added :

"I said last session, and I have said since, that if you want this whole statute concerning the use of the Army at the polls torn from your books, I will help you to do it. If you will offer a naked proposition to repeal those two sections of the Revised Statutes named in the sixth section of this bill, I will vote with you. But you do not ask a repeal of those sections. Why? They impose restrictions upon the use of the Army, limiting its functions and punishing its officers for any infraction of these limitations ; but you ask to strike out a negative clause, thereby making new and affirmative legislation of the most sweeping and dangerous character.

" Your proposed modification of the law affects not the Army alone, but the whole civil power of the United States. ' Civil officers ' are included in these sections, and, if the proposed amendment be adopted, you deny to any civil officer of the United States any power whatever to summon the armed *posse* to help him enforce the processes of the law. If you pass the section in that form, you impose restrictions upon the civil authorities of the United States never before proposed in any Congress by any legislator since this Government began. I say, therefore, in the shape you propose this, it is much the worst of all your ' riders.' In the beginning of this contest, we understood that you desired only to get the Army away from the polls. As that would still leave the civil officers full power to keep the peace at the polls, I thought it was the least important and the least dangerous of your demands ; but as you have put it here, it is the most dangerous. If you re-enact it in the shape presented, it becomes a later law than the supervisors and marshals law, and *pro tanto* repeals the latter. As it stands now in the statute-book, it is the earlier statute, and is *pro tanto* itself repealed by the marshals law of 1871, and is therefore harmless so far as it relates to civil officers. But if you put it in here, you deny the power of the marshals of the United States to perform their duties whenever a riot may require the use of an armed *posse*."

The ablest and most specious Democratic plea in behalf of the scheme of coercing the Executive was made by that distinguished jurist from Virginia, Mr. J. Randolph Tucker. He had most artfully used the deceptive and false precedent of the practice of the House of Commons of accompanying supply bills with a list of grievances to be redressed, to which Garfield replied :

" The gentleman from Virginia says, ' Unless you let us append a condition which we regard a redress of grievances, we will let the Army be annihilated on the 30th day of next June by withholding supplies.' That is legitimate argument ; that is a frank declaration of your policy. Let us examine the pro-

position.   What is the 'grievance' of which the gentleman
complains ?   He uses the word 'grievance' in the old English
sense, as though the king were thrusting himself in the way of
the nation by making a war contrary to the nation's wish.
What is the 'grievance' of which the gentleman complains ?
His 'grievance' is a law of the land—a law made by the representatives of the people—by all the forms of consent known to
the Constitution.   It is his 'grievance' that he cannot get rid
of this law by the ordinary and constitutional methods of
appeal.   [Applause.]   When he can get rid of any law by the
union of all the consents that are required to make or unmake
a law, then he can lawfully get rid of it, whether it is a grievance or a blessing.   But his method is first to call a law a
'grievance' and then try to get rid of it in defiance of the
processes which the Constitution prescribes for the law-making
power of the nation.   I denounce his method as unconstitu-
tional and revolutionary, and one that will result in far greater
evil than that of which he complains."

Through the whole of this controversy in the regular and in
the extra session, Garfield bore himself not only with courage,
which is a common attribute, but with a conscientious and independent statesmanship which refused to be controlled even
by the criticism and clamor of influential members of his own
party.   Throughout the whole he was not so much the partisan
as he was the constitutional lawyer and the patriot.   Believing
in, thoroughly comprehending, and admiring with the whole
force of his nature, the grandeur of the system of checks and
balances and distributions of powers, which characterize our
Government, he was as inflexible in the maintenance of his own
convictions of right, against the pressure of friends, as he was
fearless in meeting the assaults of political enemies who had
attempted a desperate and revolutionary scheme.   He was the
central and commanding figure in all this great controversy—
as important, in all respects, as that which Webster faced so
grandly in 1832.   As the prejudices, passions, and excitements
which clouded the minds of many of the combatants in this
period pass away, Garfield's courage and broad-minded statesmanship has become more and more the subject of admiration

on the part of those who agreed with him at the time, of those
within his own party who then differed from him, and even of
many of those whose arguments he was obliged to repel.   He
showed himself more than a mere party leader.   He rose to the
full proportions of an American statesman, whose nature, convictions, and training had rendered it impossible that he should
either surrender or cease to defend any of that beautiful and
symmetrically proportioned edifice of civil liberty which was
the product of the wisdom, the experience, and the patriotism
of the fathers.

Although it would be supposed that the duties imposed upon
him as leader of the Republican side of the House at the extra
session in opposing the coercionist and revolutionary schemes
of the Democrats would have been sufficient to engage all his
energies, it is notable that he was found prepared for every
emergency of debate on other issues of importance as they arose
for the consideration of the House.   For instance, on the 15th
of April he furnished a startling array of facts as to the number of Union soldiers who had risked everything for the cause
in the seceding States.   Five days before that he had handled
with his usual vigor the question of resumption and the currency, resisting an insidious attempt to increase the volume of
the subsidiary paper currency.   On the 17th of May he made a
brief speech on the House bill to authorize the unlimited coinage of silver, and to give the profits thereof to the owners of
bullion, which was a remarkable instance of condensation, and
was well calculated to appeal to the good sense of those advocates of silver who have some consideration for the immutable
laws of trade and currency, and warned the House that the bill
under consideration reached further and touched more vital
interests than was generally appreciated.   He called attention
to the fact that " within recent months the leading thinkers of
the civilized world had become alarmed at the attitude of the
two precious metals in relation to each other," and that " many
leading thinkers were becoming clearly of the opinion that by
some wise. judicious arrangement both the precious metals

must be kept in service for the currency of the world.'' And he called the attention of the House to the fact that in England there had been recently a decided accession to the side of those who believed that she ought to abandon the single gold standard and '' harness both silver and gold to the monetary car of the world.'' '' And yet,'' added he, '' outside of this Capitol, I do not this day know of a single great and recognized advocate of bimetallic money who regards it prudent or safe for any nation largely to increase the coinage standard of silver coin at the present time beyond the limits fixed by existing laws. France and the States of the Latin Union, that have long believed in bimetallism, maintained it against all comers, and have done all in their power to advocate it throughout the world, dare not coin a single silver coin, and have not done so since 1874. The most strenuous advocates of bimetallism in those countries say it would be ruinous to bimetallism for France or the Latin Union to coin any more silver at present. The remaining stock of German silver now for sale, amounting to from forty to seventy-five millions of dollars, is a standing menace to the exchange and silver coinage of Europe. One month ago the leading financial journal of London proposed that the Bank of England buy one half of the German surplus and hold it five years on condition that the German Government shall hold the other half off the market. The time is ripe for some wise and prudent arrangement among the nations to save silver from a disastrous break-down.''

And he continued :

'' Yet we, who during the past two years have coined far more silver dollars than we ever before coined since the foundation of the Government—ten times as many as we coined during half a century of our national life—are to-day ignoring and defying the enlightened, universal opinion of bimetallists, and saying that the United States, single-handed and alone, can enter the field and settle the mighty issue alone. We are justifying the old proverb that ' Fools rush in where angels fear to tread.'

'' It is sheer madness, Mr. Speaker. I once saw a dog on a

great stack of hay that had been floated out into the wild, over-flowed stream of a river, with its stack-pen and foundation still holding together, but ready to be wrecked. For a little while the animal appeared to be perfectly happy. His hay-stack was there and the pen around it, and he seemed to think the world bright, and his happiness secure, while the sunshine fell softly on his head and his hay. But by and by he began to discover that the house and the barn and their surroundings were not all there as they were when he went to sleep the night before ; and he began to see that he could not command all the prospect and peacefully dominate the scene as he had done before. So with this House. We assume to manage this mighty question which has been launched on the wild current that sweeps over the whole world, and we bark from our legislative hay-stacks, as though we commanded the whole world. [Applause.] In the name of common-sense and sanity, let us take some account of the flood ; let us understand that a deluge means something, and try, if we can, to get our bearings before we undertake to settle the affairs of all mankind by a vote of this House.

" To-day we are coining one third of all the silver that is being coined in the round world. China is coining another third ; and all other nations are using the remaining one third for subsidiary coin. And if we want to take rank with China and part company with all of the civilized nations of the West-ern world, let us pass this bill, and then ' bay the moon ' as we float down the whirling channel to take our place among the silver monometallists of Asia.

" What this country needs above all other things, is that this Congress shall pass the appropriation bills, adjourn, and go home [applause on the Republican side], and let the forces of business and good order and brotherhood, working in their natural and orderly way, bring us into light and stability and peace. And we want time to adjust this great international question. Now, while I am speaking, the Administration is opening negotiations with all the Western nations, to see if there cannot be some international arrangement whereby this question of bimetallism may be wisely settled. We tried it by international monetary conference. It was a preliminary recon-naissance, and—"

[Here the hammer fell.]

On the 21st of June General Garfield made a speech on the Mississippi River as an object of national care, which showed that while he was resolutely opposed to wasting the national treasure in improving mountain-trout brooks for purposes of navigation, and to river and harbor bills that consisted largely of appropriations for harbors which had no commerce and rivers which were vexed by no keels, he was perfectly willing to go the full length of a wise liberality in the improvement of great national water-ways, especially of the river which drains thirty States of the Union.

This speech attracted much attention and called out much admiration at the time, and deserves to form a part of any record of Garfield's statesmanship. Said he :

" Mr. Speaker : I should oppose this bill, very decidedly, if it committed us at this time to any plan or theory of managing the Mississippi River ; and I think the remarks of the gentleman from Indiana [Mr. Baker], warning us against committal in any such direction, are wise. But I have looked the bill over with what care I could, and it does not seem to me that by its passage we commit ourselves to anything further than the purpose to obtain accurate official information touching the present condition and needs of this great stream. I admit that we have already had examinations and explorations of the Mississippi, some of them scientific and very valuable ; but everybody will concede that one important experiment has been made, in recent years, which, though against the opinion of the majority of engineers, has proved apparently a great success : I mean the jetty system at the mouth of that river. I say ' apparently,' because it is possible that in the long run it may not prove a success ; but at the present moment it appears to be a great and striking success in the management of the mouths of that river. If it prove to be permanently so, all our calculations, and, indeed, all our theories concerning the improvement and management of other portions of that river need to be reconsidered in view of the new light that the jetty system will throw upon the question. Hence a proposition to turn on the light, to get information, and to get it from the best scientific advisers that we can call to our aid, is a step in the right direction. I have always favored measures which will result in giving us information upon all questions about which we are called upon to legislate. What shall be done with this knowledge when it comes, will be for our successors to say. We do not commit ourselves or them to any scheme at this time. But for myself, I believe that one of the grandest of our material national interests—one that is national in the largest material sense of that word—is the Mississippi River and its navigable tributaries.   It is the most gigantic single natural feature of our continent, far transcending the glory of the ancient Nile or of any other river on the earth.   The statesmanship of America must grapple the problem of this mighty stream.   It is too vast for any State to handle ; too much for any authority less than that of the nation itself to manage. And I believe the time will come when the liberal-minded statesmanship of this country will devise a wise and comprehensive system, that will harness the powers of this great river to the material interests of America, so that not only all the people who live on its banks and the banks of its confluents, but all the citizens of the Republic, whether dwellers in the central valley or on the slope of either ocean, will recognize the importance of preserving and perfecting this great natural and material bond of national union between the North and the South—a bond to be so strengthened by commerce and intercourse that it can never be severed. [Applause.]

" One of our early Presidents went so far as even to exceed his early preconceived opinions of the constitutional power of the Executive, in order to buy from France a mighty empire to be added to the Union ; and he did it for this reason chiefly, that the young Republic could not permanently endure as a nation without owning and controlling the mouths of the Mississippi.   Nearly the whole continent west of that river was bought, to make the Union perpetual by bringing every foot of the shore of the Mississippi under our flag.   If I did not think it almost unworthy of so great a theme, I would say that if there had been no patriotic impulse higher than any consideration of material welfare which moved twenty millions of Americans to resist the attempt to break the Union in pieces, and impelled them to hold it together by all the cost of blood and treasure that our late war required, if there had been no higher national sentiment inspiring them, the immense material stake which the people of the great North and West and centre of this country had in the free use of that river from its sources to its mouth, that their commerce might go southward to the sea under the one flag, unvexed by conflicting nationalities, this material stake alone would have made all the people of the upper valley of the Mississippi resist to the last the dismemberment of the Union.

" This great river, which our fathers made such sacrifices to acquire, and which the present generation made so much costlier sacrifices to redeem from disunion and to hold within the grasp of the nation, we have held, not in obedience to mere sentiment alone, not with a view of keeping it as a vast and worthless waste of water, but to utilize it by making it the servant of all the people of this country. How shall we utilize it, unless at some time, and in some wise way, we bridle it by the skill of man and make it subservient to the interests of commerce ?

" Now, Mr. Speaker and gentlemen of the House, there is another reason why I am in favor of this measure. I rejoice in any occasion which enables Representatives from the North and from the South to unite in an unpartisan effort to promote a great national interest. [Applause.] Such an occasion is good for us both. And when we can do it without the sacrifice of our convictions, and can benefit millions of our fellow-citizens, and thereby strengthen the bonds of the Union, we ought to do it with rejoicing ; for, in so doing, we shall inspire our people with larger and more generous views, and help to confirm for them and for our posterity to our latest generations, the indissoluble Union and the permanent grandeur of this Republic. I shall vote for this bill." [Applause on both sides of the House.]

On the 27th of June he made a very terse and condensed argument on the various phases of the revived doctrine of State Sovereignty, showing from the recent speeches of Democratic members that Calhounism still had prominent defenders and exponents among the leaders of that party in both branches of Congress. The declarations made by these men he summarized in this manner :

" Let me summarize them : First, there are no national elections ; second, the United States has no voters ; third, the States have the exclusive right to control all elections of members of Congress ; fourth, the Senators and Representatives in Congress are State officers, or, as they have been called during the present session, ' ambassadors ' or ' agents ' of the State ; fifth, the United States has no authority to keep the peace anywhere within a State, and, in fact, has no peace to keep ; sixth, the United States is not a nation endowed with sovereign power, but is a confederacy of States ; seventh, the States are sovereignties possessing inherent supreme powers ; they are older than the

Union, and as independent sovereignties the State Governments created the Union and determined and limited the powers of the General Government.

" These declarations embody the sum total of the constitutional doctrines which the Democracy has avowed during this extra session of Congress.   They form a body of doctrines which I do not hesitate to say are more extreme than were ever before held in this subject, except perhaps at the very crisis of secession and rebellion."

He then enumerated the attempts which had been made to embody these abstract and false theories of our Government in practice ; and met them with these broad counter-propositions, which are important in any estimate of Garfield's constitutional views :

" I affirm : First, that the Constitution of the United States was not created by the Government of the States, but was ordained and established by the only sovereign in this country—the common superior of both the States and the nation—the people themselves ; second, that the United States is a nation, having a government whose powers, as defined and limited by the Constitution, operate upon all the States in their corporate capacity and upon all the people ; third, that by its legislative, executive, and judicial authority, the nation is armed with adequate power to enforce all the provisions of the Constitution against all opposition of individuals or of States, at all times and all places within the Union."

These propositions he defended by a summary of the history of the sovereignty and government in this country as comprised in four sharply defined epochs, to wit :

" First : Prior to the 4th of July, 1776, sovereignty, so far as it can be affirmed of this country, was lodgd in the Crown of Great Britain.   Every member of every colony (the colonists were not citizens but subjects) drew his legal rights from the Crown of Great Britain. ' Every acre of land in this country was then held mediately or immediately by grants from that Crown,' and ' all the civil authority then existing or exercised here, flowed from the head of the British Empire.'

" Second : On the 4th day of July, 1776, the people of these colonies, asserting their natural inherent right as sovereigns, withdrew the sovereignty from the Crown of Great Britain and reserved it to themselves.   In so far as they delegated this national authority at all, they delegated it to the Continental Congress assembled at Philadelphia.   That Congress, by general consent, became the supreme government of this country—executive, judicial, and legislative in one.   During the whole of its existence it wielded the supreme power of the new nation.

"Third : On the 1st day of March, 1781, the same sovereign power, the people, withdrew the authority from the Continental Congress and lodged it, so far as they lodged it at all, with the Confederation, which, though a league of States, was declared to be a perpetual union.

"Fourth : When at last our fathers found the Confederation too weak and inefficient for the purposes of a great nation, they abolished it and lodged the national authority, enlarged and strengthened by new powers, in the Constitution of the United States, where, in spite of all assaults, it still remains.   All these great acts were done by the only sovereign in this Republic, the people themselves."

After illustrating the truth of his propositions, by quotations from Elliot's "Debates" and the "Decisions of the Supreme Court of the United States," he said :

"I am unwilling to believe that any considerable number of Americans will ever again push that doctrine to the same extreme ; and yet in these summer months of 1879, in the Congress of the reunited nation, we find the majority drifting fast and far in the wrong direction, by reasserting much of that doctrine which the war ought to have settled forever.   And what is more lamentable, such declarations as those which I read at the outset are finding their echoes in many portions of the country which was lately the theatre of war.   No one can read the proceedings at certain recent celebrations, without observing the growing determination to assert that the men who fought against the Union were not engaged in treasonable conspiracy against the nation, but that they did right to fight for their States, and that, in the long run, the lost cause will be victorious.   These indications are filling the people with anxiety and indignation ; and they are beginning to inquire whether the war has really settled these great questions.

"I remind gentlemen on the other side that we have not ourselves revived these issues. We had hoped they were settled beyond recall, and that peace and friendship might be fully restored to our people.

"But the truth requires me to say that there is one indispensable ground of agreement on which alone we can stand together, and it is this : The war for the Union was right, everlastingly right [applause] ; and the war against the Union was wrong, forever wrong. However honest and sincere individuals may have been, the secession was none the less rebellion and treason. We defend the States in the exercise of their many and important rights, and we defend with equal zeal the rights of the United States. The rights and authority of both were received from the people—the only source of inherent power.

"We insist not only that this is a nation, but that the power of the Government, within its own prescribed sphere, operates directly upon the States and upon all the people. We insist that our laws shall be construed by our own courts and enforced by our Executive. Any theory which is inconsistent with this doctrine we will resist to the end."

(Garfield to B. A. Hinsdale.)

WASHINGTON, May 20, 1879.

I have read your letter carefully. It is all interesting, and some of your reflections and suggestions are very valuable. I will notice your points in the order you state them.

FIRST.—You think my position in the first speech was greatly modified, if not abandoned, in the second, because, first, from the speech of March 29th, the ordinary reader would get the idea that revolution comes in on the rider, and not in insisting upon the rider when it could not command a two thirds vote ; second, that the latter point is not mentioned at all in my first speech, and no intimation is made that the rider is ever legitimate. It is no doubt true that the reader of my first speech who had not paid special attention to the transactions of Congress during the preceding month might fail to understand what was plain to my hearers, who had listened to the debate, in which the Democrats had repeatedly stated that their reason for putting their independent legislation upon the appropriation bill as a rider was because they were certain it would be vetoed if passed as an independent measure, and their only hope of success was to pass no appropriation bills without the riders.

Several of these declarations are quoted in the President's veto of the Army Appropriation Bill. But I don't think that the ordinary reader can find anything in my first speech which implies that it is revolutionary to put a rider on an appropriation bill.

It is singular that no member of Congress who replied to me attempted to show by any quotation from my speech that I had said so.

On the contrary, I think the ordinary reader will understand that I was discussing the refusal to vote supplies if the ridered bill should be vetoed.

Let me call your attention to the fact that, after developing, on pages 6, 7 and 8 of the first speech, the doctrine of the voluntary powers of the government, and that the free consent of the House, the Senate, and the President, or two thirds of the House and Senate against the President's consent is the basis of all our laws, I say at the close of page 8: "The programme announced two weeks ago was that if the Senate refused to consent to the demands of the House the government should stop. And the proposition was then, and the programme is now, that, although there is not a Senate to be coerced, there is still a third independent branch in the legislative power of the government whose consent is to be coerced at the peril of the destruction of this government. That is, if the President, in the discharge of his duty, shall exercise his plain constitutional right to refuse his consent to this proposed legislation, Congress will so use its voluntary powers as to destroy the government."

This is the proposition which we confront and we denounce as revolutionary. That is, the Democratic party in Congress, knowing it had not a two thirds majority, declared that if the President refused his signature to their independent legislation they would not vote supplies and would let the government perish of inanition. My replies to the questions of Mr. Stevens, page 11, and Mr. Davis, page 14, are to the same effect, from the beginning to the end of the speech. I was discussing their proposition, that if they could not pass their measures of independent legislation in spite of the President's veto—and they knew they could not—they would refuse to vote supplies. As Mr. Beck said : "Whether that course is right or wrong, it will be adhered to, no matter what happens to the appropriation bills."

My theme was the proposed coercion of the President and the threat of stopping the government.

I think it appears from the foregoing that I did not call riders revolutionary. I said nothing about the legitimacy of riders, because that was not my theme.

SECOND.—You think, *first*, that I used the word revolution in a loose stump-speech sense, and not in the more serious sense in which statesmen should employ it ; *second*, and you see nothing in the state of the public mind outside of Congress to indicate any general concurrence in my opinion that revolution was threatened. I know the word is sometimes loosely used in reference to changes of a quiet sort. We say, for example, there has been a revolution in the common-school system. I do not think I am open to the charge of using it either in the stump-speech or in the milder sense just referred to. Certainly we had a revolution in 1861; but before we came to blows the revolution was prepared by the attempt of the South to put in force the doctrine that a State was sovereign and had a right to secede from the Union. To put that doctrine in practice was to destroy the government, and dissolution was revolution.

Now, the Democratic programme, as announced by Thurman, Beck, and the rest, is that, whatever may be the consequence, they will not vote supplies unless certain laws are repealed; and, not having the constitutional power to repeal those laws, they have thus far refused to vote supplies. Continued persistence in that refusal destroys the government. I denounce their policy and purpose as threatened revolution. If that which inevitably destroys the government be not revolution, in the largest and most dangerous sense of that word, I am wholly mistaken.

You say you do not see signs of revolution in the country : nor do I. I saw it only in Congress. The title of my speech was "Revolution in Congress," and I resisted it there in order that it might not spread and become revolution throughout the whole Union. I do not now believe it will ripen into completed revolution, because the purposes of the Democracy having been disclosed, public opinion will break them down. I think my speech has done something toward breaking them down by disclosing their purposes. The responses of the country before I made my second speech greatly relieved my apprehensions, and I felt less for the result April 4th than I did March 29th, though the Democracy had not abandoned their scheme, nor have they done so yet.

THIRD.—Your analysis of the elements that make up the spirit of the Republican party is certainly just in the main. It would not be possible for any party to be the chief actor in the events of the past twenty-five years without being influenced by the spirit of the events themselves. Our recent history has developed a war-horse type of Republican which I agree with you in despising as a permanent element; but I do not agree with you that the present agitation is an outcome on the part of Republicans to get up a new cry. We do not get up the cry, we do not bring in this new issue. My analysis of the situation is this : Two Democratic leaders, Tilden and Thurman, are engaged in a desperate struggle for the next Presidency. Tilden hopes to be elected on the reminiscences of 1876. The Potter Committee was appointed to infuse the belief that Tilden had been counted out by fraud. Tilden had been gaining ground as a candidate, and if Thurman merely joined in this cry of fraud he carried coals to Tilden's cellar and did not help himself. He therefore raised a new issue to rally the party around him. His cry was: "No military interference with elections !" "Down with the bayonet at the polls !" "Down with national interference with elections." The only way that he and his associates could elevate this issue into prominence was by threatening to stop the government if his aggravations are not redressed. Not to have resisted this scheme would have been criminal on our part. It is true that in resisting it the war-horse type of Republican has found new employment, and many of the undesirable elements of our party are delighted that this issue has been raised. This could not be otherwise; but it is not just to say that Republicans have raised the issue to feed their taste for gore.

I note with great interest what you say about the recent history of my mind and the effect of stump-speaking upon my modes of thinking. I have no doubt that it induces a looseness and superficiality of thought, and an extravagance of expression; but, on the other hand, it has some compensations. A man addressing a great and mixed audience composed of friends and enemies is certainly impelled to be more careful in his statements of facts than one who has his audience all to himself. He is much less liable to become epigrammatical and self-confident in his own views than those who have a friendly audience, where nobody opposes or puts questions. I should be grieved indeed if I felt that political speaking was weakening my love of study and reflection in other directions. I thank you for the suggestions, and shall keep watch of myself all the more in consequence of them. But it occurs to me I have made more speeches of the kind you approve within the last six months than of the kind you disapprove. For example, the Henry speech, the speech on the Relation of the Government to Science, the Sugar Tariff speech, the speech on Mr. Schleicher, the Chicago speech, and the two articles in the *North American Review*.

(Garfield to B. A. Hinsdale.)

WASHINGTON, July 7, 1879.

The session has been a most uncomfortable one ; but, on the whole, it has been valuable in the new class of topics it has brought into discussion. The Democrats completely abandoned the main ground which they at first took, and the most sensible among them do not hesitate to admit privately that it was wholly untenable. Instead of withholding $45.000.000 of appropriations to compel the redress of grievances, they withheld only $600,000, and they did not carry as many points of legislation as were tendered them at the close of the last Congress. The course of justice can only be kept by the marshals advancing the necessary money and run the risk of Congress paying them hereafter ; but their powers and official authority are not impaired. . . .

Partywise, the extra session has united the Republicans more than anything since 1868, and it bids fair to give us 1880.

CHAPTER XIII.

SOME attempt has been made to asperse Garfield on account of his going down to New Orleans as one of the " visiting statesmen," after the Presidential election of 1876. The attempt is utterly futile, but it may be well to refer to the actual facts with regard to this visit. At the request of President Grant he went to New Orleans, and when Mr. Potter afterward came there with his investigating committee, after full inquiry he found no fault whatever with Garfield's conduct in his report. Nobody before the committee charged that he did or said any unjust or unfair thing. What he did, and all he did, was to examine very carefully the testimony in relation to the election in one parish, West Feliciana, and to write out a careful, brief, and judicial statement of the official testimony as to the conduct of the election there, and bring out his own conclusions, which formed a part of the general report ; but his report on West Feliciana was written separately. In it he analyzed the Ku-Klux Rifle Club movement in that parish which broke up the election, and confined himself to that. He is perfectly willing to stand on everything he did there as being straight and true and fair.

When the " visiting statesmen " returned, and the question of counting the electoral votes came up, an effort was finally made to constitute the Electoral Commission, on the assumption that the Vice-President had not the right to count the vote, but that Congress had the exclusive right to count it. He made a speech on this subject on the 28th of January, 1877, in which he took the ground that the Vice-President had the right under the Constitution to count the vote ; that Congress would be committing a usurpation if it undertook to count it ; that Congress was only present as a witness of a great, solemn ceremony, and not as an actor, and he voted against the bill establishing the Electoral Commission. He was opposed to it on principle. The bill itself was due largely to suggestions from the Democratic members —not of a majority, but of a few influential men. It was also supported by prominent Republicans. The Democrats joined heartily in sustaining it, and defended it as from high and patriotic principles. It afterward appeared that they believed that Judge Davis of the Supreme Court, who had be· come almost if not quite a Democrat, would hold the casting vote and count in Mr. Tilden. Mr. Henry B. Payne, of Ohio, afterward admitted, in a speech in Cleveland, that he and his Democratic colleagues would not have passed the Electoral bill had they not supposed that Judge Davis would be a member of the committee. Garfield had voted against the Electoral bill, and spoken against it, yet when it was, by common consent of some of the ablest and most patriotic members of both Houses of Congress, decided that the Electoral Commission should be constituted, and that the Republicans should have two members of the Commission from the House and the Democrats three, when the Republicans met they first and unanimously selected Garfield as the man to represent them, and then chose Mr. George F. Hoar, now Senator, and lately the chairman of the Chicago Convention. Garfield accepted the appointment to serve, but regarded it as he would service on a committee. He did not believe that the Electoral Commission was a constitutional body, but merely a select committee appointed by Congress to make a report, which was subject to rejection by both Houses of Congress ; and it is singular that the Democrats who sustained Mr. John Bigelow's able argument in favor of the absolute power of Congress to count the votes have forgotten, or failed to see, that it is entirely immaterial whether or not the Electoral Commission was either a constitutional body or a just and conscientious committee. It was the action of Congress on the report of the Electoral Commission which made the count effectual and constitutional, and on any theory whatever this action gave to Mr. Hayes a title as valid as has been possessed by any President.

On the inauguration of Hayes to the Presidency the Republican party was considerably divided and demoralized. It was reunited and vindicated by the report of the Potter Committee, which, having set out to authenticate Democratic scandals, ended by the discovery of scandals of a much more serious nature affecting their own candidate. At that period Garfield held the difficult position of a leader who was trying to protect his party from divisions, which he only succeeded in doing by keeping the minority for six months from having a caucus, except to meet and choose officers or to do some unimportant and unexciting business. There was no caucus in this period held for the purpose of declaring party principles or policies.

In this connection it is well to state, as showing the recognition of Garfield's leadership by his party associates in the House, that after Mr. Blaine went to the Senate Garfield was unanimously voted for as their candidate for Speaker. He was thus sustained three successive times—once after Kerr died, during his term as Speaker, and when Randall was elected for the short term; then when Randall was first elected, and again when he was re-elected Speaker.

There was a strong tendency in 1877, on the part of some of the Republican leaders in both Houses, to assail President Hayes as a traitor who was going to Johnsonize the party. At first the defenders of the Administration were comparatively few ; but there was perfect agreement between them that they would prevent any serious division in the party, so far as possible, and there was no party caucus of the Republican members of the House on any important question until Mr. Potter made his motion for an investigation of the title of President Hayes. That had the effect to bring all the Republican members together. A caucus was held which denounced the Potter Investigation as revolutionary, and worked together with perfect harmony ; and on this nucleus of support to one of the cleanest, purest, and ablest administrations of the Government in all its history, was gradually developed a Republican support of the administration which has been all the more notable that it has come from a quiet and steadily growing recognition by Republicans of the ability, fidelity to duty, and statesmanship with which the President and his constitutional advisers have fulfilled their duties and met their responsibilities.   Garfield's work as a pacificator of the party was very effective.   He is a natural conciliator, having no selfish or personal ends in view, absorbed entirely in strengthening his party, and leading it, through honorable paths, to lasting successes.   His ready abandonment of minor causes of difference, his generous spirit, his inspiring devotion to the true interests of the party have made him its most helpful leader, the one who has aroused the fewest antagonisms, and who has won for his party its most honorable triumphs.

(Garfield to B. A. Hinsdale.)

WASHINGTON, November 11, 1876.

Last evening the President telegraphed me from Philadelphia, requesting me to go to New Orleans and remain until the vote is counted, acting as a witness of the count.   I was a good deal embarrassed by the request for several reasons.   First, the President has no power in the case, and I could only act in a personal and irresponsible way, with the danger that I might be considered an intermeddler ; second, I did not know who else was going, and I might find myself associated with violent partisan Republicans, who mean to count our side in *per fas* or *ne fas*.   In that case I should be called upon either to assent to the injustice or to make a report which would call down upon me all the passion of this passionate hour.   Of course neither of these situations is pleasant to contemplate.   I might escape from both by declining to go, but it may be a duty of the very highest sort, which I have no right to decline on any personal ground.

8.30 P.M.—At four o'clock this afternoon I called on the President.   He showed me a list of gentlemen whom he had invited to go to New Orleans.   I have concluded to go, and shall leave at midnight.   I go with great reluctance, but feel it to be a duty from which I cannot shrink.

(Garfield to the Hon. C. C. Hill, Boston, Mass.)

NEW ORLEANS, LA., November 18, 1876.

The present political situation is a very grave one, and some of its aspects fill me with solicitude.   I think it is the duty of all good citizens to discourage all violent feeling.   The day of choice is past.   Neither you nor I have any longer any right to push our preferences.   That effort was ended on the 7th instant. Our chief concern should now be to ascertain what the choice was, and then to insist that the choice shall be our law.

It is most unfortunate that the result should turn upon the vote of a State so peculiarly and delicately situated as Louisiana. The whole stress and strain of public passion thus presses upon the weakest and worst place. The official report of the State Board of Canvassers cannot be completed in less than ten days. They begin their work to-day, and will invite a delegation of both political parties to join as spectators. I shall try to get excused from being on the delegation if possible, for I want to go home. But it now appears probable I shall be compelled to remain until the count is complete.

*   *   *   *   *   *   *   *   *   *   *   *   *   *

I started for this place on the urgent request of the President. I have been so depressed in spirit by the loss of our precious little boy that I have hardly had the heart to write at all.

(Garfield to B. A. Hinsdale.)

WASHINGTON, January 4, 1877.

When I reflect that it is now more than sixteen years since I have been for a moment free from the responsibilities of public life, I seem to have become the slave of others, and hardly at all free to follow the plans of personal culture of which I once dreamed and hoped; and so I join you in much dissatisfaction with my past, and yet I suppose we should feel the same in any course of life we might have pursued.

I appreciate what you say of the political situation. I have no doubt that whatever man is inaugurated President will go in with a cloud upon his title, in the estimation of many men, but the behavior of a great nation in the administration of its laws at a critical moment is more important than the fate of any one man or party. We have reached the place where the road is marked by no footprint, and we must make a direct line to be fit to follow after we are dead. It is only at such times that the domain of law is enlarged and the safeguard of liberty is increased. I confess to you that I do not feel adequate to the task; but I shall do my best to point out a worthy way to the light and the right.

(Garfield to B. A. Hinsdale.)

WASHINGTON, March 10, 1877.

It is due to Hayes that we stand by him and give his policy a fair trial. I understand he wants me to stay in the House. I shall see him this evening and if he is decided in his wishes on that point, I shall probably decline to be a candidate for the Senate. On many accounts I would like to take that place, but it seems to fall to my lot to make the sacrifice. It is probable, though not certain, that I could be elected if I ran.

CHAPTER XIV

IT is wonderful, considering all of his other activities and with his multifarious studies, that Garfield has found the time to deliver so many addresses of a non-political character. It is impossible to consider even a small proportion of these efforts, all of which are interesting, many of which are important, and some of which deserve to be ranked among the first class of productions of their sort.

His oration on the first great occasion of decorating the graves of Union soldiers is a type of one class of purely patriotic efforts. It was delivered at Arlington Heights, to a most distinguished audience, consisting of the President, his Cabinet, a large number of members of Congress, and eminent citizens from all parts of the country, and amid surroundings peculiarly calculated to inspire any speaker as susceptible and impressible as Garfield. It was the first considerable memorial service of the sort observed anywhere in the Union, occurring on the 30th of May, 1868. At the very opening, he admitted that he was oppressed with a sense of the impropriety of uttering words on such an occasion. Said he :

" If silence is ever golden, it must be here, beside the graves of fifteen thousand men, whose lives were more significant than speech, and whose death was a poem the music of which can never be sung. With words, we make promises, plight faith, praise virtue. Promises may not be kept ; plighted faith may be broken ; and vaunted virtue may be only the cunning mask of vice. We do not know one promise these men made, one pledge they gave, one word they spoke ; but we do know they summed up and perfected, by one supreme act, the highest virtues of men and citizens. For love of country they accepted death ;

and thus resolved all doubts, and made immortal their patriotism and their virtue.

" For the noblest man that lives there still remains a conflict. He must still withstand the assaults of time and fortune ; must still be assailed with temptations before which lofty natures have fallen.   But with *these*, the conflict ended, the victory was won, when death stamped on them the great seal of heroic character, and closed a record which years can never blot."

One oratorical passage in this beautiful tribute to the gallant dead will be appreciated by all those who have beheld the impressive scene which is spread out in front of the visitor to Arlington Heights.   Said he :

" The view from this spot bears some resemblance to that which greets the eye at Rome.   In sight of the Capitoline Hill, up and across the Tiber, and overlooking the city, is a hill, not rugged or lofty, but known as the Vatican Mount.   At the beginning of the Christian Era, an imperial circus stood on its summit.   There, gladiator slaves died for the sport of Rome, and wild beasts fought with wilder men.   In that arena, a Galilean fisherman gave up his life a sacrifice for his faith.   No human life was ever so nobly avenged.   On that spot was reared the proudest Christian temple ever built by human hands.   For its adornment the rich offerings of every clime and kingdom had been contributed.   And now, after eighteen centuries the hearts of two hundred million people turn toward it with reverence when they worship God.   As the traveller descends the Apennines, he sees the dome of St. Peter rsing above the desolate Campagna and the dead city, long before the Seven Hills and ruined palaces appear to his view.   The fame of the dead fisherman has outlived the glory of the Eternal City.   A noble life, crowned with heroic death, rises above and outlives the pride and pomp and glory of the mightiest empire of the earth."

Probably the memorial effort that gave him the greatest degree of thought and labor, and even apprehension, was the eulogy on General George H. Thomas, which he delivered to his comrades of the Army of the Cumberland, at Cleveland, on the 25th of November, 1870.   No man had a deeper appreciation of the massive and majestic character of Thomas than Garfield, for he had been associated with Thomas in the closest official and personal relations, and between them there had sprung up a friendship of extraordinary strength. It is generally conceded that this eulogy upon Thomas is by far the ablest, the justest, and the most eloquent tribute ever paid by an orator to the great Virginia soldier. As a review of Thomas's personal and military career, as a defense against malignant accusations from treasonable sources, and as a rhetorical picture of a character of singular individuality and grandeur, it is without blemish, and comes up to the highest standard. His portrait of Thomas will go down to history as a masterly description of a magnificent specimen of manhood.   Said he :

" I know that each of you here present sees him in memory at this moment, as we often saw him in life ; erect and strong, like a tower of solid masonry ; his broad, square shoulders and massive head ; his abundant hair and full beard of light brown, sprinkled with silver ; his broad forehead, full face, and features that would appear colossal but for their perfect harmony of proportion ; his clear complexion, with just enough color to assure you of robust health and a well-regulated life ; his face lighted up by an eye which was cold gray to his enemies, but warm, deep blue to his friends ; not a man of iron, but of live oak. His attitude, form, and features all assured you of inflexible firmness, of inexpugnable strength, while his welcoming smile set every feature aglow with a kindness that won your manliest affection.   If thus in memory you see his form and features, even more vividly do you remember the qualities of his mind and heart.   His body was the fitting type of his intellect and character ; and you saw both his intellect and character tried again and again in the fiery furnace of war, and by other tests not less searching.   Thus, comrades, you see him ; and your memories supply a thousand details which complete and adorn the picture.   I beg you, therefore, to supply the deficiency of my work from these living phototypes in your own hearts."

His description of the secret of Thomas's success is to so large a degree applicable to his own career that it has an autobiographical interest.   Said he :

" Thomas's life is a notable illustration of the virtue and

power of hard work ; and in the last analysis the power to do hard work is only another name for talent. Professor Church, one of his instructors at West Point, says of his student life, that ' he never allowed anything to escape a thorough examination, and left nothing behind that he did not fully comprehend ' And so it was in the army. To him a battle was neither an earthquake, nor a volcano, nor a chaos of brave men and frantic horses, involved in vast explosions of gunpowder. It was rather a calm rational concentration of force against force. It was a question of lines and positions ; of weight and of metal, and strength of battalions. He knew that the elements and forces which bring victory are not created on the battle-field, but must be patiently elaborated in the quiet of the camp, by the perfect organization and outfit of his army. His remark to a captain of artillery while inspecting a battery, is worth remembering, for it exhibits his theory of success : ' Keep everything in order, for the fate of a battle may turn on a buckle or a linchpin.' He understood so thoroughly the condition of his army, and its equipment, that when the hour of trial came, he knew how great a pressure it could stand, and how hard a blow it could strike."

Without much changing of words, this terse characterization of the sources of Thomas's adequacy to every emergency might be applied to Garfield's own readiness to meet the numerous critical occasions to which he has always and invariably shown his equality.

As is well known, each State of the Union has the right to place in the sculpture gallery of the old Senate chamber two statues representing distinguished citizens of the Commonwealth. Their reception by Congress is always the occasion of memorial speeches by those members who are supposed to be best fitted for such discourses. On the 19th of December, 1876, an occasion of this sort occurred in the House, in regard to the reception of the statues of John Winthrop and Samuel Adams from the State of Massachusetts. Garfield's speech was a brief one, but it was marked by its felicity of historical allusion and patriotic sentiment. Nothing, for instance, could be more graceful, in the way of a compliment to two great States, than this passage :

" I can well understand that the State of Massachusetts, embarrassed by her wealth of historic glory, found it difficult to make the selection. And while the distinguished gentleman from Massachusetts [Mr. Hoar] was so fittingly honoring his State by portraying that happy embarrassment, I was reflecting that the sister-State of Virginia will encounter, if possible, a still greater difficulty when she comes to make the selection of her immortals. One name I venture to hope she will not select ; a name too great for the glory of any one State. I trust she will allow us to claim Washington as belonging to all States, for all time. If she shall pass over the great distance that separates Washington from all others, I can hardly imagine how she will make the choice from her crowded roll. But I have no doubt that she will be able to select two who will represent the great phases of her history as happily and worthily as Massachusetts is represented in the choice she has to-day announced. It is difficult to imagine a happier combination of great and beneficent forces than will be presented by the representative heroes of these two great States.

" Virginia and Massachusetts were the two focal centres from which sprang the life-forces of this Republic. They were, in many ways, complements of each other, each supplying what the other lacked, and both uniting to endow the Republic with its noblest and most enduring qualities."

Nor could there be given better reasons for going back to Winthrop and Adams as the especially honored representatives of Massachusetts in the Congressional Pantheon than the following :

" Indeed, before Winthrop and his company landed at Salem, the Pilgrims were laying the foundations of civil liberty. While the Mayflower was passing Cape Cod and seeking an anchorage, in the midst of the storm, her brave passengers sat down in the little cabin and drafted and signed a covenant which contains the germ of American liberty. How familiar to the American habit of mind are these declarations of the Pilgrim covenant of 1620 :

" 'That no act, imposition, law, or ordinance be made or imposed upon us at present or to come but such as has been or shall be enacted by the consent of the body of freemen or associates, or their representatives, legally assembled.'

" 'The New England town was the model, the primary cell,

from which our Republic was evolved.   The town meeting was the germ of all the parliamentary life and habits of Americans.

" John Winthrop brought with him the more formal organization of New England society ; and, in his long and useful life, did more than perhaps any other to direct and strengthen its growth.

" Nothing, therefore, could be more fitting, than for Massachusetts to place in our Memorial Hall the statue of the first of the Puritans, representing him at the moment when he was stepping on shore from the ship that brought him from England, and bearing with him the charter of that first political society which laid the foundations of our country ; and that near him should stand that Puritan embodiment of the logic of the Revolution, Samuel Adams.   I am glad to see this decisive, though tardy, acknowledgment of his great and signal services to America.   I doubt if any man equalled Samuel Adams in formulating and uttering the fierce, clear, and inexorable logic of the Revolution.   With our present habits of thought, we can hardly realize how great were the obstacles to overcome. Not the least was the religious belief of the fathers—that allegiance to rulers was obedience to God.   The thirteenth chapter of Romans was to many minds a barrier against revolution stronger than the battalions of George III. :

" ' Let every soul be subject unto the higher powers.   For there is no power but of God : the powers that be are ordained of God.   Whosoever therefore resisteth the power, resisteth the ordinance of God.'

" And it was not until the people of that religious age were led to see that they might obey God and still establish liberty, in spite of kingly despotism, that they were willing to engage in war against one who called himself ' king by the grace of God.'   The men who pointed out the pathway to freedom by the light of religion as well as of law, were the foremost promoters of American Independence.   And of these, Adams was unquestionably chief."

His concluding paragraph might well be emblazoned in some conspicuous place in the halls of both houses of Congress. Said he :

" Mr. Speaker, this great lesson of self-restraint is taught in the whole history of the Revolution ; and it is this lesson that to-day, more, perhaps, than any other we have seen, we ought

to take most to heart.   Let us seek liberty and peace, under the
law ; and, following the pathway of our fathers, preserve the
great legacy they have committed to our keeping.''

On the 16th of January, 1878, General Garfield introduced
into the House of Representatives a resolution thanking a very
liberal, patriotic and philanthropic lady of New York, Mrs.
Elizabeth Thompson, for the presentation to Congress of
Carpenter's great painting of President Lincoln and his Cabinet
at the time of his first reading of the proclamation of emancipation, and accepting of her gift.   On the 12th of February the
formal presentation and acceptance of the painting by Congress
occurred.   General Garfield was selected by the joint order of
the Senate and the House, and on behalf of Mrs. Thompson, to
make the speech of the occasion.   It was to him a welcome
task, because of his friendship for the artist, his natural love
for all works of art, particularly those which illustrated the
history of our own country, and because of his reverent admiration of Mr. Lincoln.   His speech was not only appropriate to
the peculiar occasion which gave it birth, but contained an
estimate of the greatness of Lincoln and of his place in history
which is singularly just, truthful and appreciative ; and there-
in, without intending it, he forecast, with considerable simili-
tude, the position which he was to occupy among the leading
men of his own party.   Much that he said in this passage, of
Lincoln and his career, will be found applicable to himself and
his own career :

" Let us pause to consider the actors in that scene.   In force
of character, in thoroughness and breadth of culture, in experience of public affairs and in national reputation, the Cabinet that sat around that council-board has had no superior,
perhaps no equal, in our history.   Seward, the finished scholar,
the consummate orator, the great leader of the Senate, had
come to crown his career with those achievements which placed
him in the first rank of modern diplomatists.   Chase, with a
culture and a fame of massive grandeur, stood as the rock and
pillar of the public credit, the noble embodiment of the public

faith.   Stanton was there, a very Titan of strength, the great organizer of victory.   Eminent lawyers, men of business, leaders of States and leaders of men, completed the group.

" But the man who presided over that council, who inspired and guided its deliberations, was a character so unique that he stood alone, without a model in history or a parallel among men.   Born on this day, sixty-nine years ago, to an inheritance of extremest poverty ; surrounded by the rude forces of the wilderness ; wholly unaided by parents ; only one year in any school ; never, for a day, master of his own time until he reached his majority ; making his way to the profession of the law by the hardest and roughest road ; yet by force of unconquerable will and persistent, patient work, he attained a foremost place in his profession,

> And, moving up from high to higher,
> Became, on fortune's crowning slope,
> The pillar of a people's hope,
> The center of a world's desire.

" At first, it was the prevailing belief that he would be only the nominal head of his administration ; that its policy would be directed by the eminent statesmen he had called to his council.   How erroneous this opinion was, may be seen from a single incident :

" Among the earliest, most difficult, and most delicate duties of his administration, was the adjustment of our relations with Great Britain.   Serious complications, even hostilities were apprehended.   On the 21st of May, 1861, the Secretary of State presented to the President his draught of a letter of instructions to Minister Adams, in which the position of the United States and the attitude of Great Britain were set forth with the clearness and force which long experience and great ability had placed at the command of the Secretary.

" Upon almost every page of that original draught are erasures, additions, and marginal notes in the handwriting of Abraham Lincoln, which exhibit a sagacity, a breadth of wisdom, and a comprehension of the whole subject, impossible to be found except in a man of the very first order.   And these modifications of a great state paper were made by a man who, but three months before, had entered, for the first time, the wide theatre of Executive action.

" Gifted with an insight and a foresight which the ancients would have called divination, he saw, in the midst of darkness and obscurity, the logic of events, and forecast the result.

From the first, in his own quaint, original way, without ostentation or offense to his associates, he was pilot and commander of his administration.   He was one of the few great rulers whose wisdom increased with his power, and whose spirit grew gentler and tenderer as his triumphs were multiplied."

CHAPTER XV.

GARFIELD'S CAREER AS A LAWYER.

In undertaking a brief review of Garfield's career as a lawyer, it is impossible to avoid a feeling that it is far more difficult to impress on the public mind a fair sense of what he has achieved in this direction of activity than as to any other part of his public life. Everybody knows something of the romantic history of his early struggles for education. The prominence which he rapidly attained in the army and his brilliant record during the period of his service are equally well known. In Congress he has been, for over half a generation, conspicuous in the debates on all the living issues of the day. But there are few who know

NOTE.—It is far from my purpose to go into any elaborate exposure of the falsehoods, misrepresentations, insinuations, and misunderstandings as to Garfield's official integrity, that are kept alive through malice, and only impose on ignorance. If he is not an honest man, from core to cuticle, I do not know where to find an honest man in public life. But he has perfectly vindicated himself, and his vindication has been scattered all over the land. I have before me a copy of the Troy *Times*, whose editor would be the last man to help cover up any official shortcoming or offence of his best friend, which contains, in full, the memorable speech made by Garfield to his constituents, in the campaign of 1874, at Warren, where the headquarters of the most disaffected and hostile Republicans in his district. At every stage of this exhaustive review of these stale scandals, that are now daily served up as the nutriment of the unfortunate readers of extreme Democratic organs, he paused for questions. I never read a manlier speech. Every accusation and innuendo was frankly and fully met, and the intelligent man who reads it, and has any remaining doubt of Garfield's absolute integrity, must have a peculiar and unenviable organization. As to the De Golyer charge, it was shown to be utterly absurd and baseless. In the first place, Garfield, as a member of the Committee on Appropriations, was bound to vote for the assessments on Federal property for any pavement properly petitioned for by a certain proportion of adjacent property-holders. He simply undertook, for a conditional fee of $5000, to act as assistant counsel to Mr. Parsons, who was retained by the owners of the De Golyer pavement patent. After going into a detailed statement of all the facts in the case, covering nearly two columns, he was interrupted by a question. I give both question and

the extent of his ability and acquirements in the higher walks
of the profession which he adopted before going into the army,
but did not practice until after he had become known as a
statesman. The extent of the lack of appreciation of what Garfield has actually achieved in this arduous and exacting profession is shown in the common statements in Democratic papers,
which refer to the malicious De Golyer charge, and assume that
the fee which he received from De Golyer was not paid to him professionally, because he was not entitled to large fees as a lawyer.
Such has not been the estimate of the distinguished advocates
of both parties who have tested Garfield's high legal ability by
actual encounter or in active co-operation. On general principles it is difficult for any man to obtain a high reputation in
the law who has not ascended to eminence by regular gradation
from the lowest and most primary stages of practice. The rule
of success and eminence at the bar is generally a course of
patient apprenticeship, beginning with studying in a lawyer's

answer, to show, by a single example, how thorough was Garfield's method of
dealing with his constituents of the "Western Reserve," the New England
of the West:

   "*Question*—General Garfield, allow me to ask you one question· What
question of law was submitted to you in that case? Was it a question of law,
or a question of the difference between the payments?
   "*General Garfield*—There were questions both of law and of merit. In the
first place, there were forty-two different kinds of pavement presented. If the
government took one, there might be a question of conflicting patents—there
might be a patent lawsuit growing out of it—and I felt it to be my first duty to
inquire whether the two patents that extend into this pavement were valid
patents that could properly be sustained. I made that examination as the very
first step I took in the case. I understand that the Board of Public Works said
that they did not care very much about that, on the ground that they would not
pay a royalty in any case. But the fact was that the contractor himself—the
owner of the patent—regarded it as a valuable franchise, and the validity of the
patent was to him the first consideration.
   "Now, where there are forty patents, or nearly that, concerned, it is of some
importance to know the relative validity of the patents."

   And yet there is little likelihood that Garfield's wilful defamers will not
continue, in spite of this plain statement of the work he did, for a conditional
fee, to reiterate the falsehood that he did nothing professionally in return. But
this sort of attack has never prevented the election of any American public man
whose career had been anything like as noble, consistent, and honorable as
Garfield's has been. Mud-flinging is not only the meanest of occupations; it
is the most futile.

office, and perhaps sweeping the same for a year or two, then a period of clerkship for as much longer, then petty practice in inferior courts and subordinate positions in important cases, until, at mature age, a man finally becomes recognized as a lawyer, when admittance into the Supreme Court of the United States with a case to argue there is considered the final attestation of his professional standing. Neither as regards attaining eminence in the law nor in any other line of intellectual effort has Garfield pursued the beaten and common path. It so happened that the first case in which he ever appeared was one of the most important argued in the Supreme Court of the United States for many years. He thus, to use a sailor's maxim, "jumped in through the cabin windows," apparently. But it was not true that he attained this position by boldness or good luck. As in the case of his readiness for all great questions of statesmanship, he had done the work and pursued the studies which enabled him, on his first appearance in this new arena, to take his place among the first men in the country. He had studied law as thoroughly as any of the legal practitioners in his neighborhood—studied it in its principles and in its illustrations in English and American history, and was admitted to the bar in 1861 by the Supreme Court of Ohio. He was about to form a law partnership and to go into practice when the war broke out, but had never tried a case, nor argued one, nor had anything to do with one, until he appeared as one of the counsel in the famous Milligan case, in the Supreme Court of the United States.

On the 18th of January, 1865, Henry Winter Davis of Maryland and General Garfield made very energetic protests against the arbitrary exercise of powers by the subordinates of the Secretary of War. No two members of the House had been more devoted or energetic in the support of every measure essential to the prosecution of the war ; but in both the love of civil liberty was a controlling sentiment. Both were admirers of the tremendous working powers and efficiency of Mr. Stanton. Both were too manly to witness without indignation the tyrannical and lawless acts which were committed by some of Mr. Stanton's subordinates.   General Garfield had had his quick sympathies excited by a visit to what was known as the Old Capitol military prison, and spoke with a warmth which excited considerable attention at the time.   He spoke of the case of one officer who had been confined for five months in that prison and had not been furnished even with a copy of the charges against him, although he had frequently demanded to know with what crime he was charged.   This man bore on his person honorable scars received .n the service of his country.   He was a colonel, and was the victim of the vengeance of some unknown enemy. Garfield, alluding to the fact that there were many alleged cases where officers and citizens after being confined for a long period had been allowed to go out without a word of explanation concerning either the arrest or the discharge, made this manly appeal :

" I ask the House of Representatives whether that kind of practice is to grow up under this Government, and no man is to raise his voice against it or make any inquiry concerning it lest some one should say he is factious, he is unfriendly to the War Department, he is opposing the administration.   Gentlemen, if we are not men in our places here, let us stop our ears to all complaints.   Let every department do as it pleases, and with meekness and in silence vote whatever appropriations are asked for. I do not say, for I do not know, that the head of any department is responsible for these things, or knows them.   It may be that they have been done by subordinates.   It may be that the heads of the departments are not cognizant of the facts.   I make no accusation ; but I do say that it is our business to see that the laws be respected, and that if a man has no powerful friend in court he shall at least find the Congress of the United States his friend.   I hope the resolution will not be reconsidered, and I renew the motion to lay on the table the motion to reconsider."

On calling the roll there were 136 yeas and only 5 nays, the latter including Mr. Spalding and Thaddeus Stevens ; the im-

mediate effect of which energetic protests of Garfield and Henry
Winter Davis was a large jail delivery from the Old Capitol
prison the very next day.

Garfield based his resistance on the broad grounds which he
had learned in the history of the development of Anglo-Saxon
liberty. About that time that great lawyer, Judge Jeremiah
S. Black, as the attorney of the Indiana Democrats who had
been opposing the war, came to his friend Garfield and said that
there were some men imprisoned in Indiana for conspiracy
against the Government in trying to prevent enlistments, and to
encourage desertion. They had been tried in 1864, while the
war was going on, and, by a military commission sitting in Indiana, where there was no war, they had been sentenced to
death. Mr. Lincoln commuted the sentence to imprisonment for
life, and they were put into State prison in accordance
with the commutation. They then took out a writ of *habeas
corpus*, to test the constitutionality and legality of their trial,
and the judges in the Circuit Court had disagreed, there being
two of them, and certified their disagreement up to the Supreme
Court of the United States. Judge Black said to Garfield that
he had seen what Garfield had said in Congress, and asked him
if he was willing to say in an argument in the Supreme Court
what he had advocated in Congress, to which Garfield replied,
" It depends upon your case altogether." Judge Black sent him
the facts in the case—the record. Garfield read it over and said,
" I believe in that doctrine." To which Judge Black replied,
" Young man, you know it is a perilous thing for a young Republican in Congress to say that, and I don't want you to injure
yourself." Said Garfield, " It does not make any difference. I
believe in English liberty and English law. But," continued
he, " Judge Black, I am not a practitioner in the Supreme
Court, and I never tried a case in my life anywhere." Judge
Black asked, " How long ago were you admitted to the bar ?"
" Just about six years ago." " That will do," Black replied,
and he took Garfield thereupon over to the Supreme Court and
moved his admission. He immediately entered upon the con-

sideration of this important case. On the side of the Government was arrayed a formidable amount of legal talent. The
Attorney-General was aided by General Butler, who was called
in on account of his military knowledge, and by Henry Stan-
bery. Associated with General Garfield as counsel for the petitioners were two of the greatest lawyers in the country—Judge
Black and the Hon. David Dudley Field—and the Hon. John E.
McDonald, now Senator from Indiana. The argument submitted
by General Garfield was one of the most remarkable ever made
before the Supreme Court of the United States, and was made
under circumstances peculiarly creditable to Garfield's courage,
independence, and resolute devotion to the cause of constitutional liberty—a devotion not inspired by wild dreams of political promotion, for at that time it was dangerous for any young
Republican Congressman to defend the constitutional rights of
men known to be disloyal, and rightly despised and hated for
their disloyal practices.

Merely as a lawyer-like presentation of the case, Garfield's
argument is worthy of special study and commendation. It exhibits, not the skill and adroitness of a practiced case-lawyer,
or of a lawyer whose mind has been cramped and narrowed by
the study of mere precedents and technicalities ; but it is a logical and philosophical development of the doctrines and purposes of the Constitution, of the careful limitation of the military
as of all other powers, and of the fundamental principles of
civil liberty.

At the very outset of his masterly argument he affirmed that
every citizen of the United States is under dominion of law ;
that whether he be a civilian, a sailor, or a soldier, the Constitution provides for him a tribunal before which he may be protected
if innocent, and punished if guilty of crime. Thereupon he
proceeded to show the development of the true theory of the
Constitution by the practice of the fathers, by the decisions of
our courts, and by the precedents from the English practice.
Throughout the whole sweep of this reasoning there is shown
that mastery of English and American history which some of

our most eminent lawyers fail to attain.   After establishing his
propositions by an impregnable array of precedents, the glow
of the patriotic statesman entered into the argument of the law-
~er.   Speaking of these precedents, he said :

"They enable us to trace from its far-off source the progress and development of Anglo-Saxon liberty ; its innumerable conflicts with irresponsible power ; its victories, dearly
bought, but always won—victories which have crowned
with immortal honors the institutions of England, and left their
indelible impress upon the Anglo-Saxon mind.   These principles our fathers brought with them to the new world, and
guarded with sleepless vigilance and religious devotion.   In its
darkest hour of trial, during the late rebellion, the Republic did
not forget them.   So completely have they been impressed on
the minds of American lawyers, so thoroughly have they been
ingrained into the very fibre of American character, that notwithstanding the citizens of eleven States went off into wild rebellion, broke their oaths of allegiance to the Constitution, and
levied war against their country, yet with all their crimes upon
them, there was still in the minds of those men, during all the
struggle, so deep and enduring an impression on this great subject, that even during the rebellion the courts of the Southern
States adjudicated causes like the one now before you, in favor
of the civil law and against court-martials established under
military authority for the trial of citizens.   In Texas, Mississippi, Virginia, and other insurgent States, by the order of the
rebel President, the writ of *habeas corpus* was suspended, martial law was declared, and provost-marshals were appointed to
administer military authority.   But when civilians, arrested by
military authority, petitioned for release by writ of *habeas corpus*,
in every case, save one, the writ was granted, and it was decided
that there could be no suspension of the writ or declaration of
martial law by the Executive, or by any other than the supreme
legislative authority."

No Democratic statesman who has used the grand doctrines
of American and civil liberty as an ambush behind which to
fight the prosecution of the war for liberty and the Union has
ever stated more broadly the English and American doctrines

than this young and ambitious Republican politician stated it to the Supreme Court of the United States in the first case which ever tested his ability and his manhood. Said he :

" And yet, if this military commission could legally try these petitioners, its authority rested only upon the will of a single man. If it had the right to try the petitioners, it had the right to try any civilian in the United States ; it had the right to try your Honors, for you are civilians. The learned gentlemen tell us that necessity justifies martial law. But what is the nature of that necessity ? If at this moment, Lee, with his rebel army at one end of Pennsylvania Avenue, and Grant, with the army of the Union at the other, with hostile banners and roaring guns, were approaching this Capitol, the sacred seat of justice and law, I have no doubt they would expel your Honors from their bench, and the Senate and House of Representatives from their halls. The jurisdiction of battle would supersede the jurisdiction of law. This Court would be silenced by the thunders of war.

" If an earthquake should shake the City of Washington, and tumble this Capitol in ruins about us, it would drive your Honors from the bench, and for the time volcanic law would supersede the Constitution.

" If the Supreme Court of Herculaneum or Pompeii had been in session when the fiery rain overwhelmed those cities, its authority would have been suddenly usurped and overthrown, but I question the propriety of calling that *law* which, in its very nature, is a destruction or suspension of all law."

As to the specious and dangerous plea of necessity, he was equally explicit and fearless. Said he :

" The only ground on which the learned counsel attempt to establish the authority of the military commission to try the petitioners is that of the necessity of the case. I answer, there was no such necessity. Neither the Constitution nor Congress recognized it. I point to the Constitution as an arsenal, stored with ample powers to meet every emergency of national life. No higher test of its completeness can be imagined than has been afforded by the great rebellion, which dissolved the municipal governments of eleven States, and consolidated them into

a gigantic traitorous government *de facto*, inspired with the
desperate purpose of destroying the Government of the United
States.''

'' From the beginning of the rebellion to its close, Congress,
by its legislation, kept pace with the necessities of the nation.
In sixteen carefully considered laws the National Legislature
undertook to provide for every contingency, and arm the Executive at every point with the solemn sanction of law.   Observe
how perfectly the case of the petitioners was covered by the provisions of law.''

Then he went on to prove the baselessness of some of the
charges under which Milligan was convicted, and swept them
away with a logic and with facts that were irresistible.

His conclusion showed that the instincts of an American citizen, who valued his citizenship intensely because the institutions
of his country had enabled him to make his way upward with
such brilliant rapidity, were all-powerful and commanding over
his conduct and his enthusiasms.   Said he :

'' Your decision will mark an era in American history.   The
just and final settlement of this great question will take a high
place among the great achievements which have immortalized
this decade.   It will establish forever this truth, of inestimable
value to us and to mankind, that a republic can wield the vast
enginery of war without breaking down the safeguards of liberty ; can suppress insurrection and put down rebellion, however formidable, without destroying the bulwarks of law ; can,
by the might of its armed millions, preserve and defend both
nationality and liberty.   Victories on the field were of priceless
value, for they plucked the life of the Republic out of the hands
of its enemies ; but

'Peace hath her victories
No less renowned than war ;'

and if the protection of law shall, by your decision, be extended
over ever acre of our peaceful territory, you will have rendered
the great decision of the century.

'' When Pericles had made Greece immortal in arts and arms,
in liberty and law, he invoked the genius of Phidias to devise a
monument which should symbolize the beauty and glory of
Athens.   That artist selected for his theme the tutelar divinity

of Athens, the Jove-born goddess, protectress of arts and arms, of industry and law, who typified the Greek conception of composed, majestic, unrelenting force. He erected on the heights of the Acropolis a colossal statue of Minerva, armed with spear and helmet, which towered in awful majesty above the surrounding temples of the gods. Sailors on far-off ships beheld the crest and spear of the goddess and bowed with reverent awe. To every Greek she was the symbol of power and glory. But the Acropolis, with its temples and statues, is now a heap of ruins. The visible gods have vanished in the clearer light of modern civilization. We cannot restore the decayed emblems of ancient Greece, but it is in your power, O judges, to erect in this citadel of our liberties a monument more lasting than brass ; invisible indeed to the eye of flesh, but visible to the eye of the spirit as the awful form and figure of Justice, crowning and adorning the Republic ; rising above the storms of political strife, above the din of battle, above the earthquake shock of rebellion ; seen from afar and hailed as protector by the oppressed of all nations, dispensing equal blessings, and covering with the protecting shield of law the weakest, the humblest, the meanest, and, until declared by solemn law unworthy of protection, the guiltiest of its citizens.''

Remember that this argument was not only made by a Republican politician representing one of the most radical of Republican districts, but that it was made on the 6th of March, 1866, the year before a distinguished soldier, whose sole duty was to enforce the laws of the United States, undertook to further the schemes of the strong men who had determined to make him a Presidential candidate of the party that had opposed him in the only field where he had ever been either prominent or active, by issuing a series of proclamations which encouraged the revival of a rebellious and disorderly spirit in Texas and Louisiana, and which were not only insubordinate to the legislative branch of the Government, but to his two distinguished military superiors. Hancock, the favorite and *protégé* of Andrew Johnson, undertook the task of reversing the policy of Sheridan and of Grant, after the greatest of all Virginians since Washington, George H. Thomas, had absolutely and indignantly refused to do Johnson's work and to undo the work of the war. It was not any part of the duty of a soldier in Hancock's place to indulge in the "glittering generalities" which were a misplaced and shallow adaptation of the sound and lawyer-like doctrines of civil liberty expounded by the citizen-soldier and the defender of the rights of citizenship, James A. Garfield, who had much to fear politically from his course, while Hancock had everything to expect from adding the incongruous functions of a demagogue to the proper duties of a subordinate commander. The people of the United States can judge whether Garfield's defense of civil liberty or Hancock's, under all the circumstances and conditions, was the more creditable and patriotic.

The preparation for the argument in the Milligan case was necessarily limited in time, but the fundamental principles which underlaid Garfield's effort were all thoroughly familiar to him, and he needed only to work up the cases and make the application. Realizing fully the importance of the case, he plunged with all his vigor into the work of preparation, accomplishing, through the help of his unusually vigorous constitution and power of rapid work, an immense amount of actual achievement. In making out his argument he worked for two days and two nights, with the exception of four or five hours of sleep, and concentrated in that time what most lawyers would consider fortnight labor.

The day before the trial was to come off the counsel were assembled for consultation to determine upon the policy to be pursued, when Judge Black called upon Garfield, as the junior counsel, to give his views first. The diffidence of Garfield in responding to this request was very deep and unfeigned, in presence of some of the very ablest and most distinguished lawyers in the country, to whom he was to show his method of trying the case ; but he had done his best, and there was nothing for him to do except to state his points and the line of his argument, which having done, the senior counsel relieved him of all apprehension and anxiety by unanimously telling him, "Don't you change a line or a word of that."

The argument which passed so successfully the ordeal of such severe critics was equally effectual in court, whose decision was unanimously in favor of Garfield's clients.   It was a great triumph, one richly deserved by Garfield for his courage in assuming the risks of unpopularity with his own party, and not otherwise compensated for than in the consciousness of having defended what he believed to be the true principles of our Government.   There was certainly little outside encouragement for the work which he did in this case.   The defendants were poor and in prison.   Garfield paid for printing his own brief.   He had never seen his clients, never had any relations with them, nor ever received a cent in any way for his service.   But his argument and his success won for him immediately a high standing in the Supreme Court of the United States, and opened to him a practice before that and other high tribunals which has really afforded to him all the profit which is represented in his actual present property, as his compensation in the army and in Congress has barely paid the economic expenses of his living.

One of the pleasantest circumstances connected with his argument of the Milligan case was its effect in deepening the existing friendship between himself and his mortal enemy in politics, Judge Black, and in increasing Judge Black's already strong admiration for the intellectual, moral, and manly qualities of his young friend.   This friendship has continued under all circumstances with increasing strength and fervor to this day, and has given rise to many other acts of friendship on the part of Judge Black than his now celebrated letter defending Garfield from the charges in connection with the Credit Mobilier and other matters.   To those who know Judge Black and his unbending, uncompromising integrity of character, it is unnecessary to say that no considerations would cause him to write, in behalf even of a most beloved brother, such a letter as that which has been recently republished in regard to General Garfield and the latter's connection with the Credit Mobilier.

Among the cases in which Garfield has been retained as counsel, one of the most notable was that known as the great Alexander Campbell will case, in which he was associated with

Judge Black in defence of the will. His senior counsel was obliged to leave the conduct of the argument to Garfield entirely. Alexander Campbell, the founder of the sect known as the Campbellites, left about a quarter of a million of dollars, and his will was contested on the ground that he was mentally infirm from old age when his will was made. The trial lasted for ten days, and presented many difficult points, but Garfield was successful, and maintained the soundness of the testator's mind and the validity of the will. In this case he was well paid.

In another case he was the assistant junior counsel of that great jurist Benjamin R. Curtis, in the last case which the latter ever argued before the Supreme Court of the United States, of which tribunal he had been for many years the most distinguished ornament. The question involved in this case was one as to the effect of war on a life-insurance policy—whether a Southern policy-holder by entering the Confederate military service forfeited his policy. Judge Curtis and General Garfield maintained that he did. It was an entirely new question in the Supreme Court, and its difficulty may be judged of from the fact that as one of the nine judges happened to be sick the other eight were equally divided, and it was impossible then to arrive at a final decision.

But a year later, after Judge Curtis' death, another case came up involving the same discussion, and Garfield was chosen by the New York Life Insurance Company to manage it, and won it, the Court deciding that war vitiates and renders void a policy of life insurance.

The mention of these cases shows that General Garfield maintained the extraordinary position in the profession which he assumed at the very outset. They are mentioned only to indicate the nature of the practice into which Garfield entered, and which has been since continued in a large number and variety of important cases, some of which will be referred to elsewhere. The records of the American Bar will fail to show any parallel instance to that of his splendid beginning and of his maintenance of the elevated position to which he at first attained—a position reached by few, even among those whose whole lives have been given to the professional work, until after they have passed their meridian.   Of course he has been able to give but a small proportion of his time to the practice of the law, even for large fees. He has never sought cases, but has been obliged to decline a great deal of practice which has come to him of its own accord.   Still, his income has been materially benefited by his fees as a lawyer, and altogether they would amount, probably, to a considerable sum.   The amount he has received has varied very much in different years.   In some years his receipts from the profession would not be over a thousand dollars, while in other years they were six or seven times that amount.

(Garfield to B. A. Hinsdale.)

WASHINGTON, February 2, 1868.

You were surprised that I introduced the Hancock Bill; so was I; but the orders and proclamations which he had been issuing were of so insubordinate a character as to endanger the whole work of reconstruction in Louisiana.   It was a part of the plan by which the President seemed determined to make it appear that the reaction was going to overthrow not only our party, but all its work.   Even if we should see that the Government plan was not the best, it was manifest that a change now would be every way disastrous.   Those who clamor against the plan of Congress most are not able to say what better thing can now be done—indeed, they propose no plan.   Their only purpose is to get into power.   Seeing this so clearly, it became manifest that we must rebuke all attempts at insubordinate reaction.   We must show that our refusal to impeach the President did not arise either from want of courage, nor from any purpose to abandon our work of reconstruction on the basis of universal freedom.   With these views I introduced the Hancock Bill, not so much for the purpose of passing it as to show him how completely he was in our hands, and that he could not make political merchandise of his commission, and read lectures to the National Legislature when he ought to be executing its law.   I could readily have carried the bill through, but preferred to let it hang suspended.   I think it has had the desired effect, for the General has kept his place ever since.   So long as he continues to do so, I shall let him alone.

I sent you a copy of my remarks on the Reconstruction Bill, which will show you more at length my reasons.   I have been spending all my leisure during the past two weeks in studying the currency question—in going over again the ground—and in a week or two shall make a speech on which I expect to stand or fall, probably the latter, for I see the tide of wild and insane clamor for paper money rising higher and higher.

(Garfield to B. A. Hinsdale.)

WASHINGTON, March 8, 1868.

When your last letter came, I was in the midst of my preparation for the Campbell will case. That case kept me away from the city thirteen days. . . .

You may be interested to know that the chief burden of the will case fell upon me. The trial occupied ten days, and Judge Black left me at the end of the second day. Young Richardson, of Wheeling, was my only assistant, and he was sick part of the time. There were sixty-eight witnesses, and the lawyers on the other side spoke over eight hours. I had the closing speech, and reviewed the testimony and opposing speeches. I spoke six hours and a half. The will and codicil were sustained. I suppose it may not be immodest for me to say to you that I think I have never done a more creditable piece of intellectual work than on that trial. . . .

The State Convention at Columbus has committed itself to some financial doctrines that, if I understand them, I cannot and will not endorse. If my constituents approve them, they cannot approve me. Before many weeks my immediate political future will be decided. I care less about the result than I have ever cared before.

(Garfield to B. A. Hinsdale.)

WASHINGTON, April 30, 1874.

There is much in life to make one sad and disheartened ; but whether we maintain a cheerful spirit or not, depends largely on the way in which we view the events and outcomes of life. I think the main point of safety is to look upon life with a view of doing as much good to others as possible, and, as far as possible, to strip ourselves of what the French call egoism.

The worst days of darkness through which I have ever passed have been greatly alleviated by throwing myself with all my energy into some work relating to others. Your life is so much devoted in this direction that I think you will find in it the greatest safety from the danger of gloom.

*   *   *   *   *   *   *   *   *

Those who criticise the paving business, do so without recalling that the fee was a contingent one in which the labor went for nothing if the result was not a success. It is everywhere understood that the fee is larger in consequence of the risk the lawyer takes of getting nothing, and, when it is considered that the work the parties were to do was to amount to $700,000, the contingent fee of Parsons will not be considered an extravagant one. Judge Black charged the Phillips Bros. $10,000 for the work we did for them in Philadelphia, and he had two thirds of the fee and I one third. This was on account of the large sum involved, namely, $400,000. Nobody would criticise that as an extravagant fee under the circumstances ; and yet, the amount involved was little more than one half of that involved in the Parson's fee. If I had had any reason to suppose that the parties were employing anybody else, I would not have helped Parsons. They gave Parsons no intimation that they were employing anybody besides him.

(Garfield to B. A. Hinsdale.)

WASHINGTON, January 7, 1876.

I hardly know what to say of the last year. For many reasons it has been very unlike its predecessors. To me it has been full of work, of sickness and changes. It has brought to me the wonders of the Pacific coast. It has brought to me some good books and large thoughts. It has brought a revolution in political parties. It has brought me for the first time into a legislative minority. It has brought me to confront more seriously than ever the proposition to retire from public life, and enter upon work for myself. More than any other year of my life, it has brought to me a conviction that I have possibly so far sinned against my health by overwork that I shall never again have the capacity for work formerly enjoyed. It has brought the first death into the small and select circle of my Hiram friends in depriving us of Almeda. It is not a little surprising that so few deaths have occurred in our circle for twenty-two years, but the shaft will fall thicker and faster hereafter.

I ought to have added, the last few months have awakened in me an increased interest in the law, and I think the year has witnessed considerable increase in my power as a lawyer. I have followed this rule : whenever I have had a case, I have undertaken to work out thoroughly the principles involved in it ; not for the case alone, but for the sake of comprehending thoroughly that branch of the law. And my cases have fortunately covered a wide range.

I send you a couple of briefs which I have written within the last ten days, and which will, in part, illustrate my meaning.

(*Garfield to B. A. Hinsdale.*)

ALLIANCE, OHIO, June 13, 1877.

You know that my life has abounded in crises and difficult situations. This trip has been, perhaps, not a crisis, but certainly has placed me in a situation of extreme difficulty. Two or three months ago, W. B. Duncan, a prominent business man in New York, retained me as his lawyer in a suit to be heard in the United States Court in Mobile, and sent me the papers in the case. I studied them, and found that they involved an important and somewhat difficult question of law, and I made myself sufficiently familiar with it, so that when Duncan telegraphed me to be in Mobile on the first Monday in June, I went with a pretty comfortable sense of my readiness to meet anybody who should be employed on the other side. But when I reached Mobile I found there were two other suits connected with this, and involving the ownership, sale, and complicated rights of several parties to the Mobile and Ohio Railroad.

After two days' skirmishing, the Court ordered the three suits to be consolidated. The question I had prepared myself on passed wholly out of sight, and the whole entanglement of an insolvent railroad, twenty-five years old, and lying across four States, and costing $20,000,000, came upon us at once. There were seven lawyers in the case besides me. On one side were John A. Campbell, of New Orleans, late member of the Supreme Bench of the United States, a leading New York and a Mobile lawyer. Against us were Judge Hoadley, of Cincinnati, and several Southern men. I was assigned the duty of summing up the case for our side, and answering the final argument of the opposition. I have never felt myself in such danger of failure before, all had so much better knowledge of the facts than I, and all had more experience with that class of litigation ; but I am very sure no one of them did so much hard work, in the five nights and five days of the trial, as I did. I am glad to tell you that I have received a dispatch from Mobile that the Court adopted my view of the case, and gave us a verdict on all points.

As you may imagine, I am good deal used up.

(Garfield to B. A. Hinsdale.)

WASHINGTON, November 2, 1878.

Last evening I called on Judge Black at the Ebbett House and found him with a Bible in his hand. He said : "I don't know any one who has properly appreciated the parables of Jesus. I don't believe that the man ever lived who could have written any one of them, even the least of them. They are unlike anything in literature or philosophy in their spirit, purpose, and character. I they were all that Jesus had left us, they would be conclusive proofs of his divinity." What do you think of this ? The Judge then went on to say that he had that morning asked a lady friend to lend him some books for Sunday reading, and, among others, she had sent him a volume entitled "Alone with Jesus." "And," said he, "the title repelled me for two reasons: first, it is a piece of spontaneous egoism for any man to assume that he is of so much consequence in the universe that Christ would shut out all the rest of the world and attend to him ; and, second, I knew a bank cashier who stole everything he could lay his hands on, and then ran away in the night. He left behind him a diary full of the most pious ejaculations, and the last entry he made in it was this: 'Spent an hour of sweet communion alone with Jesus.' This remembrance spoiled the book for me, and so I have not read it."

I spent several hours with him, and found him more than usually brilliant. He said he was inclined to believe that a man rarely, after he was forty years old, fell in love with a new poet. For his own part no one later than Byron had taken much hold on him. Coleridge, Southey, and Wordsworth he had read but little, probably because Byron had so savagely denounced them as the lakers. He has no admiration for Tennyson, and says he never had the patience to wade through "In Memoriam." He was greatly pleased with my plan of going into the law, and proposed to form a sort of special partnership in the cases that he and I might have in the Supreme Court here. This may be of much service to me.

CHAPTER XVI.

IN the addresses which at various times he has delivered on the subject of education, he has disclosed the methods and workings of his own mind, with an unconsciousness of that fact which is perfectly characteristic. For instance, in an address delivered before the Literary Societies of the Eclectic Institute at Hiram on the 14th of June, 1867, he covered the whole ground of the disputed educational questions of the day, and brought out very strongly many of the theories of education which he had evolved from his own experience and reading. Take, for instance, his classification of the kinds of knowledge that should be the objects of a liberal education. This conforms largely with the classification of Herbert Spencer; but it is broader and deeper by far than Herbert Spencer's, for in giving his final definition, which is made comprehensive and sweeping, he says that " the student should study himself, his relations to society, to nature, and to art, and above all, in all, and through all these, he should study the relations of himself, society, nature, and art to God, the Author of them all."

Having started in his education with a passionate love of the classics, he had finally reached the point of enlargement by a study of the physical sciences, where he began to believe that the share of time alloted to classical studies by our colleges was too great in proportion, and not arranged in the right order of development. To illustrate his views by his own language, what he suggested as to the order of study was " that the student shall first study what he needs most to know; that the order of his needs shall be the order of his work." " Now," said he, " it will not be denied that from the day that the child's foot first presses the green turf till the day when, an old man, he is ready to be laid under it, there is not an hour in which he does not need to know a thousand things in relation to his body, ' what he shall eat, what he shall drink, and where-withal he shall be clothed.' If parents were themselves suffi-ciently educated, most of this knowledge might be acquired at the mother's knee ; but, by the strangest perversion and mis-direction of the educational forces, these most essential elements of knowledge are more neglected than any other.''

Further on he said : '' It is to me a perpetual wonder that any child's love of knowledge survives the outrages of the school-house,'' and added, '' I, for one, declare that no child of mine shall ever be *compelled* to study one hour, or to learn even the English alphabet, before he has deposited under his skin at least seven years of muscle and bone.''

Alluding to the then common college course of study, he said :

'' A finished education is supposed to consist mainly of literary culture. The story of the forges of the Cyclops, where the thunderbolts of Jove were fashioned, is supposed to adorn elegant scholarship more gracefully than those sturdy truths which are preaching to this generation in the wonders of the mine, in the fire of the furnace, in the clang of the iron-mills, and the other innumerable industries which, more than all other human agencies, have made our civilization what it is, and are destined to achieve wonders yet undreamed of. This generation is beginning to understand that education should not be forever divorced from industry ; that the highest results can be reached only when science guides the hand of labor. With what eagerness and alacrity is industry seizing every truth of science and putting it in harness !''

Reviewing the extent and variety of knowledge, scientific and practical, which the farmer needs in order to reach the full height and scope of his noble calling, he asks, '' What has our American system of education done for this controlling majority of the people ?'' Which question he answers with the single fact that '' notwithstanding there are in the United States 120,-000 common schools, and 7,000 academies and seminaries ; notwithstanding there are 275 colleges where young men may be graduated as Bachelors and Masters of the liberal arts, yet in all these the people of the United States have found so little being done, or likely to be done, to educate men for the work of agriculture, that they have demanded, and at last have secured, from their political servants in Congress, an appropriation sufficient to build and maintain, in each State of the Union, a college for the education of farmers. This great outlay would have been totally unnecessary but for the stupid and criminal neglect of college, academic, and common school Boards of Education to furnish that which the want of the people require. The scholar and the worker must join hands if both would be successful."

But it was not the lack of utility in the common courses of educational training which most awakened Garfield's indignation. He was more aroused by the neglect to provide text-books for instruction as to the nature of our own Government, and as to the history of its development and progress. Said he :

" For this defect I have neither respect nor toleration. It is far inferior to that of Persia three thousand years ago. The uncultivated tribes of Greece, Rome, Libya, and Germany surpassed us in this respect. Grecian children were taught to reverence and emulate the virtue of their ancestors. Our educational forces are so wielded as to teach our children to admire most that which is foreign and fabulous and dead. Our American children must know all the classic rivers, from the Scamander to the yellow Tiber, must tell you the length of the Appian Way, and of the canal over which Horace and Virgil sailed on their journey to Brundusium ; but he may be crowned with baccalaureate honors without having heard, since his first moment of Freshman life, one word concerning the 122,000 miles of coast and river navigation, the 6000 miles of canal, and the 35,000 miles of railroad, which indicate both the prosperity and the possibilities of his own country."

Without undertaking to give the full scope of this vigorous outline of what he regarded as a style of education adapted to the unprecedented conditions of American youth, there is one passage which is so profound and lofty in its intelligent Americanism, that it must be given without regard to its length or the lack of space :

" It is well to know the history of those magnificent nations, whose origin is lost in fable, and whose epitaphs were written a thousand years ago—but if we cannot know both, it is far better to study the history of our own nation, whose origin we can trace to the freest and noblest aspirations of the human heart—a nation that was formed from the hardiest, purest, and most enduring elements of European civilization—a nation, that by its faith and courage has dared and accomplished more for the human race in a single century than Europe accomplished in the first thousand years of the Christian Era.   The New England township was the type after which our Federal Government was modelled ; yet it would be rare to find a college student who can make a comprehensive and intelligible statement of the municipal organization of the township in which he was born, and tell you by what officers its legislative, judicial and executive functions are administered.   One half of the time which is now almost wholly wasted, in district schools, on English Grammar, attempted at too early an age, would be sufficient to teach our children to love the Republic, and to become its loyal and life-long supporters.   After the bloody baptism from which the nation has arisen to a higher and nobler life, if this shameful defect in our system of education be not speedily remedied, we shall deserve the infinite contempt of future generations.   I insist that it should be made an indispensable condition of graduation in every American college, that the student must understand the history of this continent since its discovery by Europeans, the origin and history of the United States, its constitution of government, the struggles through which it has passed, and the rights and duties of citizens who are to determine its destiny and share its glory.

" Having thus gained the knowledge which is necessary to life, health, industry, and citizenship, the student is prepared to enter a wider and grander field of thought.   If he desires that large and liberal culture which will call into activity all his powers, and make the most of the material God has given him, he must study deeply and earnestly the intellectual, the moral, the religious and the æsthetic nature of man ; his relations to nature, to civilization, past and present ; and above all, his relations to God.   These should occupy, nearly, if not fully, half the time of his college course.   In connection with the

philosophy of the mind, he should study logic, the pure mathematics, and the general laws of thought.   In connection with
moral philosophy, he should study political and social ethics, a
science so little known either in colleges or Congresses.
Prominent among all the rest, should be his study of the wonderful history of the human race, in its slow and toilsome march
across the centuries—now, buried in ignorance, superstition
and crime ; now rising to the sublimity of heroism and catch-
ing a glimpse of a better destiny ; now turning remorselessly
away from, and leaving to perish, empires and civilizations in
which it had invested its faith and courage and boundless
energy for a thousand years, and plunging into the forests of
Germany, Gaul, and Britain, to build for itself new empires
better fitted for its new aspirations ; and at last, crossing three
thousand miles of unknown sea, and building in the wilderness
of a new hemisphere its latest and proudest monuments.''

CHAPTER XVII.

It has generally happened to political parties to have at least one question that was peculiarly troublesome. The slavery question was the death of the old Whig party, whose composition was such that it was impossible that it should stand anything like a chance of success in a competition with the Democratic party for the favor and support of the South. Time has brought its revenges, however, and since the war the various phases of the slavery question and of the constitutional doctrines which were invented to buttress slavery against external assaults, have been, at various times, very ugly things for the Democratic party to deal with, and the currency question has been still fuller of dangers and disasters. But the question of Civil Service Reform has been the peculiar difficulty of the Republican Party. It is a party which, as a matter of recognized fact, contains within itself a large proportion of the best educated, the most intelligent, and politically the most conscientious and independent people in the country. While, in some of the States of the Union, twenty years of continuous power have given to what are known as the "party machines" a perfection of organization, a thoroughness of drill and discipline, and a steadiness of grip, unequalled, perhaps, in the political history of the country, there is no State in which the whole fabric of organization is not liable to be swept away at any time by an uprising of the disinterested intellectual and moral forces within the party, on sufficient provocation and with proper direction. And yet, although the party convention in Cincinnati four years ago adopted an unequivocal Civil Service Reform platform, which was received with approbation by pretty much all Republicans who were not either running political

" machines" or expecting favors and offices therefrom, it has
required three years of excellent, pure, successful, and, in some
respects, magnificent administration, for President Hayes to
secure from his party the unquestionably general honor, respect,
and support which he now enjoys.   But it would be very unsafe
to suppose that, with all the human nature there is in any great
political party, the Republican Party is anything like a unit on
the subject of Civil Service Reform.   It is one thing to be willing to fight for freedom in the Territories, or for emancipation in
all the old slave States ; it is quite another thing to fight for
purity of administration and the abolition of patronage for
political purposes, when there are so many good people in the
country who, for themselves or for their friends or relations, are
entertaining great expectations from the distribution of a hundred thousand Federal offices.   The tendency of the party unquestionably is toward Civil Service Reform ; and while the
Chicago platform, for reasons needless to mention here, ignored
this question in the way of any direct treatment, the convention
unanimously nominated a man for the Presidency whose record
on the subject of Civil Service Reform is, in itself, a platform ;
and that record, if it is not known of all men, easily can be.   I
am sure that General Garfield will not shrink from its minutest
scrutiny, or from the implied pledges that are contained in his
various public declarations on this subject.   So far as his career
as a politician is concerned, from first to last, he has been, not
so much antagonist to, as distinct from, that class of leaders whose
power has been strengthened, continued, and perpetuated by
the creation and preservation of " machines" and the judicious
disposition of patronage.   Garfield has maintained his hold on
the affections and confidence of the people of his own district
and of the State of Ohio by virtue of what he has been, and
said, and done.   He never managed a convention or a caucus in
his own interest, or for his own purposes.   He never attempted
to do so.   Even in his contest for the United States Senate, when
his opponent was a man of such large national reputation and
deserved personal popularity, he not only did not go near the

scene of the contest, he did not have there any "headquarters;" kept no "grocery;" made no pledges, bargains, or concessions; authorized and made no personal attacks on his great competitor, Judge Thurman, and quietly and without excitement awaited the result.

He has been repeatedly and continuously honored by his fellow-citizens with their confidence, not because of what he has done directly to insure that support, but by virtue of what he has uniformly said and done in the interests of his party and of his country. He therefore has, and can have, no sympathy with those who oppose Civil Service Reform, because it is inconsistent with the maintenance of despotic political "machines," run for their own benefit. But he is also an exceedingly practical man. As a member of Congress unusually familiar with the wants and the relative merits of his constituents, he has long acted as their friend, their mouthpiece, and their mediator, with the appointing power. He knows how utterly impossible it is for executive officers in Washington to understand, unaided by Congressional advice, the relative merits of competing applicants for office, all over the vast extent of this country; and yet he has a constitutional aversion to acting as an intermediary between office-seekers and the Executive. Even the slightest glimpse into the activities of a public character which have distinguished him ever since he took his seat in Congress would show any one how he must begrudge every moment of time given to the mere details of providing constituents with offices, no matter how fit they may have been for Executive favor.

But it is far better to allow General Garfield to define his own views on a subject so delicate, difficult, and important. He has done this in a contribution to the *Atlantic Monthly* for July, 1877, which is, perhaps, as clear and comprehensive a statement of the views of an enlightened and practical statesman, who has been in thorough accord with the spirit of the Hayes Administration, while he has opposed or criticised many of its methods, as could possibly be found.

" This brings me to consider the present relations of Congress to the other great departments of the Government, and to the people. The limits of this article will permit no more than a glance at a few principal heads of inquiry.

" In the main, the balance of powers so admirably adjusted and distributed among the three great departments of the Government have been safely preserved. It was the purpose of our fathers to lodge absolute power nowhere ; to leave each department independent within its own sphere ; yet, in every case, responsible for the exercise of its discretion. But some dangerous innovations have been made.

" And first, the appointing power of the President has been seriously encroached upon by Congress, or rather by the members of Congress Curiously enough, this encroachment originated in the act of the Chief Executive himself. The fierce popular hatred of the Federal party which resulted in the elevation of Jefferson to the Presidency led that officer to set the first example of removing men from office on account of political opinions. For political causes alone he removed a considerable number of officers who had recently been appointed by President Adams, and thus set the pernicious example. His immediate successors made only a few removals for political reasons. But Jackson made his political opponents who were in office feel the full weight of his executive hand. From that time forward the civil offices of the Government became the prizes for which political parties strove ; and, twenty-five years ago, the corrupting doctrine that ' to the victors belong the spoils ' was shamelessly announced as an article of political faith and practice. It is hardly possible to state with adequate force the noxious influence of this doctrine. It was bad enough when the Federal officers numbered no more than eight or ten thousand ; but now, when the growth of the country, and the great increase in the number of public offices, occasioned by the late war, have swelled the civil list to more than eighty thousand, and to the ordinary motives for political strife this vast patronage is offered as a reward to the victorious party, the magnitude of the evil can hardly be measured. The public mind has, by degrees, drifted into an acceptance of this doctrine ; and thus an election has become a fierce, selfish struggle between the ' ins ' and the ' outs,' the one striving to keep and the other to gain the prize of office. It is not possible for any President to select, with any degree of intelligence, so vast an army of office-holders without the aid of men who are acquainted with the people of the various sections of the country. And thus it has become the habit of Presidents to make most of their appointments on the recommendation of members of Congress.   During the last twenty-five years it has been understood, by the Congress and the people, that offices are to be obtained by the aid of Senators and Representatives, who thus become the dispensers, sometimes the brokers of patronage.   The members of State Legislatures who choose a Senator, and the district electors who choose a Representative, look to the man of their choice for appointments to office.   Thus, from the President downward, through all the grades of official authority, to the electors themselves, civil office becomes a vast corrupting power, to be used in running the machine of party politics.

"This evil has been greatly aggravated by the passage of the Tenure of Office Act of 1867, whose object was to restrain President Johnson from making removals for political cause.   But it has virtually resulted in the usurpation, by the Senate, of a large share of the appointing power.   The President can remove no officer without the consent of the Senate ; and such consent is not often given, unless the appointment of the successor nominated to fill the proposed vacancy is agreeable to the Senator in whose State the appointee resides.   Thus it has happened that a policy, inaugurated by an early President, has resulted in seriously crippling the just powers of the Executive, and has placed in the hands of Senators and Representatives a power most corrupting and dangerous.

"Not the least serious evil resulting from this invasion of the executive functions by members of Congress is the fact that it greatly impairs their own usefulness as legislators.   One third of the working hours of Senators and Representatives is hardly sufficient to meet the demands made upon them in reference to appointments to office.   The spirit of that clause of the Constitution which shields them from arrest ' during their attendance on the session of their respective houses, and in going to and from the same,' should also shield them from being arrested from their legislative work, morning, noon, and night, by office-seekers.   To sum up in a word : the present system invades the independence of the Executive, and makes him less responsible for the character of his appointments ; it impairs the efficiency of the legislator by diverting him from his proper sphere of duty, and involving him in the intrigues of aspirants for office ; it degrades the civil service itself by destroying the personal independence of those who are appointed ; it repels from the service those high and manly qualities which are so necessary to a pure and efficient administration ; and, finally, it de-

bauches the public mind by holding up public office as the reward of mere party zeal.

"To reform this service is one of the highest and most imperative duties of statesmanship. This reform cannot be accomplished without a complete divorce between Congress and the
Executive in the matter of appointments. It will be a proud
day when an administration Senator or Representative, who is
in good standing in his party, can say as Thomas Hughes said,
during his recent visit to this country, that though he was on
the most intimate terms with the members of his own administration, yet it was not in his power to secure the removal of the
humblest clerk in the civil service of his government.

' This is not the occasion to discuss the recent enlargement of
the jurisdiction of Congress in reference to the election of a
President and Vice-President by the States. But it cannot be
denied that the electoral bill has spread a wide and dangerous
field for Congressional action. Unless the boundaries of its
power shall be restricted by a new amendment of the Constitution, we have seen the last of our elections of President on the
old plan. The power to decide who has been elected may be
so used as to exceed the power of electing.

"I have long believed that the official relations between the
Executive and Congress should be more open and direct. They
are now conducted by correspondence with the presiding officers of the two Houses, by consultation with committees, or by
private interviews with individual members. This frequently
leads to misunderstandings, and may lead to corrupt combinations. It would be far better for both departments if the members of the Cabinet were permitted to sit in Congress and par-
ticipate in the debates on measures relating to their several departments, but, of course, without a vote. This would tend to
secure the ablest men for the chief executive offices ; it would
bring the policy of the administration into the fullest publicity
by giving both parties ample opportunity for criticism and defense."

CHAPTER XVIII.

THE reader will have realized before reading this chapter, how hard it is to grapple with all the aspects of Garfield's public career, to illustrate which adequately half a dozen volumes would be needed. It will only be possible to deal in generalities, with a few salient features of Garfield's public activities and private life since he entered Congress. His record as a party leader, to begin with, has been exceptional. At every stage of his rapid, and yet steady, advance toward the culmination and crowning of his leadership, by the spontaneous and unanimous action of the assembled representatives of his party, at Chicago, he has developed, in growing measure, the rare combination of powers and qualities that made him the most honored and popular student at Williams, then President at Hiram College, and State Senator, and afterward the Chief of Staff of the Army of the Cumberland. The reasons for his success have been in him, and not in his circumstances or in any adroit scheme to capture it. His courage, inherited on both sides, developed by his early life, and under fire and amid disaster, in the army, has been of that high moral order that dares the censure or criticism of associates or constituents, when his clear intuitions of right and justice have commanded his action, as they always have. His unreserved, confidential letters to Hinsdale and Rockwell and other intimate friends, which he never dreamed would see the light, show this with the utmost clearness. From his first entrance on public life until the Chicago Convention, these letters show him to have been almost continually acting on convictions not shared by some of his best friends in Congress, and unpopular with many of his constituents and with politicians. When President Lincoln, in the terrible winter of 1863-4, wanted

Congress to pass an efficient draft law, and begged members to pass it, as the only means by which our armies could even be kept in the field, there came an occasion when Garfield stood up, solitary and alone, and voted in accordance with Lincoln's entreaties.   When, in the heat of the desperate conflict between the majority in Congress and President Johnson, there was exhibited, on the part of the former, some disregard of the spirit of the Constitution, Garfield, the Representative of the most radical, anti-Johnson district in the country, called a halt. When some Republican Congressmen failed to see that justice and policy demanded that the South should have a fair chance to show its acceptance of the results of the war, he was not afraid to use the language of prudence, moderation, and wisdom.   And then, when the "solid South," whose "Brigadiers" ruled the Democratic Congressional caucus, had determined to "starve the Government" unless the Executive should surrender his constitutional prerogatives, he was the leader of the fight that required the highest degree of moral courage ever demanded of a party leader in Congress.

In all the sectional and partisan discussions which have afforded chances for the display of his powers in Congress, he has retained the esteem, confidence, and personal good-will of the best and ablest of his antagonists.   Among his warmest friends are to be found some of the most pronounced representatives of extreme Southern and Democratic sentiment.   They know the man, and so transparent, ingenuous, and outspoken a man is easily known.   They know that he has no political passions whatever.   They know that there is not a legitimate Southern interest which would not be certain of justice and liberality at his hands ; that sectional hates have no place in his generous heart, nor sectional ideas in his broad nature.   It is impossible to conceive of his enduring for a day the misery of a grudge or a jealousy.   Least of all, is it possible for him to cherish ill-feelings or suspicions toward party associates who have sought the same ends that he has, by different methods.   The feeling of "comradeship" with party associates in public life who are actuated by any high sense of the mission and duties of the party, is peculiarly warm and strong—no matter what their attitude toward him or his policy may have been. He is the best friend of the greatest number of men, and the poorest and most inefficient enemy, of any man whom I know in politics. In fact, the very exuberance of his own activities and the fruition thereof, render him largely unconscious of and apathetic toward inter-party contentions and rivalries.

It is a characteristic of Garfield, as it is of every man whose intellectual and moral growth has been healthful, spontaneous, symmetrical, and consistent, that whatever thing has once absorbed his interest and his energies, has so possessed his whole nature that from that time forward only opportunities and occasions have been needed to develop the views and the purposes, with larger knowledge and stronger faith, that had become part of his existence.

In fact, the prelude and key to his whole public career can be found in those terribly hard-working days when he was alternately teacher and pupil ; when his mind was grasping out in all directions with an ambition as broad as Bacon's, when he wanted to '' possess all knowledge'' as his '' province,'' but under limitations, amid difficulties, and with a poverty of facilities which the nature of Bacon never would have surmounted. The athletic young teacher, who was the comrade of his pupils and the devoted friend of his most accomplished teacher, found the full fruition of his functions in his noble and heroic experience at Hiram. He was the teacher then in all his instincts, with all his force, with all his winning affectionateness of nature, with all his swift-growing capacity to communicate. He has been, ever since and simultaneously, the teacher and the pupil. He has been able to illustrate every one of the themes which he has been obliged to develop in Congress as a teacher ; because no application has been too great, no press of official duties too arduous, to prevent him from sitting reverently at the feet of the wisest teachers of all times and filling himself up with the abundance from which he has instructed others.

Being such, it was most natural that one of his early and earnest efforts in Congress was to make a plea for the establishment of the National Bureau of Education, which owes its existence to his energetic and persuasive advocacy, and which has done more good, at less cost, than any other bureau established by our own or any other government.

His speech delivered on the 8th of June, 1866, passed in view the magnitude of the interests involved in the establishment of the proposed bureau. In a brief space it covered the progress of general education in our own and other countries, and the increase of the facilities of knowledge, and cited eloquent passages from the great men of our own and other lands.

In behalf of extending educational privileges, he said, in conclusion : " I know that this is not a measure which is likely to attract the attention of those whose chief work is to watch the political movements that affect the results of nominating conventions and elections. The mere politician will see in it nothing valuable, for the millions of people to be benefited by it can give him no votes ; but I appeal to those who care more for the future safety and glory of this nation than for any mere temporary advantage to aid in giving to education the public recognition and active support of the Federal Government."

It was natural that he should keep up and widen his culture and his acquaintance with, and friendship for, literary and scientific men, even during the very thick of thronging public duties. Mr. Spofford, the Librarian of Congress, will testify that no other member has made such large and constant use of the Library as Garfield. He has not been a promiscuous and desultory reader, except in periods of illness, convalescence, or rest, but has taken special themes or fields of inquiry and study, and followed them out in all directions. At one time, to illustrate, he collected everything he could find in regard to Goethe, his development, surroundings, relations to German thought, and influence on his contemporaries and successors. I have seen the large blank book which is nearly filled with the rich gleanings of this comprehensive search, in his own handwriting. So he got from the Library its rarest and most valuable treasures of Horatian literature, which he never tires of exploring. One of his letters to Colonel Rockwell shows that even in a rough and hasty rhythmical transfer of one of Horace's odes he was able to display a keen application of the subtle beauties of the most artistic of Latin poets. One of the most valued treasures in his library is a beautiful Paris edition of Horace, sent to him by his distinguished and scholarly friend, Secretary Evarts, for whose commanding ability as a jurist, advocate, and statesman he cherishes an admiration that has been deepened by the intimacy growing out of like literary tastes and of common high objects of a political character.

In all his official, professional, and literary work, Garfield has pursued a system that has enabled him to accumulate, on a vast range and variety of subjects, an amount of easily-available information such as no one else has shown the possession of by its use. His house at Washington is a workshop, in which the tools are always kept within immediate reach. Although books overrun his house from top to bottom, his library contains the working material on which he mainly depends. And the amount of material is enormous. Large numbers of scrap-books that have been accumulating for over twenty years, in number and in value—made up with an eye to what either is or may become useful, which would render the collection of priceless value to the library of any first-class newspaper establishment— are so perfectly arranged and indexed that their owner, with his all-retentive memory, can turn in a moment to the facts that may be needed for almost any conceivable emergency in debate. These are supplemented by diaries that preserve Garfield's multifarious political, scientific, literary and religious inquiries, studies, and readings. And, to make the machinery of rapid work complete, he has a large box containing sixty-three different drawers, each properly labelled, in which he places newspaper cuttings, documents, and slips of paper, and from which he can pull out what he wants as easily as an organist can play on the stops of his instrument. In other words, the hardest and most masterful worker in Congress has had the largest and most scientifically arranged of workshops.

Having been entirely contented with the congenial activities and pleasant social relations and warm friendships of his career as member of the House, he has not exerted himself for official promotion.   The position of United States Senator would have been congenial to him, for the reason that it would have given him greater leisure for study and culture, and opportunity for more preparation in the way of speech-making.   But he not only never did anything to secure it—intriguing for it would have been impossible for him —he declined to accept the candidacy for it, when it was within his reach, because President Hayes and others urged on him the duty of remaining in the House, where he was most needed.   When his election to the Senate did come, it was the spontaneous and unforced result of nearly twenty years of good and great service, for his party and his country, of which every detail was known to the people of Ohio.   His great antagonist, Judge Thurman, who, two years before, had publicly testified his deliberate judgment as to the baselessness of the now revived slanders and scandals, was so fairly beaten, and by such an overpowering sentiment in favor of Garfield, that his supporters, moved by his own lofty spirit, joined in support of the motion to make Garfield's nomination unanimous, and he was elected without a dissenting vote.   By this unprecedented vote, the State of Ohio, which knows Garfield from the beginning, and has sifted all the slanders that malice and ignorance have combined to invent and keep alive, has cast her broad and protecting mantle over the greatest of her sons.   The prophet that is thus honored " in his own country" must have a record that will stand the minutest scrutiny, and those who know less of him than his own fellow " Buckeyes" should learn all the facts known to Ohioans about Garfield, before attempting to reverse Ohio's judgment.

NOTE.—A week after his election, Garfield had a reception in the House of Representatives, at Columbus, and, before the assembled Legislature and a large number of other citizens, delivered a speech which was a model of

Which inevitably brings me to a few allusions to the only portion of Garfield's public career which has ever given him serious annoyance. It was that in which arose the wholly inadequate foundations for what are known as the "Crédit Mobilier," "De Golyer," and "Back Pay" scandals. As to them, he has made the fullest and most satisfactory explanations to those who were most directly interested in ascertaining the exact degree of his culpability, if any at all existed. His defences were published and widely circulated at the time when our newspapers and people were in the habit of condemning public men as soon as the latter were accused, and then considering whether the condemned could "prove themselves innocent," which neither the law nor the everlasting principles of justice require any man to do. But after epidemics of official corruption there always follow epidemics of promiscuous censure and flaming

eloquence. It contained one paragraph which would not have been spoken by any man, under the circumstances, to men of both parties who had known him his whole life-time, had he not enjoyed "a conscience void of offence." Said he : "And now, gentlemen of the General Assembly without distinction of party, I recognize this tribute and compliment made to me to-night. Whatever my own course may be in the future, a large share of the inspiration of my future public life will be drawn from this occasion and these surroundings, and I shall feel anew the sense of obligation that I feel to the State of Ohio. Let me venture to point a single sentence in regard to that work. During the twenty years that I have been in public life, almost eighteen of it in the Congress of the United States, I have tried to do one thing. Whether I was mistaken or otherwise, it has been the plan of my life to follow my conviction at whatever personal cost to myself. I have represented for many years a district in Congress whose approbation I greatly desired ; but though it may seem, perhaps, a little egotistical to say it, I yet desired still more the approbation of one person, and his name was Garfield. [Laughter and applause.] He is the only man that I am compelled to sleep with [laughter], and eat with, and live with, and die with ; and if I could not have his approbation, I should have bad companionship. [Renewed laughter and applause.] And in this larger constituency, which has called me to represent them now, I can only do what is true to my best self, applying the same rule. And if I should be so unfortunate as to lose the confidence of this larger constituency, I must do what every other fairminded man has to do—carry his political life in his hand and take the consequences. But I must follow what seems to me to be the only safe rule of my life ; and with that view of the case, and with that much personal reference, I leave that subject."

virtue. The drift-wood of a wave of fierce and ill-considered newspaper comment on Garfield is still preserved and displayed by malignant partisan organs, probably to the annoyance of the respectable journals that have seen and admitted how unjust were their hasty contemporary criticisms. Thus the very dregs of the Past are cherished and thrust into the living waters of the Present.

There is nothing new or strange about these reiterations of charges that have been fully met and answered, even to the satisfaction of so independent, critical, and almost cynical a judge of public men as the *Nation*. The charges against Garfield are mild, tame, and colorless compared with those that were persistently brought against Washington, Jefferson, the two great Adamses, Jackson, and Clay. Even without the conclusive testimony of the man who knew all about the facts on which these charges rest, and who has always been a bitter political foe of Garfield, Judge Jeremiah S. Black ; without the testimony of Judge Poland, the chairman of the committee that investigated the "Credit Mobilier" scandals ; without the comprehensive defences made by Garfield himself, which satisfied a most exacting and enlightened constituency ; without the testimony in his behalf of such an able representative of the most aggressive Democracy of the South, Henry Watterson ; no man who knows Garfield well—his history, his opportunities for making fortunes by the undiscoverable and unpunishable exercise of his official opportunities as chairman of the Committee on Appropriations ; the constant narrowness of his means for a plain though generous style of living ; his struggles with debt ; the ingenuousness of his nature and its utter freedom from guile, craft, or deceit—would listen with patience, much less with credence, to the stale scandals that can no more affect the people's judgment of his character for integrity, than would any sort of scandals as to the courage of Grant or Sheridan, the honor of Bayard, the truthfulness of Washington, or the purity of Channing, affect the people's judgment as to the traits assailed. Whoever knows Garfield knows that corruptionism could no

more taint his blood than cowardice could have blanched the
cheeks of Sir Philip Sydney. And if I have succeeded in im-
parting to my readers any tolerable conception of the sort of
man that he, by his ancestry, breeding, habits, life, and trials,
has become, they would be offended by any elaborate defence
of his character against scandals that cannot be made to stick
to it.

[Mr. George William Curtis, in *Harper's Weekly*, has pierced the heart of the
" Crédit Mobilier" slander with a single arrow from a full quiver. Says he :
" The authors of the report—[the Poland Report]—may have thought it necessary
to show their impartiality by sacrificing some of their own party friends. But
whatever the reason of their action, the whole case, so far as Mr. Garfield is concerned, is a question of veracity between him and Oakes Ames. Comparing
Ames's testimony regarding Mr. Garfield with that in reference to others, it will
be seen that when he testified from memory, he acquitted Mr. Garfield entirely,
and afterward, in every case except that of Mr. Garfield, he produced some doc-
umentary evidence, certificates of stock, receipts of money or dividends, checks
bearing the full names or the initials of the persons to whom they purported to
have been paid, or entries in his diary of accounts, marked 'adjusted and closed.'
No such evidence, or any other but Mr. Ames's assertion and his diary was produced in Mr. Garfield's case, and nobody ever pretended or supposed that such
evidence exists or ever existed. The admitted facts of the transaction, and the
character of Mr. Garfield, never before or since impeached by friend or foe, and
impeached in this case only by a man engaged in bribery, but who confesses that
he may be mistaken, who cannot explain why he did not give Mr. Garfield the
stock which he said Mr. Garfield had paid for, and who does not pretend to say
why Mr. Garfield did not ask for the rest of the money which was due to him.
have already completely acquitted Mr. Garfield in every candid mind.'']

(*Garfield to B. A. Hinsdale.*)

HIRAM, October 26, 1865.

I do not remember to have claimed that St. Cyril was tinctured with Neo-
platonism ; but I did say that the Church at Alexandria was considerably influenced by the doctrines of that sect. I have looked into it a little and find a considerable variety of opinions among different authors. Gibbon speaks of it as
an attempt to reconcile the doctrines of Plato and Aristotle, and says that as a
philosophy it is unworthy of notice. It is only important as connected with
Christianity. The bigotry and folly of the Church persecuted it. Gibbon's com-
mentator says the Neoplatonists were not at war with Christianity, but desired
to apply their philosophy to the religion of Christ. Gibbon speaks of it also as
an attempt to revive Paganism. See also his interesting account of Julian the
Apostate, who was a Neoplatonist for a while.

(*Garfield to B. A. Hinsdale.*)

WASHINGTON, February 2, 1871.
I appreciate all the difficulties of the Governorship question as you present them. I have answered our friends in the Legislature by positively refusing to be a candidate, and have tried to explain to them the grounds of my refusal.

I think there is great danger of my giving offence by this course, but I cannot help it. I may see the case differently hereafter, but I think not.

(*Garfield to B. A. Hinsdale.*)

WASHINGTON, January 1, 1872.
In regard to the authenticity and purity of the Shakespeare text I have made some considerable study, and with what I have already done, I hope to be able to get something for you at the library either in the way of a loan or of reference, and I will attend to it soon. . . .

Have you seen the new book on Physical Geography by the French writer Reclus ? A translation has just been published in New York. I have looked over it, and think it a remarkably valuable book. The *Evening Post* has said of it within the past two or three days that it is the completest work extant on that subject.

(*Garfield to B. A. Hinsdale.*)

WASHINGTON, January 11, 1872.
The Senatorship went as I expected it would. I may say to you, however, that the Democrats tendered to me their unanimous vote, and enough Republicans to elect with the help of the Democrats expressed themselves willing to bolt from the caucus nomination. It was, I confess, some temptation with some risk. A position obtained in that way would have been an independent one. But, on the whole, though the Democrats did not demand any conditions, I felt I would be considered as placed under obligations, and therefore declined. What say you, was it wise or otherwise ?

(*Garfield to B. A. Hinsdale.*)

WASHINGTON, February 22, 1872.
Yours of the 16th instant is received. I am glad to know that somebody has related the subject of the Holy Roman Empire in an intelligent way. It has always been to me one of the dark points in European history. I shall get the book without delay, and read it as soon as I can steal time enough from work and sleep.

Since I wrote you last I found a book which interests me very much. You may have seen it ; if not, I hope you will get it. It is entitled "Ten Great Religions," by James Freeman Clarke. I have read the chapter on Buddhism with great interest. It is admirably written, in a liberal and philosophical spirit, and I am sure will interest you. What I have read of it leads me to believe that we have taken too narrow a view of the subject of religion.

(Garfield to B. A. Hinsdale.)

WASHINGTON, December 31, 1872.

The astonishing reverses of political life during the past year mark an epoch in our history and tend to sadden one's views of that kind of a career. There is something so touching, so pathetically tragic in the last days of Mr. Greeley, that it throws a shadow over all the walks and ways of public men.

We are in a singular condition here in Congress. There is virtually no opposition to the Republican party. The Democracy are stunned, perhaps killed, by their late defeat, and there seems to be no limit to the power of the dominant party. If to its great strength it shall add, as I fear, arrogance and recklessness, it will break in two before the next administration goes far.

The Credit Mobilier scandal has given me much pain. As I told you last fall, I feared it would turn and that the company itself was a bad thing. So I think it will, and perhaps some members of Congress were consciously parties to its plans. It has been a new form of trial for me to see my name flying the rounds of the press in connection with the basest of crimes. It is not enough for one to know that his heart and motives have been pure and true if he is not sure but that good men here and there, who do not know him, will set him down among the lowest men of doubtful morality. There is nothing in my relation to the case for which the tenderest conscience or the most scrupulous honor can blame me. It is fortunate that I never fully concluded to accept the offer made me ' but it grieves me greatly to have been negotiating with a man who had so little sense of truth and honor as to use his proposals for a purpose in a way now apparent to me. I shall go before the committee, and in due time before the House, with a full statement of all that is essential to the case so far as I am concerned. You and I are now nearly in middle life, and have not yet become soured and shrivelled with the wear and tear of life. Let us pray to be delivered from that condition where life and nature have no fresh, sweet sensations for us.

(Garfield to B. A. Hinsdale.)

WASHINGTON, January 27, 1873.

You have seen the second testimony of Mr. Ames is utterly in conflict with his first, and clearly inspired by a desire to protect himself against the threatened suit of the company to account to them for the stock he did not sell as pretended. I am involved, as the whole subject now is, in a storm of general obloquy and in the falsehoods which Mr. Ames has thrown into it. No one can tell the extent of damage it will work to individual reputations. It is clear to my mind that I shall suffer to some extent in consequence of his wickedness.

He has produced a pretended memorandum of an account with me—a memorandum of his own making—which he says he copied from his books ; but these he has not produced.

The only course for me to take for the present is to bear in silence whatever is cast upon me until the investigation is concluded. Then I shall speak. The condition of panic into which the public mind is thrown makes it nearly impossible either to speak or listen with calmness and judicial fairness. In the meantime I bespeak the patience of my friends.

(Garfield to B. A. Hinsdale.)
WASHINGTON, February 8, 1873.

Nothing new has transpired since you wrote except that Ames has been ordered to bring his original books and memoranda. None of the papers that he presented to the committee in the form of accounts were original except the receipts in Patterson's case. He does not pretend to have any receipts from me, nor any other evidence of the points in which our testimony conflicts. The committee themselves have been stampeded by the general spirit of panic that has prevailed, and, though some of them are good lawyers, they have not applied the rules of evidence to this investigation. I think the indications are that the men here are recovering their balance a little, and begin to think with more calmness on the merits of the case. But it is, even yet, too early to tell into what conclusions the public judgment will settle down. . . . .

I expect Judge Black in town to-day, and I have no doubt that he will remember that I gave him three years ago the same account of my relation to the Credit Mobilier as I have given in my testimony.

(Garfield to B. A. Hinsdale.)
WASHINGTON, February 15, 1873.

Ames has come and made whatever exhibition his memorandum-book enabled him to make. I cannot see that he has added anything to the strengthening of his case by the production of the book. The impression here is beginning to prevail that he fixed up his memorandum for use with his company, to make them believe he had effected sales of his stock.

I think it is clear that Ames intended to get members of Congress interested in this company without saying anything to them to indicate his purpose. He does not pretend to have any receipt of mine or any other evidence but his statement in his book of the transaction which he alleges took place between us.

The investigation is really done now, and the report will probably be finished in the course of three or four days.

(Garfield to B. A. Hinsdale.)
WASHINGTON, March 19, 1873.

I am thoroughly disgusted with the way my vote on the salary question is treated, and I feel as if there was but little use in attempting to resist the senseless and wicked clamor which is being raised on the subject.

It is very singular to notice how differently the subject is treated in different parts of the country. In some, at least, the increase of salaries, together with the retroactive clause, is stoutly defended, and but little criticism is made.

I feel this morning, though I would not say this except to you, like throwing up my position in disgust and retiring from a field where ten years of honest work goes for naught in the face of one vote, of which, at the very most, it can be said to be only a mistake honestly made, and which could not possibly have changed the result.

Were it not for the Credit Mobilier I believe I would resign.

I have not drawn the additional salary, and do not know that I shall. Certainly, I shall not for the present, and probably not at all. But this I will not say in the midst of this storm.

(*Garfield to B. A. Hinsdale.*)

WASHINGTON, March 21, 1873.

When I find that I voted no less than fifteen times against motions made in favor of the salary amendment, and did all in my power, both by speech and vote, to prevent it, I feel keenly the injustice with which the public are treating me on this subject, and I begin to get really angry over it.

(*Garfield to B. A. Hinsdale.*)

WASHINGTON, April 4, 1873.

I agree in all you say on the question of back-pay; but neither truth nor ability seemed to avail anything in the face of this temptation. I not only have never drawn the extra pay, but, nearly two weeks ago, I ordered the Sergeant-at-Arms to close my account, and directed my back-pay due me, $4500, to be covered into the Treasury beyond my reach, or that of my heirs in case of my death. That has been done; but I felt that under no circumstances would I allow it to be known publicly, at least for the present. It may, however, be necessary by and by to let the fact come out. What do you think?

*   *   *   *   *   *   *   *

One phase of this case is most singular. Here in Washington, among all the men who most earnestly opposed the salary clause from the start, I have none who attack me for the course I have taken, while at home the condemnation seems to be universal. You know that I have always said that my whole public life was an experiment to determine whether an intelligent people would sustain a man in acting sensibly on each proposition that arose, and in doing nothing for mere show or for demagogical effect. I do not now remember that I ever cast a vote of that latter sort. Perhaps it is true that the demagogue will succeed when honorable statesmanship will fail. If so, public life is the hollowest of all shams.

(*Garfield to Col. A. F. Rockwell.*)

WASHINGTON, May 21, 1873.

After many years of prosperity and success, it has been my fortune to try the discipline of disaster, without any fault or wrong on my part. My name has been dragged into the whirlpool of calumny, and I have been defending myself against assault.   enclose you a copy of my review of the Credit Mobilier rascality, and shall be glad to know how it strikes you. I think of you as away, and in an elysium of quiet and peace, where I should love to be, out of the storm and in the sunshine of love and books. Do not think from the above that I am despondent. There is life and hope and fight in your old friend yet.

(*Garfield to Col. A. F. Rockwell.*)

WASHINGTON, January 15, 1874.

Permit me to transcribe a metrical version which I made the other day of the third ode of Horace's first book. It is still in the rough:

TO THE SHIP WHICH CARRIED VIRGIL TO ATHENS.

I.

So may the powerful goddess of Cyprus,
So may the brothers of Helen, twin stars,
So may the father and ruler of tempest
(Restraining all others, save only Iäpix),

II.

Guide thee. O ship, on thy journey, that owest
To Attica's shores Virgil trusted to thee.
I pray thee restore him, in safety restore him,
And saving him, save me the half of my soul.

III.

Stout oak and brass triple surrounded his bosom
Who first to the waves of the merciless sea
Committed his frail bark. He feared not Africus,
Fierce battling the gales of the furious North.

IV.

Nor feared he the gloom of the rain-bearing Hyads,
Nor the rage of fierce Notus a tyrant than whom
No storm-god that rules o'er the broad Adriatic
Is mightier, its billows to rouse or to calm.

V.

What form, or what pathway of death him affrighted,
Who faced with dry eyes monsters swimming the deep,
Who gazed without fear on the storm-swollen billows,
And the lightning-scarred rocks, grim with death on the shore ?

VI.

In vain did the prudent Creator dissever
The lands from the lands by the desolate sea,
If o'er its broad bosom, to mortals forbidden,
 Still leap, all profanely, our impious keels.

VII.

Recklessly bold to encounter all dangers,
Through deeds God forbidden still rushes our race ;
The son of Iapelus, Heaven-defying,
By impious fraud to the nations brought fire.

VIII.

When fire was thus stolen from regions celestial
Decay smote the earth and brought down in his train
A new summoned cohort of fevers o'erbrooding,
And Fate, till then slow and reluc ant to strike,

IX.

Gave wings to his speed and swift death to his victims.
Bold Dædalus tried the void realms of the air,
Borne upward on pinions not given to mortals.
The labors of Hercules broke into Hell.

X.

Naught is too high for the daring of mortals,
Even Heaven we seek in our folly to scale :
By our own impious crimes we permit not the thunder
To sleep without flame in the right hand of Jove.

I can better most of these verses, but send to you as I left them in the first rough draft.

(*Garfield to B. A. Hinsdale.*)

WASHINGTON, July 30, 1873.

In the course of thinking over your life and mine, I was strongly impressed with the conviction that you and I ought to study German and master it. I had considerable knowledge of it some years ago, but have neglected it and should need to begin the work almost anew. French has been more important to me, for the reason that more financial discussion appears in French than in German. But to profound theological scholarship German is indispensable. I think your mind is rather of the Teutonic type, and you would be immeasurably bene-fited were you to draw from the great German storehouse of criticism. It is a large undertaking to master a foreign language ; but I think you ought to under-take it at once.

(*Garfield to B. A. Hinsdale.*)

WASHINGTON. October 27, 1873.

I have read the paper of Mr. Warren, as reported in the *Methodist*, and have stopped to consider the marked passage. The statement of the author in refer-ence to the part played by Whitefield in laying the foundation of colonial unity, is new to me. I do not know that it is historically true ; but it bears many external evidences of truth. If it is true, it is a very important element in the history of this Republic, and shows that religion played even a broader part in the forma-tion of our nation than I had supposed. After reading the article, I read a brief sketch of Whitefield's life in Brown's Encyclopædia, and find some discrepancies between that and Warren. For example, Warren says that Whitefield crossed the Atlantic nineteen times. The Encyclopædia mentions each of his voyages by date, and says that his seventh was his last. This would make thirteen times across the Atlantic. The Encyclopædia seems to have viewed Whitefield's life mainly from an English standpoint, and it may be for that reason that his American work does not stand out in such prominence in the Encyclopædia as in Warren's article.

If I had had time in my lecture last evening, I should have spoken of the struggle between Protestantism and Catholicism for the possession of this conti-nent. Warren's article informs us how striking was the contrast between the unity of the eccl siastical power of France and Spain on the one hand, and the discord of the English Protestants on the Atlantic slope on the other. If White-field brought about ecclesiastical union, he prepared the way for the colonial triumph of England over France in 1763, and the triumph of the colonies over England in 1783.

(*Garfield to B. A. Hinsdale.*)

WASHINGTON, January 8, 1874.

I can't see that he (John Stuart Mill) ever came to comprehend human life as a reality from the actual course of human affairs beginning with Greek life down to our own. Men and women were always, with him, more or less of the nature or abstractions ; while, with his enormous mass of books, he learned a wonderful power of analysis, for which he was by nature surprisingly fitted. But his education was narrow just where his own mind was originally deficient. He was educated solely through books ; for his father was never a companion. His brothers and sisters bored him. He had no playfellows, and of his mother not a word is said in his autobiography.

(*Garfield to B A. Hinsdale.*)

WASHINGTON, March 31, 1874.

I have sent you by to-day's mail copies of such of my pamphlet speeches as I have on hand that are not in the list you sent me. This is not all, but it is nearly all : Argument before Supreme Court, March 6th, 1866 ; Public Debt and Specie Payments, March 16th, 1866 ; Freedman's Bureau, February 1st, 1866 ; In Memoriam Abraham Lincoln, April 14th, 1866 ; Rebel States under Military Control, February 8th, 1867; College Education, June 14th, 1867 ; Reconstruction, January 17th, 1868 ; Impeachment of Andrew Johnson, March 2d, 1868 ; Oration at Wilmington, May 30th, 1866 ; Elements of Success, June 29th, 1869 ; Public Expenditures and Civil Service, March 14th, 1870 ; The Tariff, April 1st, 1870 ; The McGarrahan Claim, February 20th, 1871 : Public Expenditures, January 23d, 1872 ; National Aid to Education, February 6th, 1872 : Campaign on the Reserve, July 31st, 1872; Increase of Salaries, March 27th, 1873 . Credit Mobilier Company, May 8th, 1873 ; Revenues and Expenditures, March 5th, 1874.

(*Garfield to B. A. Hinsdale.*)

WASHINGTON, April 20th, 1874

The latest news from Columbus seems to indicate that the re-districting scheme has broken down. Still, it may possibly succeed, and George H. Ford writes me he believes it will before the session ends. Personally, I shall be glad to be districted out, so that I can have a good excuse for quitting public life : but I am still receiving requests to change my residence, so as to stay in the old Nineteenth.

(*Garfield to B. A. Hinsdale.*)

WASHINGTON, November 14, 1874.

I have commenced work again on my committee, but still I may find time to do some reading. My reading, however, is like the wanderings of a man in a pleasant forest, without much plan or purpose. I am now, however, trying to get a better view of the literature and intellectual life of Germany connected with Goethe and his times.

(*Garfield to B. A. Hinsdale.*)

WASHINGTON, January 4, 1875.

With me the year 1874 has been a continuation and in some respects an exaggeration of 1873. That year brought me unusual trials, and brought me face to face with personal assaults and the trial that comes from calumny and public displeasure. This year has perhaps seen the culmination, if not the end, of that kind of experience. I have had much discipline of mind and heart in living the life which these trials brought me. Lately I have been studying myself with some anxiety to see how deeply the shadows have settled around my spirit. I find I have lost much of that exuberance of feeling, that cheerful spirit which I think abounded in me before. I am a little graver and less genial than I was before the storm struck me. The consciousness of this came to me slowly, but I have at last given in to it, and am trying to counteract the tendency.

So far as individual work is concerned I have done something to keep alive my tastes and habits. For example, since I left you I have made a somewhat thorough study of Goethe and his epoch, and have sought to build up in my mind a picture of the state of literature and art in Europe, at the period when Goethe began to work, and the state when he died. I have grouped the various facts into order, have written them out, so as to preserve a memoir of the impression made upon my mind by the whole. The sketch covers nearly sixty pages of manuscript. I think some work of this kind outside the track of one's every-day work is necessary to keep up real growth.

(Garfield to B. A. Hinsdale.)

WASHINGTON, July 8, 1875.
ı am taking advantage of this enforced leisure to do a good 'deal of reading. Since I was taken sick I have read the following : Sherman's two volumes ; Leland's " English Gipsies ;" George Borrow's " Gipsies of Spain ;" Borrow's " Rommany Rye ;" Tennyson's " Mary ;" seven volumes of Froude's England ; several plays of Shakespeare, and have made some progress in a new book, which I think you will be glad to see, " The History of the English People," by Prof. Green, of Oxford, in one volume.

(Garfield to B. A. Hinsdale.)

WASHINGTON, October 22, 1877.
Since receiving your postal card I have read Godwin Smith's essay on the Decline of Party Government. To me it is altogether a disappointing paper. Many of his facts and suggestions are interesting, but his suggestions of substitution for party government are too vague to be of any value, while there are grave differences of opinion among men on questions of vital importance, whether in church or state, in social life or in science. There will be parties based upon those conditions, and the thing most desired is not how to avoid the existence of parties, but how to keep them within proper bounus.

(Garfield to B. A. Hinsdale.)

WASHINGTON, November 14, 1877.
It is in the power of the Democratic Party to make the whole country rejoice in the President's Southern policy ; but I fear their usual reactionary spirit will go far to increase public dissatisfaction.

(Garfield to B. A. Hinsdale.)

WASHINGTON, January 9, 1878.
Concerning the future I feel no great certainty. On many accounts I prefer to retire from public life, and may do so ; but the present struggle for honest money seems to make a very imperative demand on me to stand by my post a little longer.

If it were certain that the Democrats are to come into power—and that seems to be probable—both in the National Government and to continue in power in

Ohio, I would not feel like continuing. It will take the next election to determine Ohio's future.

On the whole, it is probable I will stand again for the House. I am not sure, however, but the Nineteenth District will go back on me on the silver question. If they do I shall count it an honorable discharge.

(*Garfield to D. A. Hinsdale.*)

WASHINGTON, October 12, 1878.

The result of our election shows the value of a sturdy fight for principle. The party that makes that will always win in the long run.

(*Garfield to B. A. Hinsdale.*)

MENTOR, OHIO, November 16, 1878.

I have read with great interest and satisfaction your little volume on the Christian Jewish Church. I know of no work which contains within such small compass so complete and thorough a discussion of the subject. Your analysis of the early struggle between the Jewish and Greek Christians, and the peculiar influences of the Jewish and Greek mind upon the historical development of Christianity throws a strong and clear light upon many portions of the New Testament, and affords valuable assistance to the study of church history. The whole book is pervaded with the spirit of thorough and reverent scholarship, and you deserve, and doubtless will receive, the gratitude of a wide circle of readers.

(*Garfield to B. A. Hinsdale.*)

WASHINGTON, January 30, 1879.

I have long recognized the class of citizens whom you designate as the "left centre," that occupy that broader line of the two parties, and hold slack allegiance to the organization of which they are members. I have no doubt they exercise a valuable conservative influence upon the conduct of public affairs by resisting extreme measures on the part of their party. Of course, they exercise their power as voters and writers. I think, however, there never has been any such prominent class in Congress. Of course, we have had men in both parties who were less partisan than the majority of their associates, and who have, in a measure, represented the voters referred to. Perhaps it would be well if we had a recognized party of the left centre in Congress ; but I doubt if that would be possible under our institutions.

(*Garfield to B. A. Hinsdale.*)

WASHINGTON, April 21, 1880.

I share your regret that I am so much absorbed in political work ; but the position I hold in the House requires an enormous amount of surplus work. I am compelled to look ahead at questions likely to be sprung upon us for action, and the fact is, I prepare for debate on ten subjects where I actually take part in but one. For example : it seemed certain that the Fitz-John Porter case would be discussed in the House, and I devoted the best of two weeks to a careful re-examination of the old material and a study of the new.

There is now lying on top of my bookcase a pile of books, revisions and manuscripts three feet long by a foot and a half high which I accumulated and examined for a debate which certainly will not come off this session, and perhaps not at all. I must stand in the breach to meet whatever question comes. . . .

I look forward to the Senate as at least a temporary relief from this heavy work. . . . I am just now in antagonism with my own party on legislation in reference to the election law, and here also I have prepared for two discussions, and as yet have not spoken on either. . . .

Doubtless you are right in supposing that the government is, in some cases, the most imperfect part of the social organism. That is so because all free governments are managed by the combined wisdom and folly of the people. Perhaps, as a mere matter of government, a good despot would make a better government; but for the education of the people governed, a good despotism is worse than freedom with its admixture of folly. . . .

I am sorry you did not write me in regard to my going to Chicago. I have refused to be a delegate from my district, but I think it likely that the State Convention will elect me as delegate at large. I prefer not to go at all, but, if I am chosen, I suppose I had better go.

(*Garfield to B. A. Hinsdale.*)

WASHINGTON, January 18, 1880.

At first, let me say that among the 1200 letters and telegrams that have come to me since my nomination to the Senate, no one has touched all the points of the case so perfectly as you have in your letter of the 13th instant. I need not say a word about the nomination and election and my relations to it, for you have said it all. This, however, I may say on another phase of the subject: on many accounts my transfer to the Senate brings sad recollections. Do you remember the boy "Joe" in one of Dickens' novels who said that everybody was always telling him to "move on," that, whenever he stopped to look in at a window to long for gingerbread, or catch a glimpse of the pictures, the voice of the inexorable policeman made him "move on?" I have felt something of this in the order that sends me away from the House. It is a final departure.

CHAPTER XIX

GENERAL GARFIELD is one of the most domestic of men. Fortunate in the home of his early life, where love, self-sacrifice, a cheerful religious sentiment and perfect purity made the atmosphere of his life a constant source of healthful inspiration ; engaged early to a woman who has been his fellow-student, best counsellor and friend, sharer of all his nobler ambitions, activities, joys, and sorrows, and helpmeet in every sense of the word ; with his heroic mother as companion and friend, in his growing household ; with children who are worthy scions of noble stocks—intelligent, promising, loving and lovely in character ; with a nature simple in its tastes, affectionate, hospitable, averse to social display and fashionable distractions, and utterly incapable of enjoying vicious or undomestic pleasures— how could such a man's home help being filled with the warm sunlight of his generous nature, or be other than a well-spring of happiness to all under its roof-tree ? Of necessity Garfield has had two homes since he entered Congress. From his limited means his domestic life in both places has been plain, and only until within a few years past has he been able to live in both places in a style suitable even for a family so quiet and simple in its tastes and social ambitions as his own. In fact, it has only been within a very few months that the Ohio home—that in which Garfield's free and farm-bred nature feels most at ease —has been at all sufficient for its master's needs. And this Mentor home, which the name "Lawnfield" aptly describes, owes its enlargement and architectural transformation to the taste and contriving skill of his thoughtful and planning wife, who, like many others who saw his proportions before the people and his natural destiny, long before he realized or thought of either, barely got her graceful and enlarged conceptions realized in the new home, in time to have its generous capacity tested to the uttermost by the throngs of visitors and guests, of high and low degree, who have compelled General Garfield, in the language of Governor Foster, to "keep a country hotel"

GEN. GARFIELD'S WASHINGTON HOME.

ever since the Presidential lightning struck the biggest head there was at the Chicago Convention.

To the Washington home I have already alluded. It is plain, well arranged, roomy, comfortable, and economical. When the family are in it, there is no limit to its hospitality: it is always open to friends, new and old, high and humble, plain and cultured. It is filled with the mingled atmosphere of politics, literature, sociality, family culture and sports, and general good-nature. One might say it was a literary and political workshop and headquarters, if it were not such a centre of social gatherings and pleasures. Fortunately it is not a large house. In that case Garfield would have been a bankrupt before this ; for he is as free in his hospitalities as he is disinclined and unfitted for making money by any other way then by honestly earning it, which he always has done, " by the sweat of his brow." But his old and intimate friends have long felt that there was but one house in Washington that was adequate for a man of his nature, means, and popularity. It is very large, and surrounded by fine grounds, that afford pleasant prospects and breathing-room for the big-lunged and Nature-loving farmer of Mentor. It is nobly situated between the Treasury building and that occupied by the State, War, and Navy Departments, with the business and occupants of which he has become so familiar that the location of the house I speak of seems to be better suited to his probable needs than to those of any other man in the country, and certainly no other man has been better trained for the business to which a large part of the house has always been devoted. Popularly this is called " the White House."

The new Mentor home, however is, the most notable and visited place in the country, and all the housekeeping tact and ability of Mrs. Garfield are put to their severest test by the crowd of visitors. That she was equal to every emergency, and seemed at the end of each day's " country hotel " keeping as fresh, undisturbed, and free of care-marks as though the daylight hours had passed in elegant leisure, I can testify from an experience of an eight days' visit in the latter part of June and the first of July, when " Lawnfield " was busiest and most populous. In that eventful period for the Garfield household I failed to see that Governors and Senators and Congressmen and Generals and committeemen fared any better or were treated with more courtesy than " common people." If Governor Foster's arrival was hailed with unusual fervor it was not be-

LAWNFIELD.

cause of his title, but because he was greeted as the old friend "Charles" or "Charlie Foster" by the older, and as "Uncle Charlie" by the younger members of the family. His response to all these greetings was hearty, but especially to the last.

Driving along the wide, pleasant, well-kept, tree-shaded road, for six miles from the lovely town of Painesville, with lawn-surrounded houses worthy of the finest suburbs of New York, the first impressions of "Lawnfield" are decidedly attractive. The aspect of the large, well-proportioned and home-like product of Mrs. Garfield's skill and taste is that of the country place of a family who want plenty of room, in-doors and under piazzas. Although costing far less than would be thought economical for a carriage-house up the Hudson, it is by no means an ordinary or uninteresting structure. To be particular : with its sixty feet of front and fifty of depth ; with its three stories, including that under the high and picturesque roof ; with its commodious piazzas without and wide hallways within, and graceful proportions generally, it is a piece of architecture that grows in one's esteem, especially as it so admirably fits in to a lovely landscape and is dignified by the number of the out-buildings, large and small, all suggesting the uses of actual farming and also perfect arrangement. With en-closed grass fields in front and on the south-western side ; with the croquet lawn between it and the road ; with the orchard and garden on the east, and a lane in the rear through which the sunset glories transfigure the bordering trees, and with the book and desk and table filled little house near and to one side of the rear, it suggests truthfully the living and working place of a family enjoying Nature's most human aspect—that in which she responds to all of healthy, hard-working, simple human nature's needs and tastes. Its interior arrangements show care-ful and thoughtful provision for the several and various de-mands of the family, especially the cosey and cheerful up-stairs "snuggery" of the General, and the delightful room, on the ground floor, with the front piazza on one side, the garden on another, and the parlor on another, devoted to the uses of the most important and one of the busiest members of the household, independent, individual, and unique "Mother" Garfield, who is as bright and vigorous as most old ladies of sixty or less, and between whom and her "James" there is a comradeship which is only abandoned when, in her judgment, the compliments of distinguished guests seem likely to make him unmindful of his proper filial subordination. And yet, six months before the Chicago Convention, this mysterious and prophetic old lady one day startled her son by entering his room, saying oracularly, "James, you will be nominated for President next June," and departing without saying or waiting for another word. She knew what she and Providence had been training him for, as only a mother, and such a mother, can know by the mingled intuitions of heart and head.

The household was enlivened by the presence of the General's two eldest boys, Harry A. and James, just returned from the famous St. Paul's School, at Concord, New Hampshire, the former bringing a well-earned prize for English declamation. There were, besides, Mollie, a bright, joyous, beautiful girl just in her "teens;" Irvin McDowell, next younger, and Abram, the youngest and most peculiar of a flock that has in it no "black sheep," together with the son and daughter of Colonel Rockwell, of about the ages of Harry and Mollie. These are not mentioned by way of mere chronicling of personalities, but to illustrate the spirit that pervades the household of which they were the life and light. With all their varied studies and sports the father and mother seemed to sympathize, and fully entered into, as though the latter were but "children of a larger growth." Love took the place of authority on the one side, and of fear on the other, and I believe the father had a more realizing and prouder sense of his boy Harry's success and manly promise than of his own triply accumulated political honors. Nor could I see that any member of the family seemed to be put at all out of his or her spiritual gear by the constant and inevitable allusions of visitors to the probable destiny of the plain head of the household. One might have supposed that it had " run in the family" to have Presidential honors, to which, be it added, few allusions were made by any of its members, though all were pervaded with a pleased consciousness of the future, except the General himself, who does not welcome the approaching close of the free and unfettered activities that have so long been the joy of his vigorous life. And he did welcome every good chance to escape from the work of dealing with thousands of letters and dispatches and continual political calls and conferences, to talk over old times and incidents and to discuss questions far removed from politics. If ever a Presidential candidate was free from self-consciousness, and regarded himself only as the standard-bearer and representative of a great party and great principles, James A. Garfield is the man.

And he is best seen and known at his Mentor home, which he began to "make" three years ago last spring. He had felt a growing longing for his old-time relations with Nature, when by hard labor he earned his support from her bounties. He wanted the soul-resting labor of actual farming, and to get fresh vigor from actual contact with "Mother Earth." So he bought part of the farm he now owns, and has added until it comprises about one hundred and fifty acres. Like most of the farms that border the old turnpike, or "ridge-road," near the shore of Lake Erie, it has a small frontage, only fifty rods, and runs back, across the "ridge," about a quarter of a mile in the rear, which was the old and wave-beaten shore of the lake, down across the low and spring-moistened alluvial soil of the beautiful valley, in the middle of which, on the tracks of the Lake Shore Railway, the long and thundering trains, bearing the mighty traffic of twenty States, suggest the heavy pulsations of a nation's vigorous life. As his wife enlarged and gave beautiful proportions to the home-nest, so he mixed his practical and scientific farmer brains with the soil he set out to master. A wet and uncultivable field between the "ridge" and the railroad was scientifically drained and made capable of big corn crops ; a hydraulic ram was put in the low land near the ridge, which received and was worked by the copious and pure spring water from the gravelly ridge, and made to send a constant and abundant supply for house and out-houses, for people and for their dumb servants. A workshop, a tool-shop, a root-house, improved agricultural machinery, and the other outfits of a good farm were added. And in all the farm work the master easily took the lead, working with a will and until tired nature brought the solid rest that is not given to brain toilers. By this sort of actual companionship with Nature he has recuperated from the prodigious overwork of legislation and politics, got renewed strength, and preserved his old simplicity of tastes. He has got a more valuable crop out of that farm than is harvested from the largest of the famous Minnesota wheat domains, that rival principalities in size and value.

Two quite different opportunities of seeing Garfield in his relations with his fellows, outside of politics, were afforded during my visit. The first was the Fourth of July celebration at Painesville whose peculiar interest drew out the largest and best attendance of " Western Reserve" people ever known in that handsome town, for there was to be witnessed the formal dedication of a noble " Soldiers' Monument," in the park-like " Public Square," which had been many years in course of completion, and then everybody wanted to see and hear their own long-trusted and beloved representative, as of old, before the nation claimed him. There was a long and interesting procession, and there were several good speeches. Ex-Governor Cox, the main orator, was scholarly and eloquent, of course; the Hon. A. G. Riddle recalled, by his off-hand short speech, the memories of old-time irresistible pleas before " Western Reserve" juries, and *Tribune* correspondent E. V. Smalley, as one of the first company of Painesville volunteers, warmed up into a most effective style of reminiscence. But no one had a fair chance of securing the full attention of the thousands of intelligent and earnest people who swarmed around the speakers' stand and back out of ear-shot, save the pride and glory of the " district," Garfield. And, moving around the crowd that hung breathlessly on every glowing and thrilling utterance of the "citizen-soldier," I could see how the "old Western Reserve" "rises at" Garfield and holds him in its heart of hearts, as greater than Giddings, yet unspoiled by success and unconscious of the fulness of his powers.

"The Fourth" came on the third, at enterprising Painesville. The next day, Sunday, afforded a totally different experience. I was asked to go to the "Disciples" meeting-house, about a mile toward Painesville, and attend the worship there, and went, as did pretty nearly all the Garfield family. The meeting-house is a small, old-fashioned rural New England sort of temple, built of boards and painted white, with commodious horse-sheds around. The attendance was not large, but of people who looked earnestly religious, in their plain and primitive way. There was no "preacher," in the usual sense of that word. But in the preacher's seat was General Garfield's practical, original and independent old friend and adviser, one of the most noted characters in the "Reserve," Dr. J. P. Robison, who, when young Garfield first seriously contemplated the task of getting a college education, carefully examined the brawny and brainy youth, at the latter's request, and told him that he "had the brain of a Webster," and lung power and muscle to support it. In his younger career the doctor was a famous and successful lay preacher, but with his large and varied business and farm interests, and advanced years, he confines his public exhortations to his own neighborhood church. His discourse was a plain and pungent and sometimes sarcastic and humorous attack on all human substitutes for, and additions to, the revealed word of God. He classed the complex modern "theologies" with the "mythologies" of old, and, while admitting the value of a thorough theological training, could not help alluding to the learned doctors of divinity whose preaching yielded few converts, while "Paul stole out of jail, converted a whole family, and got back so quickly that he was not missed." I confess that the plain and powerful talk

of this vigorous old man, whose grip on worldly realities and
business is remarkable, and who seemed so equally sure of the
" eternal verities" of the Gospel, with his unconsciously splendid contempt for any human assumptions of divine authority,
gave me an impression not at all unfavorable to the " Disciples" persuasion. After the preaching was over he asked
the congregation to " sing a song," and proceeded, with the aid
of two deacons, to administer the " Lord's Supper," as is done
every Sunday by the " Disciples." The ceremony was impressive by its very simplicity and evident sincerity. After the
broken bread had been blessed and partaken of, the doctor
asked " Brother Garfield " to ask a blessing on the wine, and
the latter did so, with the manner of one who was performing a simple and customary duty. Altogether the services
were exceedingly suggestive of the apostolic times and of the
notion that much might be learned from the misunderstood and
humble " Campbellites." They gave me a much clearer conception of the natural and normal character of Garfield's
" preaching," in his early manhood, and for this reason had
special value and significance. And it seemed to me that when
a man so brilliantly successful in politics is so endeared to all
his old neighbors, and moves them so deeply, one day, by
his thrilling expressions of eulogy for the dead heroes of the
war in which he freely exposed his own life, and the next day,
among those with whom he has long worshipped in simplicity,
is an earnest and devotional leader, he has a largeness and
wholeness of nature and life that inevitably draw to him the
best sentiments of the people who know him best.

(*Garfield to B. A. Hinsdale.*)

WASHINGTON, D. C., February 14, 1875.

I don't remember whether I have ever called your attention to a book which
has given me a great deal of pleasure, and which I think is an admirable help
to young people in laying the foundation of a knowledge of Shakespeare. You
may be familiar with it, but I never saw it until this winter. It is Shakespeare
written in a condensed and attractive form, by Charles and Mary Lamb, and
published in Bohn's Library. It gives but eighteen pages to each play, and puts
the story in so plain a way that a very young child can understand it. The volume contains sketches of about half of the plays. About twice a week I read

one of these stories to the children, and even Mollie gets a pretty fair under-standing of the story. Not only this, but they give older and much clearer notions of the plot of the play than the reading of the whole play ordinarily gives.

(*Garfield to B. A. Hinsdale.*)

MENTOR, OHIO, May 13, 1877.

You can hardly imagine how completely I have turned my mind out of its usual channels during the last four weeks. You know I have never been able to do anything moderately, and, to-day, I feel myself lame in every muscle with too much lifting and digging. I shall try to do a little less the coming week.

CHAPTER XX.

LET us, in conclusion, consider a few of the remarkable features of Garfield's character and public career.

In the first place, his career may be said to be, perhaps, the most remarkable illustration of the developing power of our institutions that was ever afforded. Exception to this might be taken as regards two instances : first, that of Franklin ; but Franklin accomplished by far the most important achievements of his life after he had passed the age of fifty, which Garfield has not yet reached ; second, that of Lincoln, who is considered by many profound thinkers to have been the greatest man ever begotten on this continent ; but Lincoln was one of those rare natures which seem to be peculiarly inspired for great emergencies ; and although he rose from the lowest origin, through a life of comparative poverty and great toil, to the highest honors of the Republic, yet his greatness seems to have been more a special gift of Heaven than the result of the steady development, improvement, and culture of a great brain.

The stories about the toils and privations endured by Garfield in his boyhood and early manhood will deservedly endear him to the popular heart, for the lesson they afford is one full of cheer and inspiration to the millions of young Americans whose circumstances compel them to meet like hindrances to culture and development. But it is quite possible that too much may be made of these popular illustrations, which tend to divert from consideration the fact that from the age of seventeen until he graduated from Williams the determination, energy, inflexible purpose, and lofty resolves of young Garfield were concentrated on higher objects than those which command the ambition of most of that large class of men who are known as " self-

made men," and whose successes are purely selfish in their
character.   Garfield's spirit and whole life during this heroic
period of struggle were of a totally different sort from those
which have been displayed by men who have sprung from poverty and obscurity into a wealth or political power that was
made the ultimate end of life.   He pursued culture and knowledge for the sake of developing the powers he felt within him
—largely for the sake of culture, but also in order to enable him
to fulfil, in some worthy sphere of usefulness, the highest functions of his nature, and to exercise the widest scope of his
powers.   In all human probability, he has been, since the age
of seventeen, the "growingest" specimen of human nature
under process of development in this country.   Whoever will
undertake faithfully to go through the various evidences and
products of his activity for a little over a generation will fully
coincide with this proposition.   No subject of human interest
has been foreign to the searchings, sympathies, and thinking of
this athletic student.   An American of Americans, he has absorbed, in the generous juices of his soul, all the elements of
knowledge, culture, faith, and aspiration which come most
definitely within the broad domain of American history, patriotism, philosophy, and forecast.   Living near the shore of one
of the chain of lakes that constitute our Mediterranean, and
in a region central to the better settled parts of the Union, his
sympathies have been as broad as the continent ; his consum-
ing love of nationality has been that of a man who desires,
not to extend the power of the nation over any portion of it as
a despotism, but that every portion shall equally and to the
fullest extent enjoy all the privileges and advantages of the
National Government which he believes the fathers established
" to promote the general welfare."

As to Garfield's political career, there are many points of sin-
gularity.   It has been seldom in the history of this country that
a young man elected to the House of Representatives has maintained himself in the confidence and affections of his constituents to such a remarkable degree.   Elected nine successive

times, with such growing popularity, especially during the last three campaigns, that he could have been re-elected again and again, to all human appearance, as long as he chose to remain in the House—he has maintained this length and eminence of public service without having had to depend on the methods by which other statesmen have continued for long periods in one or the other branch of Congress. To illustrate: The early founders of the Republican Party who served in Congress for long periods won their popular strength mainly by the zeal, ardor and constancy with which they devoted themselves to the one idea which was the animating purpose of the Republican Party up to the beginning of the war. After the war began, most of these men continued their hold upon the public confidence and that of their constituencies by continuing their old war cries. Other members of Congress who have served several terms have been able to do so by the support of large financial or other interests, which they have made it their peculiar mission to aid. Still others have achieved the same sort of success by their adroitness, care, skill, tact or boldness in manipulating caucuses and managing conventions. From all these public men, many of them worthy and useful statesmen, Garfield has been widely differentiated. He has had no special hobby in Congress, but has impartially and energetically devoted himself to the advocacy of what he has regarded as the right side of every great and living issue that has been presented since he entered that body. His speeches have been as remarkable for the great scope of subjects which they embraced as was the course of studies which he pursued in obtaining the knowledge and culture that were to be the main elements of his success.

There has been a steady *crescendo* in his career which impresses every one who realizes its peculiar nature, with the conviction that it cannot be thwarted or arrested in its development. There have been plenty of heroic and romantic incidents in it, and a wealth of varied honors, but each successive step has seemed so natural to so strong a will and to so stalwart and unceasingly and variously active a brain, that it is taken as a matter of course. It is what would be " the unexpected " to most men that has been " happening" to him pretty much all his life. That the poor canal boy should become a college President was romance enough for one career. That the college President should be spontaneously chosen a State Senator and become a leader in critical times was a fresh marvel. That the preaching and legislating college President should jump from his chosen avocations into the new business of fighting and begin military life as acting Brigadier-General, win the title by a series of rapid and brilliant operations, become Chief of Staff of a large army by another jump and win a Major-General's commission by pure moral and intellectual courage and power, was something to which the history of our great war offers no parallel. That the youngest member of Congress, coming from the army in mid-war times should be the first to give the best energies of his nature to a determined grapple with questions of finance and lay the foundations of the most consistent and fruitful career in the development of sound theory and wise practice in dealing with problems of taxation, tariff and currency, was, again, enough to distinguish any public man. And so we might go on, carving out of the achievements and successes of Garfield material enough to answer for several distinct and distinguished careers and biographies.

All of which unconsciously led him to, and prepared him for, the unsought, unplanned triumph at Chicago, which was not only the most wonderful event in all political history, but the most perfect instance of the resistless strength of a man developed by all the best and purest impulses, forces, and influences of American institutions into becoming their most thorough and ablest embodiment, in organic and personal activity, aspirations, and character. The finest feature of the English form of government, the virtual crowning of victorious leadership, was reproduced in the Convention of the party that has wielded the greatest powers for twenty years, and has learned how to govern as no other party ever did learn. The whole history of

Garfield's relations with the Convention, which he entered as the sincere and single-minded friend of Sherman, is full of significance. Day after day it became unconsciously more and more convinced that the nominator, and not one of the distinguished nominees, was the man of the hour, for the time, for the official leadership of the party whose existence was exactly coeval with the political activity of Garfield, and whose rank and file he had most fully represented on every field of conflict. When the party crowned with its highest honors the most perfect type of American development, by American processes, methods and institutions, it gained a fresh lease of life and power by recognizing the solid foundations of our institutions and became the most genuine Democracy, as well as the wisest, ever organized anywhere. There is not a nobly ambitious poor boy in the land who should not feel that Garfield's election would be the pledge of another century of unlimited openings and chances for youth of like poverty and hard fortune. And so long as poor American boys may feel that the highest of earthly offices is attainable by such methods as Garfield has followed, so long the boldest of all experiments in government will continue to baffle all the evil predictions of its enemies, and to surpass in its beneficence the most glowing dreams of its friends.

END.

APPENDIX.

———◦◆◦———

GARFIELD'S CHICAGO CONVENTION SPEECH.

(*New York Times, June 10th.*) .

General Garfield's speech nominating Sherman at Chicago last Saturday evening was not telegraphed. It is a fair specimen of his eloquence :

" Mr. President : I have witnessed the extraordinary scenes of this convention with deep solicitude. No emotion touches my heart more quickly than a sentiment in honor of a great and noble character, but as I sat on these seats and witnessed these demonstrations, it seemed to me you were a human ocean in a tempest.

" I have seen the sea lashed into fury and tossed into spray, and its grandeur moves the soul of the dullest man, but I remember that it is not the billows but the calm level of the sea from which all heights and depths are measured. When the storm has passed and the hour of calm settles on the ocean, when the sunlight bathes its smooth surface, then the astronomer and surveyor takes the level from which he measures all terrestrial heights and depths.

" Gentlemen of the convention, your present temper may not mark the healthful pulse of our people. When our enthusiasm has passed, when the emotions of this hour have subsided, we shall find that calm level of public opinion below the storm from which the thoughts of a mighty people are to be measured, and by which their final action will be determined. Not here in this brilliant circle, where 15,000 men and women are assembled, is the destiny of the Republican Party to be decreed. Not here, where I see the enthusiastic faces of seven hundred and fifty-six delegates, waiting to cast their votes into the urn and determine the choice of the Republic, but by four million Republican firesides, where the thoughtful voters, with their wives and children about them ; with the calm thoughts in-

spired by love of home and love of country ; with the history
of the past, the hopes of the future and the knowledge of the
great men who have adorned and blessed our nation in days
gone by—there God prepares the verdict that shall determine
the wisdom of our work to-night. Not in Chicago, in the heats
of June, but in the sober quiet that will come to them between
now and November, in the silence of deliberate judgment, will
this great question be settled. Let us aid them to-night.

" But now, gentlemen of the convention, what do we want ?
[A voice, ' Garfield !' followed by applause]. Bear with me a
moment, hear me for this cause, and for a moment, ' be silent,
that you may hear.' Twenty-five years ago this republic was
wearing a triple chain of bondage. Long familiarity with traffic
in the bodies and souls of men had paralyzed the consciences of
a majority of our people. The baleful doctrine of State sovereignty had shackled and weakened the noblest and most beneficent powers of the National Government, and the grasping
power of slavery was seizing the virgin Territories of the West
and dragging them into the den of eternal bondage. At that
crisis the Republican Party was born ; it drew its first inspiration from that fire of liberty which God has lighted in every human heart, and which all the powers of ignorance and tyranny
can never wholly extinguish. The Republican Party came to
deliver and save the republic. It entered the arena where the
beleaguered and assailed Territories were struggling for freedom,
and drew around them a sacred circle of liberty, which the
demon of slavery has never dared to cross. It made them free
forever. Strengthened by its victory on the frontier, the young
party, under the leadership of that great man who, on this
spot, twenty years ago, was made its leader, entered the national
capital, and assumed the high duties of the Government. The
light which shone from its banner dispelled the darkness in
which slavery had enshrouded the capital, melted the shackles
of every slave, and threw its rays into the darkest corner of
every slave-pen within the shadow of the Capitol. Our great
national industries, by an unprotected policy, were themselves
prostrated, and the streams of revenue flowed in such feeble
currents that the Treasury itself was well-nigh empty. The
money of the people was the wretched notes of two thousand
uncontrolled and irresponsible State banking corporations, which
were filling the country with a circulation that poisoned rather
than sustained the life of business.

" The Republican Party changed all this. It abolished the
Babel of confusion and gave the country a currency as national

as its flag and based it upon the sacred faith of the people. It threw its protecting arm around our great industries, and they stood erect, as with new life. It filled with the spirit of true nationality all the great functions of the Government ; it confronted a rebellion of unexampled magnitude, with slavery behind it, and, under God, fought the final battle of liberty until the victory was won. Then, after the storms of battle, were heard the sweet, calm words of peace spoken by the conquering nation, and saying to the conquered foe that lay prostrate at its feet : ' This is our only revenge, that you join us in lifting into the serene firmament of the Constitution, to shine like stars forever and ever, the immortal principles of truth and justice that all men, white or black, shall be free and stand equal before the law.' Then came the questions of reconstruction, the public debt, and the public faith.

" The Republican Party has finished its twenty-five years of glory and success, and is here to-night to ask you to launch it on another lustrum of glory and victory. How shall you do it ? Not by assailing any Republican. [Cheers.] The battle this year is our Thermopylæ. We stand on the narrow isthmus, and the little Spartan band must meet all the Greeks whom Xerxes can bring against them, and then the stars in their courses will fight for us. [Applause.] To win the victory we want the vote of every Grant Republican, and of every Blaine man, and of every anti-Blaine man. We are here to take calm counsel together, and to inquire what we shall do. We want a man whose life and opinions embody all the achievements of which I have spoken.

" I am happy to present to you and to name for your consideration a man who was the comrade, the associate, and the friend of nearly all those persons whose faces look down upon us in this building to-night ; a man who began his career in the politics of this country twenty-five years ago ; whose first service was done in the days of peril on the plains of Kansas, when the first red drop of that blood-shower began to fall, which increased into the deluge of gore in the Rebellion. He stood by young Kansas then and returned to his seat in the national legislature. Through all the subsequent years his pathway has been marked by the labors which he had performed in every department of legislation. If you ask me for his monument, I point to twenty-five years of the National Statutes. There is not one great, one beneficent statute on your books within that time that has been placed there without his intelligent and powerful aid. He was one of the men who formulated the laws that raised our great armies and navies and carried us through the war. His hand was in the workmanship of the statutes which brought back the unity and married calm of these States. His hand was in all that great legislation which created the great wark currency that carried us through, and in the still greater work that redeemed the promise of the Government and made it good. [Applause.]

" At last he passed from the halls of legislation into a high executive office, and there he displayed that experience, intelligence, firmness, and power of equipoise which throngs a stormy period of two and a half years, with half the public press howling and crying ' Crucify him,' carried him through unswerved by a single hair from the line of duty. He has improved the resources of the Government and the great business interests of the country, and has carried us through in the execution of that law without a jar, in spite of the false prophets and Cassandras of half the continent. [Applause.] He has shown himself able to meet in the calmness of statesmanship all the great emergencies of government. For twenty-five years he has trod that perilous height of public duty, and against all the shafts of malice he has borne his crest unharmed, and the blaze of that fierce light which has been upon him has found no flaw in his honor, no stain on his shield. I do not present him as a better Republican or a better man than thousands of others whom we honor and revere ; but I present him for your deliberate consideration. I nominate John Sherman, of Ohio."

GARFIELD'S INFORMAL ACCEPTANCE.

CHICAGO, June 7.—About midnight the committee appointed to wait on Garfield and Arthur, and inform them of their nomination, found them at the Grand Pacific Hotel, and Senator Hoar, as chairman made an appropriate speech. Garfield responded :

" Mr. Chairman and Gentlemen : I assure you that the information you have officially given me brings the sense of very grave responsibility, and especially so in view of the fact that I was a member of your body, a fact that could not have existed with propriety had I had the slightest expectation that my name would be connected with the nomination for the office.

" I have felt, with you, great solicitude concerning the situation of our party during the struggle ; but believeing that you are correct in assuring me that substantial unity has been reached in the conclusion, it gives me a gratification far greater than any personal pleasure your announcement can bring.

" I accept the trust comitted to my hands.

" As to the work of our party and as to the character of the campaign to be entered upon, I will take an early occasion to reply more fully than I can properly do to-night.

" I thank you for the assurance of confidence and esteem you have presented to me, and hope we shall see our future as promising as are the indications to-night."

GARFIELD IN THE LIGHT OF PHRENOLOGY.

(From the New York Tribune of August 1st.)

THE August number of *The Phrenological Journal* contains a sketch of General Garfield which begins with the following analysis of his mental characteristics, based upon an examination from the phrenologist's point of view. As many persons attribute no little value to such phrenological statements, this analysis will undoubtedly be read with interest :

" James A. Garfield is a man of very strong physical constitution, with broad shoulders, deep chest, and a good nutritive system, which serve to sustain with ample vigor his uncommonly large brain ; standing fully six feet high, and weighing 220 pounds. The head, which is twenty-four inches in circumference, seems to be very long from front to rear, and then the length seems extreme from the centre of the ear to the root of the nose ; it is also long from the opening of the ear backward. The whole back-head is large, and the social group amply indicated, but the reader will observe the extreme length anterior to the opening of the ears, especially across the lower part of the forehead, in which are located the organs of the perceptive intellect, those which gather and retain knowledge, and bring a man into quick sympathy with the external world, and also with the world of facts as developed in science and literature.

" Perhaps there are not two men in a hundred thousand who are intelligent and educated, who will see as much and take into account so many of the principles involved in what he sees as the subject before us. Nothing escapes his attention ; he remembers things in their elements, their qualities, and peculiarities, such as form, size, and color. He would make an excellent judge of the size of articles, and also of their weight, by simple observation. He has a talent for natural science, especially chemisty and natural philosophy. His memory, indicated by the fulness in the middle of the forehead, is enormously developed, aiding him in retaining vividly all the impressions that are worth recalling.

"The superior portion of the forehead is developed more prominently in the analogical than in the logical. His chief intellectual force is in the power to elucidate and make subjects clear ; hence he is able to teach to others whatever he knows himself.

"He has the talent for reading character ; hence he addresses himself to each individual according to his peculiar characteristics, and reaches results in the readiest and best way. His language is rather largely indicated ; he would be known more for specific compactness than for an ornate and elaborate style, because he goes as directly as possible from the premises to the conclusion, and never seems to forget the point at issue.

"The side-head is well developed in the region of Order, Constructiveness, sense of the beautiful and of the grand. It is also strongly marked in the region of Combativeness and Destructiveness, which give force and zealous earnestness in the prosecution of that which he attempts to do. He is able to compel himself to be thorough, and to hold his mind and his efforts in the direction required until he has made himself master of the subject. Industry is one of his strong traits.

He is firm, positive, determined, and the middle of the top-head indicates strong religious tendency. We seldom see so large Veneration ; he is devout, respectful toward whatever he thinks sacred, whether it relates to religion or to subordinate topics ; he would reverence ancient places made memorable in story and song ; he is respectful to the aged, polite to his equals, and especially generous and friendly toward those who are his inferiors in age or culture. Thus, young men and even children have ready access to him by his invitation and permission. His strong social affection makes his face and his voice a standing invitation toward confidence, and he has great familiarity in his treatment of the young.

"His method of studying subjects is instinctive ; he considers all the facts, every condition, that will be brought into question, and combining these by means of his logical force, his conclusions seem clear, are vigorously stated and influential. He has a strong physiognomy ; that broad and high cheek-bone indicates vital power ; that strong nose indicates determination, courage and positiveness ; the fulness of the lips shows warmth of affection and of sympathy.

" There are few men who are as well adapted to comprehend the length and depth and details of business, and hold their knowledge where it will be ready for use when it is required ; hence, as a lawyer or statesman, he should be able to impart to people his knowledge effectively and exhaustively whenever required. He is naturally qualified to be master of turbulent men, and to meet force by force, and to stand his ground in the midst of hardships, difficulties and opposition."

THE ATLAS SERIES OF ESSAYS.

www.ingramcontent.com/pod-product-compliance
Lightning Source LLC
Chambersburg PA
CBHW030805020726

47499CB00006B/1774